THE MAN OF FEELING

broadview editions
series editor: L.W. Conolly

Portrait of Henry Mackenzie by Sir Henry Raeburn, circa 1810.
By courtesy of the National Portrait Gallery, London.

THE MAN OF FEELING

Henry Mackenzie

edited by Maureen Harkin

broadview editions

Library and Archives Canada Cataloguing in Publication

Mackenzie, Henry, 1745–1831.
    The man of feeling / Henry Mackenzie ; edited by Maureen Harkin.

(Broadview editions)
Includes bibliographical references.
ISBN 1-55111-468-2

    I. Harkin, Maureen II. Title. III. Series.

PR3543.M2M328 2005   823′.6   C2005-900769-9

Broadview Editions
The Broadview Editions series represents the ever-changing canon of literature in English by bringing together texts long regarded as classics with valuable lesser-known works.

Advisory editor for this volume: Kathryn Prince

Broadview Press Ltd. is an independent, international publishing house, incorporated in 1985. Broadview believes in shared ownership, both with its employees and with the general public; since the year 2000 Broadview shares have traded publicly on the Toronto Venture Exchange under the symbol BDP.

We welcome comments and suggestions regarding any aspect of our publications — please feel free to contact us at the addresses below or at broadview@broadviewpress.com.

North America
Post Office Box 1243, Peterborough, Ontario, Canada K9J 7H5
3576 California Road, Orchard Park, NY, USA 14127
Tel: (705) 743-8990; Fax: (705) 743-8353;
email: customerservice@broadviewpress.com

UK, Ireland, and continental Europe
NBN Plymbridge, Estover Road, Plymouth PL6 7PY UK
Tel: 44 (0) 1752 202301   Fax: 44 (0) 1752 202331
Fax Order Line: 44 (0) 1752 202333
Customer Service: cservs@nbnplymbridge.com Orders: orders@nbnplymbridge.com

Australia and New Zealand
UNIREPS, University of New South Wales
Sydney, NSW, 2052 Australia
Tel: 61 2 9664 0999; Fax: 61 2 9664 5420
email: info.press@unsw.edu.au

www.broadviewpress.com

Typesetting and assembly: True to Type Inc., Mississauga, Canada.

PRINTED IN CANADA

Contents

Acknowledgements

I would like to acknowledge the financial assistance of the Reed College Faculty Research Fund in preparing this edition, and to thank the research librarians at both Reed and the Green Library of Stanford University for their help. I would also like to thank Julia Gaunce at Broadview for her assistance with the project.

Introduction

Mackenzie and the Sentimental Novel

> I remember so well its first publication, my mother and sisters crying over it, dwelling upon it with rapture! And when I read it, as I was a girl of fourteen not yet versed in sentiment, I had a secret dread I should not cry enough to gain the credit of proper sensibility.
>
> —Lady Louisa Stuart, writing about *The Man of Feeling* in 1826.[1]

It takes quite an effort of historical imagination to reconstruct a literary culture in which the term "sentimental" was not automatically understood as a pejorative, when admissions of weeping over a novel did not mark one as an unsophisticated reader. Yet in the middle and later decades of the eighteenth century, as Stuart's quote intimates, a tearful response to the novel of sentiment so popular at the time—provided one wept *enough*—could be read as a sign that one "got" the novel, grasped its ambition and felt the full power of its effects. This epoch in British and European literature, spanning the decades of the 1740s to the 1780s, and authors including Sarah Fielding, Jean Francois Marmontel, Samuel Richardson, Jean-Jacques Rousseau, Oliver Goldsmith, Sarah Scott, Laurence Sterne, Mackenzie, and Johann Wolfgang von Goethe, was one in which the sentimental novel was one of the most important genres in prose fiction. Though the sentimental as an element in literary texts is not confined to this period, remaining important in the works of nineteenth-century novelists such as Dickens, for example,[2] the sentimental novel of the eighteenth century is unique in making the spectacle of pathos, which it typically stages over and over in its pages, and the responses of observers to that spectacle its central concern.

Mid-century sentimentalism is also a phenomenon that extends well beyond the borders of fiction, to poetic, dramatic, essayistic and philosophical texts, part of the culture's fascination with the relation between emotion and judgment, and the nature of the human ability to comprehend and imaginatively recreate the

---

1 Lady Louisa Stuart, letter to Walter Scott, 4 September 1826, in *The Private Letter-Books of Sir Walter Scott*, ed. Wilfred Partington (New York: Frederick Stokes, 1930) 273.

2 See Janet Todd, *Sensibility: An Introduction* (London: Methuen, 1986) 147.

experiences of others. The tremendous popularity of sentimentalism as an attitude at this time is famously attested to by the novelist Samuel Richardson's correspondent, Lady Bradshaigh. In a wondering letter to Richardson in 1749 Bradshaigh describes a veritable cult of the sentimental: "Pray Sir, give me leave to ask you ... what, in your opinion is the meaning of the word *sentimental*, so much in vogue among the polite, both in town and country? ... Everything clever and agreeable is comprehended in that word. I am frequently astonished to hear such a one is a *sentimental* man; we were a *sentimental* party; I have been taking a *sentimental* walk."[1] The danger of the term's expanding to a point of near-meaninglessness is clearly in view, but sentimentalism as a particularly rich vein for novelists was not exhausted for several decades more.

Henry Mackenzie's *The Man of Feeling* marks the high point of the sentimental novel in English. Published in April 1771, it initially received little notice and lukewarm reviews (see Appendix D) but went on to phenomenal popularity and dozens more editions in Britain and the United States between 1771 and 1824.[2] Up to that point, Mackenzie, a twenty-five-year-old Edinburgh lawyer and aspiring man of letters, had published only a few poems and completed an unpublished tragedy. He went on to write two subsequent novels (*The Man of the World*, 1773, and *Julia de Roubigné*, 1777), various dramatic pieces (including *The Prince of Tunis*, performed 1773), and acted as editor and principal author of the two Edinburgh periodical papers *The Mirror* (January 1779-May 1780) and *The Lounger* (February 1785-January 1787). In this latter role as editor, social observer, and contributor to Edinburgh literary and cultural life Mackenzie achieved considerable renown, and it was in recognition of his status as the "Scottish Addison" that Walter Scott famously dedicated his first novel *Waverley* (1814) to him. Yet it was his first novel and its impact which dominated the literary career and subsequent reputation of Henry Mackenzie. He carried the sobriquet of "the man of feeling" from 1771 until the end of his life, long after he had stopped writing sentimental fiction, and indeed long after he had effectively given up his literary career amidst the

---

1   Undated letter to Samuel Richardson, *The Correspondence of Samuel Richardson*, ed. Anna Laetitia Barbauld (London: 1804) 282-83.

2   See list of editions in Harold William Thompson, *A Scottish Man of Feeling* (London: Oxford UP, 1931) 417-18.

claims of his active law practice and other professional responsibilities, his considerable property holdings as a member of the landed Scottish gentry, and his large family.

Mackenzie's text captured the imagination of the reading public in part through its masterful, economical deployment of what were by 1771 the well-established conventions of sentimental fiction, and in order to appreciate Mackenzie's relation to the genre we need to briefly catalogue those conventions. Sentimental novels typically focus on scenes of sympathy and suffering. They stage numerous scenes of distress in order to provoke a sympathetic response from the protagonist who witnesses the scene. The hero's, or, more rarely, heroine's, compassion is drawn forth by such spectacles; and often, though not always, this leads to an offer of financial or other practical assistance. Hence the novels abound in scenes set in prisons and madhouses, in encounters with beggars and innocent yeomen ruined by others' greed and intrigue, and with women driven mad by thwarted love or imprisoned for thwarting the lusts of their pursuers. Sympathy, however, is not confined to feeling for those in distress: as Hume observes, it is the principle "by which we enter into the sentiments of the rich and poor [alike], and partake of their pleasure and uneasiness,"[1] and the novels also feature, though somewhat less prominently, scenes of shared joy.

Sentimental novels also privilege the visible, somatic expression of the sympathy evoked by their various spectacles, condemning verbal language as an inadequate means of communicating the emotions of the feeling heart. This mistrust of language motivates the recourse to the more immediate means of expression provided by tears, blushes, sighs, gestures and even physiognomy so characteristic of the novels: a focus on visibility which frequently lends the texts' central scenes an air of pageant or theater.[2] True sentimental heroes, as George Starr has observed, are always "more or less tongue-tied"[3] while villains are glibly articulate. Linked to this bodily or visual sign as guarantee of authenticity is the resort to a number of formal

---

1 David Hume, *A Treatise of Human Nature*, ed. P.H. Nidditch, second ed. (Oxford: Clarendon, 1978) 362-64.
2 See David Marshall's discussions of theatricality in the work of Adam Smith, Pierre de Marivaux, and Jean-Jacques Rousseau in *The Figure of Theater: Shaftesbury, Defoe, Adam Smith and George Eliot* (New York: Columbia UP, 1986) and *The Surprising Effects of Sympathy: Marivaux, Diderot, Rousseau and Mary Shelley* (Chicago: U of Chicago P, 1988).
3 George Starr, "Sentimental Novels of the Later Eighteenth Century," in John Richetti *et al.*, ed., *The Columbia History of the English Novel* (New York: Columbia UP, 1994) 182.

means, not exclusive to the sentimental novel but characteristic of it, used to assert the truthfulness and artfulness of these texts.[1] Hence the numerous found manuscripts, interruptions to the story, and interpolated fragments which imply the work's status as direct transcripts of a feeling heart.

The encounters which set in play these scenes of sympathy and deciphering are often initiated by the various journeys undertaken in the sentimental novel, journeys which, whatever their ostensible purpose, function to reveal the profound bonds of sympathy between the protagonist and the strangers he meets, bonds often explicitly asserted to be as strong as those of consanguinity. The purpose of these travels in every case is very evidently to make new scenes and personages familiar, not to introduce unassimilable difference. Despite what might first appear unbridgeable gaps between characters of different social rank, nationality, gender, and/or religion, all such social and cultural differences are ultimately shown to be mere surface phenomena, easily and quickly swept away in the moments of common goodwill and sympathy that are the central events of sentimental novels. In new surroundings the sentimentalist, through his experiences of the bonds created by sympathy, is always recognizing the familiar. Yorick's reflections on his own practice as a "sentimental traveller" in Sterne's *A Sentimental Journey* (1768) stands as epigraph to the genre: "I go translating all the way."[2]

In addition to these characteristic *situations* of the sentimental novel, two other features stand out. One is the evident emphasis on instructing the reader how to react, how to feel: a sense of mission as moral education which marks the genre as strongly as its scenes of pathos. And finally, in addition to these positive characteristics, we can note what *absences* or negatives distinguish them from other contemporary works: their tendency to repeat certain plot situations,[3] and their lack of character development or suspenseful turns. These are, in sum, works in which essentially fixed characters confront starkly distressing situations in prisons, madhouses, or humble cottages, not to alter the circumstances, or to be changed by them in the manner of the *Bildungsroman*, but to

---

1   Leo Braudy, "The Form of the Sentimental Novel," *Novel* 7 (1973): 5-13.
2   Laurence Sterne, *A Sentimental Journey Through France and Italy* (London: Penguin, 1986) 79.
3   See Margaret Cohen's observations on the French sentimental novel of the early nineteenth century in *The Sentimental Education of the Novel* (Princeton: Princeton UP, 1999) 22.

establish a sense of communality with the victims, and to model the correct, sympathetic response for the reader.

Mackenzie's novel is both a compendium of these situations and a highly conscious distillation of the peculiar air of intense emotion and the futility of effort that emerges in sentimental fiction. The plot of *The Man of Feeling* centers on the adventures of Harley, an impoverished aristocrat. At the urging of friends, but against his own inclinations, he visits London in an attempt to gain the lease of some government-owned lands. On his journey, and while waiting in the capital for word on his undertaking, he encounters various types: a beggar, London confidence-men, an inmate of a madhouse, a young woman driven into prostitution after being abandoned by her seducer, a misanthropic philosopher. His quest for the lease fails, and he returns to his rural estate, encountering more characters en route, notably an older man, Ben Silton, with whom he discourses on poetry and the manners of the age, and a former acquaintance, "Old Edwards" whose long tale of distress takes up considerable space in this short novel. These encounters and exchanges, along with Harley's musing conclusions, constitute most of the action of the novel. In the concluding chapters, the novel focuses on Harley's attachment and assistance to Old Edwards and his family, and on his hopeless love for a wealthy young woman from the district, Miss Walton. Ultimately Harley succumbs to a mysterious, hysterical illness ("though he had no formed complaint, his health was manifestly on the decline," p. 135) and is mourned by the narrator of the tale as well as Miss Walton.

As this brief summary suggests, the novel's basic strategy is to pit Harley against the forces of modern commercial life. This is an unequal struggle, and one that Harley is bound to lose. The text repeatedly reiterates the opposition between Harley as a principled and superlatively sensitive respondent to others' suffering, and the people surrounding him who are concerned exclusively with acquisition and social status. From servants to local merchants to British traders abroad, Mackenzie represents the spirit of the age as a restless and avaricious one, indifferent to any considerations but those of profit and vulgar display. In this climate the sentimentalist is something of an anachronism, however noble, whose powerlessness and marginalization is drummed home in episode after episode. He laments, but usually can do little to prevent or redress the wrongs he observes.

Take for example Harley's outraged response to "the mouldering walls of a ruined house" that had formerly sheltered a village school:

> "Oh heavens!" he cried, "what do I see: silent, unroofed, and desolate! Are all thy gay tenants gone? do I hear their hum no more? Edwards, look there, look there! The scene of my infant joys, my earliest friendships, laid waste and ruinous! That was the very school where I was boarded when you were at South-hill; 'tis but a twelvemonth since I saw it standing, and its benches filled with cherubs: that opposite side of the road was the green on which they sported; see it now ploughed up! I would have given fifty times its value to have saved it from the sacrilege of that plough ... I shall never see the sward covered with its daisies ... I have sat ... within ... and been more blest—Oh! Edwards, infinitely more blest, than ever I shall be again." (Ch. XXXV)

The scene contains obvious echoes of the greed of the lordly "improving" landscapers attacked in Goldsmith's poem "The Deserted Village" (1770), which Mackenzie had read and admired, and, like it, comments on the displacements brought about by the many Enclosure Acts transforming the British countryside through the course of the eighteenth century.[1] But its main impact is to demonstrate both the intensity of the man of feeling's wishes that things were otherwise, and the equally strong conviction that he cannot do anything about it.

As this scene demonstrates, *The Man of Feeling* is remarkable both for showcasing the situations and attitudes of the sentimental novel, and for suggesting a certain weariness—even despair—at the inadequacy of the form to the task of righting the many social wrongs it observes. The tone is set with the powerful and

---

1 Enclosure Acts legalizing the appropriation by single land-owners of land formerly held by the community for its common use, or transferring control of open fields to various forms of cooperative or shared farming, were not new; but the pace and extent of enclosure increased dramatically between 1750 and 1820, when thousands of separate Enclosure Acts were passed, affecting a substantial percentage of the entire acreage of England and Wales. On the social upheaval and suffering that accompanied this reorganization of the countryside, see Roy Porter, *English Society in the Eighteenth Century*, revised edition (London: Penguin, 1990) 208-13, and Paul Langford, *A Polite and Commercial People: England 1727-1783* (Oxford: Oxford UP, 1992) 435-37.

strangely evocative melancholy of Mackenzie's introduction to the novel, in which the narrator's disappointment with a fruitless hunting expedition, the heat and stillness of the day, a solitary croaking bird and (again) some nearby ruins, "haunted" by a young woman, combine in a mournful tableau of decay and desolation.

The sight of ruins or abandoned houses in the text is indeed a general cue for passionate discourses against the forces of historical change, forces Mackenzie invariably represents as destroying the traditional structure and cohesion of social life. The introductory and schoolhouse scenes are representative episodes; the natural and social landscape of the novel are dotted with ruins, marked by absences. No modern advances improve the lives of the inhabitants. Instead we are given instances of the hardships wrought by improving landlords: Edwards, for example, has been forced off a farm that his family had occupied for generations because the owner, "who had lately got a London-attorney for his steward," decides to reapportion and consolidate his properties (ch. XXXIV). Nor do any hopeful youths rise up to replace the worthy old men—the human ruins—to whom Harley is apparently drawn, whose advanced age and broken-down state (Edwards) or death (Silton) signal the passing of a better time. The narrator makes of the empty chair of Ben Silton, now occupied by "my young lady's lap-dog," both a domestic memorial to the passing of such men and a further illustration of the frivolous practices and fashions of modern commercial society. The novel habitually, even obsessively, tends to characterize all forms of change in terms of loss and the decadence of modern manners. The death of Harley takes place in this atmosphere of general decline, and is its primary symptom.

On one level we can see Mackenzie here displaying that "*sentiment des ruines*" and intensity of feeling for a lost historical past associated with his slightly later Romantic contemporaries[1] and the work of his younger admirer Walter Scott. We will return below to this issue of historical consciousness and nostalgia, a particu-

---

1 The *sentiment des ruines* (a feeling for ruins), which finds deeper meanings and more profound effects in fragments and in broken, torn, or incomplete forms than in completeness, is not confined to Romanticism, but, according to Thomas MacFarland, reached a "special pitch of intensity" then. See MacFarland, *Romanticism and the Forms of Ruin: Wordsworth, Coleridge, and Modalities of Fragmentation* (Princeton: Princeton UP, 1981) 13-45. See also Christopher Woodward, *In Ruins* (New York: Pantheon, 2001).

larly compelling issue for eighteenth- and early nineteenth-century Scottish intellectuals. But there is also a more specific literary or novelistic dimension to the novel's insistent looking backwards. *The Man of Feeling* in particular, and sentimental fiction more broadly, in the determined preference for time past, define the sentimental novel itself as a kind of anti-*Bildungsroman*. The *Bildungsroman*, or novel of formation, developed in the later years of the eighteenth century to become, alongside the courtship novel, the dominant form of fictional prose narrative in the nineteenth century. Following the adventures and misadventures of a young and inexperienced protagonist like that of Goethe's *Wilhelm Meisters Lehrjahre* (1795-96), or Charles Dickens' *Great Expectations* (1860-61), the *Bildungsroman* shows how, in the course of time, experience, and reflection, the protagonist ultimately learns how to make his or her way in the world, adjusts or accommodates to its existing order, and finds a place in it. If, as Franco Moretti suggests, the *Bildungsroman* tends to represent as a norm a certain conciliation or adjustment of the individual's original ideals to match external requirements, to endorse "maturity" even if it indicates fairly radical compromise,[1] the sentimental novel is notably, even defiantly, dedicated to a refusal of such accommodation. Instead of a narrative of gradual growth toward maturity, the sentimental novel typically recounts, sympathetically, the experience of a character who does *not* wish to "grow up and find an active place in society."[2] Where the *Bildungsroman* represents the passage of time as a benign process, both marking and producing the individual progress(es) it celebrates, in the sentimental novel—and nowhere more dramatically than in the example of Mackenzie—the passage of time brings only loss and changes that are unquestionably for the worse.[3]

At the level of form, this results in certain distinctive strategies. Both Mackenzie and Laurence Sterne, for example, break up the flow of their narratives with gaps in the supposed manuscript (*The Man of Feeling* has fewer than twenty-five chapters and "fragments" out of a purported original fifty-six), interruptions, asides and interpolated fragments. Such features of the texts have multiple uses, helping to produce the air of spontaneity and authenticity that only

---

1 Franco Moretti, "Kindergarten," in *Signs Taken for Wonders: Essays in the Sociology of Literary Forms*, tr. Susan Fischer *et al.* (Verso: London, 1997) 174-78.
2 Starr 181-82.
3 Starr 182.

"a bundle of little episodes, put together without art" can guarantee, an effect that, as suggested earlier, is so important to the claim of sentimental fiction. Moreover, especially in the case of Sterne, such disruptions to the narrative also challenge realist conventions of representation, which demand a consistent chronology. But it also helps to disrupt the sense of time as progress or a factor in development of character. As Starr observes, the sentimental novelist is driven to such disruptions, "since narrative is always threatening to imply progress simply by unfolding in time" (181-82). Sterne's and Mackenzie's breaks and digressions work to undermine the importance of time to character or ideas of progress/improvement. What is a positive feature of time in the *Bildungsroman*, its status "as agent of growth and development— becomes in the sentimental novel its most malign feature: the power of time to transform boys into men and sons into husbands is the very thing that the sentimental novel tries to elude or deny."[1]

Mackenzie ensures that Harley does not succumb to this fate. Harley not only articulates a good deal of the novel's forceful critique of the forces of change and modernization he encounters on his rounds, but also himself appears immobilized in a position from which no change is possible. Marriage to Miss Walton would be a contradiction of his general principle of withdrawal, of living "sequestered from the ... multitude," (p. 119) and an entrance into the kinds of compromise and domestic trivia that is foreign to his constitutive, somewhat self-absorbed, gentle melancholy.[2] Instead,

---

1 Starr 181.
2 Hegel comments on the incompatibility and inevitable conflict between individual values and social reality that the *Bildungsroman* is in part created to negotiate and solve—thus:

"But in the modern world these fights are nothing more than 'apprenticeship,' the education of the individual into the realities of the present, and thereby they acquire their true significance. For the end of such apprenticeship consists in this, that the subject sows his wild oats, builds himself with his wishes and opinions into harmony with subsisting relationships and their rationality, enters the concatenation of the world, and acquires for himself an appropriate attitude to it. However much he may have quarrelled with the world, or been pushed about in it, in most cases at last he gets his girl and some sort of position, marries her, and becomes as good a Philistine as others. The woman takes charge of household management, children arrive, the adored wife, at first unique, an angel, behaves pretty much as all other wives do; the man's profession provides work and vexations, marriage brings domestic affliction—so here we have all the headaches of the rest of married folk." Hegel, *Aesthetics: Lectures on Fine Art*. Tr by T.M. Knox (Oxford: Clarendon, 1975, 2 vols.) I: 593.

he gently declines into unspecified illness and death: a conclusion which has an air of inevitability and appropriateness for the sentimentalist too sensitive and unbending to endure the harshness, corruption, and compromise of the world. The novel's concluding lines are indeed something of a manifesto on this irresolvable opposition of world and sentimentalist:

> I sometimes visit his grave; I sit in the hollow of the tree. It is worth a thousand homilies! Every nobler feeling rises within me! Every beat of my heart awakens a virtue!—but it will make you hate the world—No: there is such an air of gentleness around, that I can hate nothing; but as to the world—I pity the men of it.

Mackenzie and The Decline of Sentimentalism

As the preceding makes clear, and as the slightly later rise and success of the *Bildungsroman* itself attests, the sentimental novel was hardly a form calculated to educate readers in "the way of the world" in the manner, say, of the great nineteenth-century novels of Balzac or Dickens.

This unworldliness was an element that alarmed readers and critics of sentimental fiction, even those otherwise susceptible to its charms. Mackenzie's younger contemporary and admirer, Robert Burns, though he claimed to have honored *The Man of Feeling* to the point of wearing out two copies,[1] also testified to a certain unease about the possible effects of the novel on its readers. In a letter from 1790 he comments:

> From what book, moral or even Pious, will the susceptible young mind receive impressions more congenial to Humanity and Kindness, Generosity and Benevolence ... than from the simple affecting tale of poor Harley? Still, with all my admiration of Mckenzie's [sic] writings, I do not know if they are the fittest reading for a young Man who is about to set out ... to make his way into life ... [T]here may be a purity, a tenderness, a dignity ... which are of no use, nay in some degree, [are] absolutely disqualifying, for the truly important business of making a man's way into life."[2]

---

1 Anon., "Some Account of the Life and Writings of Robert Burns," *Scots Magazine* LIX (1797): 3.
2 Letter of 10 April 1790, in *The Letters of Robert Burns*, second edition, ed. G. Ross Roy, 2 vols. (Oxford: Clarendon P, 1985) 2:25.

The concern expressed by Burns and others among Mackenzie's admirers[1] was that a sentimental turn, however ennobling, tends to discourage the more necessary, practical attention to business matters necessary in an era of commercial expansion and social mobility. At least, necessary to the male subject: Burns' emphasis on the novel's "purity" and "tenderness" suggests there may be a place for it in the feminine, domestic sphere, where the model of heightened sensitivity to others' distress offered by sentimental fiction is not at odds with contemporary social ideals of femininity.[2]

The date of Burns' letter is significant. By the 1790s the dominance of sentimentalism as a literary form and as a mode of response was over, and by the 1820s it was something of a joke. Louisa Stuart's 1826 letter to Walter Scott, quoted below, added to her reminiscences about the tremendous impact of Mackenzie's novel on its first publication an account of the disappointments of a re-encounter some fifty-five years later. Rereading it with a group of friends, she comments, "I am afraid I perceived a sad change in it, or myself—which was worse; and the effect altogether failed. Nobody cried, and at some of the passages, the touches that I used to think so exquisite—Oh Dear! They laughed!... This circumstance has led me to reflect on the alterations of taste produced by time.... "[3]

A number of reasons have been adduced for the decline in popularity of the sentimental novel after 1790 or so. These include concerns among radicals and conservatives alike that it promoted an excessive sensibility which, according to the political perspective, either distracted readers from rational analysis and action, or fomented unrest, and its association with a foreign, French style

---

1   See, for example, Walter Scott observing, with a certain air of relief, of Henry Mackenzie in 1825: "No Man is less known from his writings. We would suppose a retired, modest somewhat affected man with a white handkerchief and a sigh ready for every sentiment. No such thing. H.M. is alert as a contracting tailor's needle in every sort of business—a politician and a sportsman." W.E.K. Anderson, *The Journal of Sir Walter Scott*, fourth edition (Oxford: Clarendon P, 1972) 26.

2   See Starr's discussion of gender in sentimental protagonists and his argument that in narratives centering on female characters embodying social ideals—for women—of innocence and sensibility, a "merging" of the sentimental novel and the *Bildungsroman* occurs (195-97).

3   In the *Private Letter-Books of Sir Walter Scott*, 273.

of delicacy (Mackenzie himself makes this connection in his *Lounger* no. 20 paper; see Appendix C) that became suspect especially after 1789 and the French Revolution. There is also an evident rejection of the idea of fiction needing to justify itself as a transparent form of moral education in the wake of the novel's rise in respectability and prestige in the late eighteenth and early nineteenth centuries, a development we will examine below.

Whatever the factors to which we ultimately ascribe the demise of sentimentalism, it is a fact that this rejection of sentimental literature remains in force to this day. We are in a distinctly post-sentimental age, at least as far as public discourse on literature goes, and while sentimentalism has remained a resource used with some power by writers like Dickens and film-makers like Spielberg, most readers, or at least most academically trained readers, do not seek opportunities to advertise their taste for or susceptibility to its tableaux of suffering. Modern critical response, until the last fifteen or so years, frequently showed a clear aversion to what was evidently perceived as the texts' tendency to spurious moralizing. In most surveys of the eighteenth-century novel before 1990 or so, sentimental fiction was dismissed for opening up no new or important path for the development of the novel, and disparaged for a sermonizing evidently perceived as irritating or hypocritical by scholars.[1] At the level of grand theory rather than specific historical studies of particular authors and moments there has been even more reluctance or distaste to deal with sentimental or moving literature. As Franco Moretti observed in 1981, "For over a century European intellectuals have been ashamed to talk about tears.... although there are numerous theories of the comic, many of them sired by prestigious names, silence reigns over the 'moving.'"[2] Only with the turn to a more historically-oriented form of criticism in the late 1980s, and a more active engagement on the part of critics with a broader range of non-canonical works and material culture, has sentimen-

---

1   See for example J.M.S. Tompkins, *The Popular Novel in England 1770-1800* (Lincoln: U of Nebraska P, 1961; first published 1932) v-vi, 1-5; and Ian Watt, *The Rise of the Novel* (Berkeley: U of California P, 1957) 174-75, 290. More recently Michael McKeon approvingly quotes comments on the "false morality" of the sentimental novel by some of its contemporary critics, in his *The Origins of the English Novel 1600-1740* (Baltimore: Johns Hopkins UP, 1987) 125-26.
2   Moretti, "Kindergarten" 157.

talism benefitted from more sustained, serious, and indeed sympathetic critical treatment.[1]

In describing reactions to sentimentalism we should acknowledge that the distaste for sentimental response is not only an aftereffect of the popularity of novels like *The Man of Feeling*. Even in the moment of sentimentalism's greatest popularity there was evident unease among readers of sentimental novels with the easy displays of emotion that have so clearly become a major barrier to audiences since the 1790s. Adam Smith (1759) and Anna Laetitia Barbauld (1773) both criticize sentimentalism's tendency to indulge readers' feelings of moral correctness while doing little to challenge the conditions under which its pitiable figures live.[2] Moreover, sentimental authors themselves frequently demonstrate ambivalence about what they are doing. Sterne constantly undercuts some of the most affecting and pathetic scenes in *A Sentimental Journey* by making them into jokes—fulsomely mourning a dead ass for example. Goldsmith retreats from the novel altogeth-

---

1   Some notable recent works in this scholarly reconsideration include John Mullan, *Sentiment and Sociability* (London: Oxford UP, 1988); Barbara Benedict, *Framing Feeling: Sentiment and Style in English Prose Fiction 1745-1800* (New York: AMS Press, 1994); Michael Bell, *Sentimentalism, Ethics and the Culture of Feeling* (New York: Palgrave, 2000) as well as the books by Janet Todd and Margaret Cohen cited above. G.J. Barker-Benfield's major historical study, *The Culture of Sensibility* (Chicago: U of Chicago P, 1992), has also given impetus to critical enquiry. In addition to this new wave of interest in sentimentalism, earlier works that gave serious attention to the phenomenon include R.F. Brissenden's *Virtue in Distress: Studies in the Novel of Sentiment from Richardson to de Sade* (London: Macmillan, 1974) and Ronald Paulson's study of satire and sentimentalism in *Satire and the Novel in Eighteenth-Century England* (New Haven: Yale UP, 1967).

2   Anna Laetitia Barbauld warns of the dangers of dulling readers' concerns about real-world suffering through the experience of repeatedly having "sensibility ... strongly called forth [in writings picturing distress] without any possibility of exerting itself in virtuous action.... Nothing is more dangerous.... at length the mind grows absolutely callous." J. Aikin and A.L. Aikin (Anna Laetitia Barbauld), "An Enquiry into Those Kinds of Distress which excite Agreeable Sensations," in Ioan Williams, ed. *Novel and Romance 1700-1800: A Documentary Record*, (New York: Barnes and Noble, 1970) 289. Adam Smith, in *The Theory of Moral Sentiments* (1759) also caustically refers to the "whining and melancholy moralists" who promote simply "an affected and sentimental sadness which [is] perfectly useless to social life." Smith, *The Theory of Moral Sentiments*, ed. D.D. Raphael and A.L. Macfie (Oxford: Oxford UP, 1976) 140.

er after writing *The Vicar of Wakefield* and turns to poetic and dramatic composition quite different in tone from his novel. In Mackenzie's case there is a similar career move—an abandonment of fiction by 1777 for other forms, chiefly journalism.

In this new role Mackenzie composed a damning critique of sentimental fiction and its effects. Writing in *The Lounger* in 1785 he argues, with some debt to his predecessors Smith and Barbauld, that:

> In the enthusiasm of sentiment there is much the same danger as in the enthusiasm of religion, of substituting certain impulses and feelings of what may be called a visionary kind, in the place of real practical duties, which in morals, as in theology, we might not improperly denominate good works. In morals, as in religion, there are not wanting instances of refined sentimentalists, who are contented with talking of virtues which they never practise, who pay in words what they owe in actions; or, perhaps, what is fully as dangerous, who open their minds to impressions which never have any effect upon their conduct ... That creation of refined and subtile feeling, reared by the authors of the works to which I allude, has an ill effect, not only on our ideas of virtue, but also on our estimate of happiness. That sickly sort of refinement creates imaginary evils and distresses, and imaginary blessings and enjoyments, which embitter the common disappointments, and depreciate the common attainments of life.
>
> (*The Lounger* no. 20, Saturday 18 June 1785; see Appendix C)

The work of Mackenzie in particular and sentimentalism in general thus provides an especially dramatic demonstration of the ways in which fictional genres come into being, attract an audience, achieve a certain (tenuous) stability, and eventually decay. Having mentioned several possible factors in this decline, from the success of the *Bildungsroman* as a narrative model more effective in representing an idea of self-formation in the newly mobile societies of late eighteenth- and nineteenth-century Western Europe, to the distrust of emotionalism in the socio-political climate of the 1790s, we should also acknowledge the clash between sentimentalism and the dominant narrative style of the early nineteenth century: realism.

Sentimentalism vs. Realism and the Hierarchy of Genres in Eighteenth-Century Literature

Histories of the eighteenth- and nineteenth-century British novel have had a pronounced tendency to grant a special status to the emergence of realist narrative techniques—those which produce the sense of complex, evolving characters existing in continuous time, securely located in a physical world, and creating the semblance of an authentic account of individual experience—and in large part to conflate the fortunes and history of the early novel with that of realism. This critical tendency to identify the early novel with an effort to reach the goal of realist representation is not without historical support. Its reference points and justification can be found in the prefaces and essays of many eighteenth-century authors in Britain who frequently, and often militantly, affirmed their sense of historical newness and their objective mission as offering, precisely, a more realist representation of the world than their seventeenth-century predecessors. Virtually all of Daniel Defoe's novel prefaces, for example, present the explicit claim that his stories are worth reading because they are actually true. In the struggle of the early novel to gain acceptance and legitimacy as a genre, the claim that its tales were true (and therefore offered the kind of instruction and edification that only "true histories" could provide) was a powerful rhetorical maneuver. By 1750, this identification of the modern novel with realism, as opposed to the seventeenth-century romance, had become almost axiomatic in the criticism of writers like Samuel Johnson, who famously sets out the comparison between the fabulous romances of old and the familiar characters and settings of the new novel in his essay for the fourth issue of *The Rambler* (31 March 1750). There he contrasts "the romances formerly written, [in which] every transaction and sentiment was so remote from all that passes among men, that the reader was in very little danger of making any applications to himself," to the modern novel which had eliminated this gap between the world of fiction and the world of the reader, with readers now actively judging and regulating their behavior in reference to novelistic heroes. This sense of the novel as primarily concerned with an imitation of reality has been tremendously influential in the subsequent critical tradition of eighteenth-century novel criticism, for example in the the widely disseminated accounts of the novel before 1800 of J.M.S. Tompkins (1932) and, especially, Ian Watt (1957).[1]

However, as non-realist forms such as sentimental and gothic fiction attest, realism should not be identified with the genre of

---

1   For Tompkins and Watt see note 1, p. 20; for Samuel Johnson see his
      Selected Writings (London: Penguin, 1986) 149-53.

the novel itself. The domination of realism in discussions of the early English novel until quite recently has had the effect of pushing non-realist works to the margins, locating them as deviations from the task of developing convincing representations of reality rather than as separate, complex and compelling solutions to the diverse literary and social problems facing writers in the period. The problem of the dominance of the realist model is that in consigning other novelistic genres, like the sentimental, to marginal status, it has made it difficult to see the particular merits, meanings, and problematics of these other works. When we read literature of this sort, what Margaret Cohen (in describing French sentimental literature) calls literature "out of circulation," the barrier we are up against is that the readings we generate depend on an internalized "set of aesthetic expectations derived precisely from a history of reading the works that have *not* fallen out of circulation"[1]—that is, from works that largely fall in the canon of realist fiction: Defoe, Austen, Balzac and so on.

From our sampling of episodes (for example the schoolhouse scene, and the conclusion's lines on the intensity of emotions triggered in visiting Harley's grave) the primary difference between realism and sentimentalism is quite evident. Instead of making the (realist) claim that "this is how things are," the sentimental novel says, in effect, "this is how to feel," or perhaps, "this is how to derive a certain aesthetic pleasure from the experience of sympathy." The assumption in sentimental literature is that life and literature are linked, not through imitation, but through the belief that literature can shape and direct the way we live[2] and teach its readers what kind of response to produce in reaction to distress. What sentimental fiction offers is a literary practice that emphasizes a notion of sympathetic bonding and shared humanity, a sameness between observer and sufferer, rather than a representation of varied experience and reactions; an emphasis on conveying depth of feeling rather than on creating the impression of objective reportage; and a much greater focus than we find in other contemporary novels on getting the reader to feel the same way.

In its heyday the sentimental novel's tendency to instruct and model correct (emotional) responses for its readers had been a real force in the literary world. Presumably this ensemble of situations and techniques arose in response to particular social and formal

---

1 Cohen, *The Sentimental Education of the Novel* 21.
2 Todd, *Sensibility* 4.

problems,[1] and indeed the question of which intertwined social and literary factors led to the rise of sentimentalism has attracted even more commentary than the reasons for its decline. Perhaps the most frequently-cited recent explanation for the rise of the form has identified its emphasis on community and fellow-feeling or universal brotherhood as motivated by mid-century anxieties about social fragmentation in writers like David Hume, Adam Smith, Samuel Richardson and Mackenzie. Barker-Benfield has suggested a gradual replacement of male and aristocratic ethical standards and forms of public conduct by middle-class and feminine notions of propriety. Other sources frequently invoked include the ascent of Latitudinarian theology, with its emphasis on beneficence and goodwill, in the Church of England from the seventeenth century on; the influence of the works of Shaftesbury; the recognition of the importance of nerves in sensation in late seventeenth-century physiology, with a corresponding fascination with the integration of moral and physiological study; and the development of a culture of organized philanthropy in eighteenth-century England. Not to be provincial, there is also the example of the French: between 1750 and 1770 ten of the top-selling thirty authors in English were French, including major proponents of the sentimental style such as Rousseau and Marmontel, the latter explicitly invoked as exemplar by Mackenzie in the introduction to *The Man of Feeling*.[2]

All of these explanations for the rise of the genre of sentimental

---

1   For a discussion of the general problem of the genesis of genres see Cohen, *The Sentimental Education of the Novel*, 7ff. On this and broader issues of genre and struggles dividing the literary field see Pierre Bourdieu, *The Rules of Art: Genesis and Structure of the Literary Field*, tr. Susan Emanuel (Stanford: Stanford UP, 1992).

2   On sentiment as a response to the anxieties of establishing community, see Mullan, *Sentiment and Sociability*. On bourgeois and feminine challenges to aristocratic and male standards of conduct and response see Barker-Benfield, *The Culture of Sensibility*. On the influence of Latitudinarianism see R.S. Crane, "Suggestions toward a Genealogy of the 'Man of Feeling,'" *ELH* 1:3 (1934): 205-30; on the impact of Shaftesbury see the early statement by C.A. Moore, "Shaftesbury and the Ethical Poets in England," *PMLA* 31 (1916): 264-325; for the physiological thesis see G.S. Rousseau, "Nerves, Spirits and Fibres: Towards Defining the Origins of Sensibility," *Studies in the Eighteenth Century* III, ed. R.F. Brissenden and J.C. Eade (Toronto: U of Toronto P, 1976) 137-57; on the link to organized philanthropy see R.F. Brissenden, *Virtue in Distress* 79-81. The figures for translations of French literary works in eighteenth-century England are James Raven's, quoted in Franco Moretti, *Atlas of the European Novel* (1999) 156.

fiction and writing on sympathy generally have considerable substance, though questions still remain, for example about the long gap between some of these phenomena and the appearance of a sentimental literature in the middle decades of the eighteenth century. More importantly, these explanations tend to say little about what we have identified as the sentimental novel's distinguishing feature: not simply the fascination with representing distress and the response of the beholder, but its stress on using these situations to *educate* the reader and mold his or her response. To illuminate this dominant feature of sentimental fiction, it is instead more helpful to turn to another discourse closely intertwined with eighteenth-century fiction, contemporary aesthetic theory.

When we look at mid- to late-century theoretical commentaries on literature and aesthetics, one of the most frequently canvassed topics is that of the hierarchy of genres of prose narrative. One of the more obvious differences between the eighteenth-century literary field and our own is the way in which fictional texts, despite the dominant position they have since come to attain, were by no means the most prestigious form of narrative writing in the period. In prose narrative before 1800 the pre-eminent form is *history*, not fiction. Though "the modern restriction of literature to works of imagination has [now] divided history and other non-fiction genres from a redefined literary field," we should keep in mind, as Mark Salber Phillips argues, the central importance of historical texts to the literary system of our period.[1] In this hierarchy of prose genres, history writing is accorded a value far in excess of any novel or fictional text. Mackenzie's friend Adam Smith, for one, lays out the reasons why in his *Lectures on Rhetoric and Belles Lettres* (1762-3):

> The design of historicall writing is not merely to entertain ... besides that it has in view the instruction of the reader. It sets before us the more interesting and important events of human life, points out the causes by which these events were brought about[,] and by this means points out to us by what manner and method we may produce similar good effects or avoid Similar bad ones.[2]

---

1 Mark Salber Phillips, *Society and Sentiment: Genres of Historical Writing in Britain, 1740-1820* (Princeton: Princeton UP, 2000) xiii.
2 Adam Smith, *Lectures on Rhetoric and Belles Lettres*, ed. J.C. Bryce. Vol. IV of *The Glasgow Edition of the Works of Adam Smith* (Oxford: Oxford UP, 1983) 90.

Smith's account stresses that the privileged status of history does not, or does not *only*, lie in its truth claims, its account of how things really were. This truthfulness itself is accorded a value precisely insofar as it, and it alone, reliably provides moral instruction for the reader. Its power and importance lie in its ability not to accurately report the world (the claim of realist fiction), but to mold the future conduct of that reader. This reader is understood to be a future actor in the public life of the nation and events of historic significance; the content of his reading therefore is of some import.

Smith continues:

> In this ... [history] differs from a Romance the Sole view of which is to entertain ... a well contrived Story may be as interesting and entertaining as any real one: the causes which brought about the several incidents that are narrated may all be very ingeniously contrived and well adapted to their severall ends, but still as the facts are not such as have really existed, the end proposed by history will not be answered. The facts must be real, otherwise they will not assist us in our future conduct, by pointing out the means to avoid or produce any event. Feigned Events and the causes contrived for them, as they did not exist, can not inform us of what happened in former times, nor of consequence assist us in a plan of future conduct.[1]

Future conduct then is the mark by which narratives must be judged, and fiction, understood as committed to entertainment rather than instruction, naturally rates low. But Smith's assertion—that only histories can *help* guide our future behavior, is rather disingenuous in implying that fiction, because it does not deal with actual lives, therefore exerts no influence on reader conduct. Most eighteenth-century writers on aesthetic questions believed that fictional narratives, and especially contemporary novels, were highly likely to affect the future conduct of many of their readers, indeed that they were more likely than any other form of writing to do so—especially if those readers were young and/or female. There is an entire body of literature on this topic, of which the anxious reactions to Samuel Richardson's two great novels of the 1740s, *Pamela* and *Clarissa*, and the 1750 *Rambler*

---

1 Smith, *Lectures* 91.

essay by Samuel Johnson cited above are but two of the many examples that could be quoted.[1]

What we encounter here, in short, is the effective privileging of history, granted social force through its association with "active, adult male reader[s] whose interests, ... capacities [and social role] were contrasted to the youthful, female, and private readership ascribed to the novel"—even if, in practice, the readership for the two genres overlapped.[2] Historical literature, Smith and others claim, possesses an educative, improving, transforming force which fictive tales lack; but it would seem that this is more of an assumption related to who is reading history and fiction than anything innate to the genres themselves.[3]

The point I want to make in this brief excursus into the history-fiction nexus as Smith and other mid-century theorists see it, is how important the value of history's education of its reader was understood to be. Historical narratives thereby claimed seriousness and status at a time when the novel was frequently dismissed as merely "women's reading." This educational claim proves to be crucial in reconstructing the logic of sentimentality, describing the status and condition that sentimental texts aspire to. Like history in Smith's rendering, sentimental fiction too takes as its highest goal the molding of its readers, teaching them, through its repeated staging of scenes of suffering mediated through the reactions of the sentimental observer, how to respond to suffering, how to regulate their feelings, develop an appropriate sensibility to the experiences of others, and form "a plan of future conduct." Literally meant as a sentimental education, the sentimental novel in its characteristic efforts to direct the response of its readers is essentially attempting to follow the lead of the prestigious, mas-

---

1   For a brief sampling see Charlotte Lennox's satirical novel *The Female Quixote* (1752), the numerous works excerpted in Ioan Willams' *Novel and Romance 1700-1800* (see note 2, p. 21), and John Tinnon Taylor's *Early Opposition to the English Novel* (New York: Columbia UP, 1943).

2   Phillips, *Society and Sentiment* 103.

3   Smith's and Mackenzie's contemporary and fellow Scot Lord Kames, for example, in his widely influential *Elements of Criticism* (1762), explicitly dismisses the idea that there is any difference between real and fictional narratives in terms of their emotional impact on the reader. See Kames' discussion of "Emotions caused by Fiction" in *Elements of Criticism* (London: Routledge/Thoemmes Press, 1993; reprint of 1785 edition. 2 vols.) I: 88-104.

culine-coded genre, history, developing both from the literary possibilities of sympathy *and* as a solution to the problem of establishing the novel itself as a legitimate genre.

The consequence of this for writers like Mackenzie, Sterne, Sarah Scott and others is that the direction of a reader's future behavior—not the faithful report of experience of the realist aesthetic—is understood as the ultimate and most honorable goal of the novelist. The fiction-history link and its gender associations helps explain why we see this insistent emphasis on educating the reader's feelings in sentimental novels, and, equally, is at least a partial explanation for its decline in popularity toward the end of the century, as novelists' stock rose. When we read the newly self-confident assessments of the cultural place of the novel in later writers such as Frances Burney and Jane Austen—the latter of whom famously contrasts the sophistication and brilliance of the novelist with the dreariness of the "nine-hundredth abridger of the History of England" in the fifth chapter of *Northanger Abbey* (written in the late 1790s, first published in 1818)—we are seeing an epochal shift of literary hierarchies. The combination of rich social observation, elegance of style, and originality which Austen describes as the major concern of the contemporary novelist[1] clearly marks the end of the sentimental conception of novel as moral preceptor.

In describing this rivalry of genres I don't mean to suggest that the literary or novelistic field of the late eighteenth century can be understood as territory contested simply by two combatants, sentimentalism and realism. Rather than this kind of opposition, the literary field at any time is no doubt more of a struggle of multiple possibilities, styles, sub-genres (in this period including, for

---

1 "[W]hile the abilities of the nine-hundredth abridger of the History of England ... are eulogized by a thousand pens,—there seems almost a general wish of decrying the capacity and undervaluing the labour of the novelist, and of slighting the performances which have only genius, wit, and taste to recommend them.... 'It is really very well for a novel.'—Such is the common cant ... 'It is only Cecilia, or Camilla, or Belinda;' [novels, the first two by Frances Burney, the third by Maria Edgeworth] or, in short, only some work in which the greatest powers of the mind are displayed, in which the most thorough knowledge of human nature, the happiest delineation of its varieties, the liveliest effusions of wit and humour, are conveyed to the world in the best chosen language." Jane Austen, *Northanger Abbey* (second edition) ed. Claire Grogan (Peterborough, ON: Broadview Press, 2002) 59-60.

example, the gothic, the comic epic of Henry Fielding, the satiric social observation of Tobias Smollett, the pornographic fantasy of John Cleland, as well as the options of sentimentalism and realism).[1] Instead, my goal in counterposing these two examples is to show just how a certain set of expectations about the historical role or tendency of the eighteenth-century novel as essentially to do with establishing realism has contributed to the difficulty of seeing how non-realist genres like the sentimental actually work, and what the latter's literary historical situation and value are.

Sentimentalism and Colonialism: Mackenzie as Social Critic

Sentimentalism, then, is above all concerned with educating the reader, taking as a primary goal the formation of a newly sensitized subject whose bonds of sympathy with other members of his or her community are reinforced by meditations on the sympathetic spectacles they encounter in the pages of the sentimental text. Mackenzie and his fellow novelists essentially created idealized fictional communities where the difficulties created by differences and inequities between class, gender, and race could be played out and resolved, transcended by sentimental communion. However, there is an internal feature of the genre, one especially noticeable in *The Man of Feeling*, that puts a strain on this notion of community and also, I would suggest, makes the genre particularly susceptible to collapse from within. This is what one critic calls the "plot of fracture"[2] which runs through the genre. Despite the commitment to communality and bonds of sympathy that are so important to the genre, the sentimental novel also frequently

---

1   The first gothic novel in English, *The Castle of Otranto* by Horace Walpole (1717-97), was published in 1764; a flood of gothic fictions followed. The novels of Henry Fielding (1707-54), including *Joseph Andrews* (1742) and the immensely popular *Tom Jones* (1749), were avowed attempts to establish a new literary form, the "comic epic-poem in prose" whose features were described by Fielding in his preface to *Joseph Andrews*. The enormous success of *Memoirs of a Woman of Pleasure*, also known as *Fanny Hill* (1748-49), by John Cleland (1709-89) made it the best-known pornographic novel of its time. Tobias Smollett (1721-71) published half a dozen satiric novels from the late 1740s on, culminating in his final work, *The Expedition of Humphry Clinker* (1771).
2   For a discussion of this dynamic in French sentimental literature of the early nineteenth century see Cohen, *The Sentimental Education of the Novel*, 10f.

features a sentimental protagonist whose relations to the social collective are strained and who is prevented by his extreme sensibility from participation in practical social life.[1] The contradiction embedded in this phenomenon—between the understanding of the sentimental novel as mechanism of social bonding and education, and the problem of an excessive sensibility that unfits the sentimental individual for life in society—is nowhere more evident than in *The Man of Feeling*, and in Harley's odd status as both exemplary observer and marginalized misfit.

Mackenzie's novel is remarkable in the degree to which it tends both to support Harley's critiques (his speculations on why the local schoolhouse was razed for example, quoted above, turn out to be correct), and to subvert their effectiveness by suggesting their futility, excessiveness, or error. This is an observable feature of other sentimental fictions—the essential "goodness" negated by the hopeless naïveté and smugness of Goldsmith's Primrose in *The Vicar of Wakefield* comes to mind, for example—but is pushed to its limit in *The Man of Feeling*. Needless to say, such a combination poses certain problems for evaluating the status of Harley's fairly frequent criticisms of contemporary British society. He may clearly be right in his indignation at the destruction of the schoolhouse, or in his assessment of his fellow travelers in the carriage back to Scotland; but his overly trusting acceptance of the stories of various characters and sharpers he meets in London, including an inmate of the Bethlehem hospital for the insane (Bedlam), and the comical errors he makes based on his supposed ability to read character from faces, make it clear that Harley is a well-intentioned but often wildly inaccurate interpreter of character and situation. His assessments simply can't be accepted at face value. This is a general problem in the text, but one which becomes particularly telling in connection with Harley's, and Mackenzie's, critique of British colonialism in the latter part of the novel.

The British empire grew prodigiously over the course of Mackenzie's lifetime, losing its American colonies after 1776 to be sure, but retaining or gaining control in India, Australia, eastern Canada, and Jamaica, for example. The domestic reaction to these facts was complex, ranging from extreme anxiety about the problem of British identity in a new empire and a feared drain on the national population by emigration, to a delighted sense of vastly

---

1 Todd, *Sensibility* 95-104.

increased global power and commercial opportunity. The role of literature and culture in what might be considered primarily military and economic developments, as Edward Said has famously pointed out, was to make it possible to imagine colonialism as an established fact: "the enterprise of empire depends upon *the idea of having an empire*, ... and all kinds of preparations are made for it within a culture."[1] In Said's view, the creation of an empire depended on a certain control of narrative:

> The main battle in imperialism is over land, of course; but when it came to who owned the land, who had the right to settle and work on it, who kept it going, who won it back, and who now plans its future—these issues were reflected, contested, and even for a time decided in narrative. As one critic has suggested, nations themselves *are* narrations. The power to narrate, or to block other narratives from forming and emerging, is very important to culture and imperialism, and constitutes one of the main connections between them.[2]

The contribution of sentimental literature to the imagining of empire, and especially to the issue of slavery in British colonies (not abolished till 1833), has recently begun to draw considerable critical attention, most notably by Markman Ellis. Ellis shows that pro-slavery interests and abolitionist discourse in the period do not fully account for the range of Enlightenment-era positions on slavery. Between these two opposing views is a third position, "amelioration," that "argues for the mitigation of the conditions of slavery but not its abolition" (87) and Ellis shows fairly persuasively that this is the position that most sentimental fiction-writers adopt, including Mackenzie in his later novel *Julia de Roubigné*, (see excerpts in Appendix C), Sarah Scott, and Laurence Sterne. One might be surprised to think that a fictional genre apparently dedicated to honoring bonds of universal brotherhood and the quality of distress of others could make its peace with the institution of slavery. However, as close readings of the texts reveal, the sentimental novel as a genre, with its habit of drawing attention to the feeling heart of the observer rather than victim in spectacles of distress, focuses on the reluctant colonial

---

1 Edward Said, *Culture and Imperialism* (New York: Vintage Books, 1993) 11.
2 Said xii-xiii.

master and his sufferings rather than on the experience of the slave.[1] The kind of master we see in Sarah Scott and Mackenzie, taking a deep interest in the welfare of his slaves, presumably permitted the reader to simultaneously acknowledge slavery as a problem while showing how individual slave-owners were exempt from blame. Such a procedure, clearly, is likely to do less to challenge the conditions under which its victims suffer than to reassure those who look on and respond with sympathy of their moral sensitivity, a criticism leveled at sentimental literature from the eighteenth century to the present.

The claim that the fiction of Mackenzie and other sentimental writers is simply a mildly hand-wringing acceptance of colonialism and slavery rather than a forum for real exploration hits home in the instance of *Julia de Roubigné* and the other examples Ellis proposes. However, though this last novel may indeed suggest a rather complicitous relation to the darker facts of British colonial expansion, Mackenzie's general response to British colonialism is actually more complicated than this. His case is especially compelling because all three of his novels feature analyses, often highly critical ones, of Britain's colonial role. In *Julia de Roubigné*, set in France and its colonies, the heroine's lover Savillon leaves France to make his fortune and travels to his uncle's plantation in Martinique, where his first reactions to the cruelties of slavery are sharply critical, even if the narrative plots his rapid acceptance of the "necessity" of slavery. Mackenzie's second novel, *The Man of the World* (1773), incorporates a detailed and admiring portrait of the fortitude and dignity of Native Americans, contrasted with the shabby behavior of their English masters, given by an unfortunate convict, Billy Annesley (see Appendix C). *The Man of Feeling* itself includes a couple of lengthy protests against Britain's crude exploitation of her subjects in India and the West Indies, offered both by Harley and his friend, Old Edwards. Edwards' tale of British rapacity and brutality confronting the dignity, generosity and self-command of the natives of the East Indies in Chapter XXXIV is amplified by Harley a couple of chapters later when he launches a scathing critique of British colonial policy in India (no doubt partly influenced by coverage of the recent trial, in 1767, of

---

1   See Ellis's reading of Laurence Sterne's correspondence with Ignatius Sancho, Mackenzie's *Julia de Roubigné* (1777), and Sarah Scott's *Sir George Ellison* (1766) in *The Politics of Sensibility* (Cambridge: Cambridge UP, 1996), chs. 2 and 3 (49-128).

Robert Clive for corruption and abuse of power in India—see note 1, p. 118)

"Edwards," said he, "I have a proper regard for the prosperity of my country ... but I cannot throw off the man so much, as to rejoice at our conquests in India. You tell me of immense territories subject to the English: I cannot think of their possessions, without being led to enquire by what right they possess them. They came there as traders, bartering the commodities they brought for others which their purchasers could spare; and however great their profits were, they were then equitable. But what title have the subjects of another kingdom to establish an empire in India? to give laws to a country where the inhabitants received them on the terms of friendly commerce? You say they are happier under our regulations than the tyranny of their own petty princes. I must doubt it, from the conduct of those by whom these regulations have been made. They have drained the treasuries of Nabobs, who must fill them by oppressing the industry of their subjects. Nor is this to be wondered at, when we consider the motive upon which those gentlemen do not deny their going to India. The fame of conquest, barbarous as that motive is, is but a secondary consideration [to wealth] ... When shall I see a commander return from India in the pride of honourable poverty?—You describe the victories they have gained; they are sullied by the cause in which they fought: you enumerate the spoils of those victories; they are covered with the blood of the vanquished!

"Could you tell me of some conqueror giving peace and happiness to the conquered? ... did he use his power to gain security and freedom to the regions of oppression and slavery? did he endear the British name by examples of generosity, which the most barbarous or most depraved are rarely able to resist? ... These were laurels which princes might envy—which an honest man would not condemn! (117-19)

Harley's attack on British colonial policy in India refers to the recent violent annexation of India, transforming it from trading partner to subjugated nation with the Battle of Plassey in 1757, and to the profiteering and cruel treatment of native Indians by the British East India Company that led to public scandals and trials in England in the 1760s and '80s. Mackenzie here gives a sample of the intense opposition at home to British imperial expansion, even at the moment of what seems, retrospectively, its apparently inevitable acceleration, among the many British citizens and intellectuals unconvinced of the purported "civilizing" mission of colonialism.

As a Scot, of course, Mackenzie's critique of colonialism has a particular charge, for since the 1707 Act of Union with Great Britain which merged the legislatures of the two countries, with Scots representatives henceforth sitting as a small minority in Westminster, Scotland occupied an uneasy place in relation to England and the entity of Great Britain. Both part of Britain, with great hopes of modernizing and prospering alongside its much wealthier southern neighbor, and frontier, part of the "Celtic fringe" eliciting mixed fascination and fear among metropolitan English writers like Samuel Johnson, Scotland's peculiar situation gave rise to an intense series of reflections on cultural identity and political domination among its writers and philosophers from David Hume, Adam Smith and Lord Kames to Mackenzie, Robert Burns and Walter Scott. In this atmosphere of enquiry, and of ambivalence about Scotland's true status and ties to England, Mackenzie's insistent return to the question of the goals and nature of British colonialism in all three of his novels is a significant reminder of the urgency and complexity of these issues for late eighteenth- and early nineteenth-century Scottish intellectuals.

The conclusions of this enquiry however remain ambiguous. While Mackenzie's depictions of colonial misrule and greed in *The Man of Feeling* and *The Man of The World* show a distinctly cold-eyed analysis of the gap between Britain's imperial rhetoric and its actual practices, overall it must be said that Mackenzie tends to undercut the force of the critiques his characters offer. In the instance quoted above from *The Man of Feeling*, for example, the fact that the critique of the British in India is articulated by Harley, a figure the text has clearly established as too virtuous and principled for this world, already slightly weakens the force of the attack; and to intensify the ambiguity as to where he stands on the issue even further, Mackenzie places the critique in a chapter entitled "The Man of Feeling Talks of What he does not Understand." Similarly, the unflattering comparison between grasping European colonizers and noble native Americans in *The Man of the World* is made by a relatively minor character who is otherwise represented as extremely naive and rather ineffectual. Most strikingly, Savillon, in *Julia de Roubigné*, loses his horror at slavery in a project of improving his uncle's slaves' working conditions, the logic of the text suggesting that it is not the institution of slavery so much as the poor regulation of plantations that should be the target of critique and reform.

This last text indeed goes beyond ambiguity into an apparent acceptance of the institution of slavery, the reason for its targeting by Ellis. One factor that should be acknowledged here is, of course, that of race. The fellow-feeling, however ambiguously expressed, that Mackenzie shows his various characters experiencing for oppressed Indians and native peoples of the New World, seems not to exist for African slaves, reminding us that in an Enlightenment largely committed to ideas of European racial superiority[1] Africans are frequently ranked lower, and seen as more culturally distant, than other non-European peoples. The figure of the noble Indian and islander haunts the contemporary writings of Jean-Jacques Rousseau, the Pacific explorer Captain James Cook, and, in an especially relevant example, Adam Smith. Smith's respect for the hardiness and primitive self-sufficiency of the "North American Savage" is a notable feature of his reflections on history in his 1759 *Theory of Moral Sentiments*, a work widely circulated in the decades after its publication and which Mackenzie appears to have read attentively. A sense of kinship with, and admiration for, ancient virtues ("a heroic and unconquerable firmness") emerges in Smith's comments on North American Indians as living reminders of a lost, honorable way of life. In Smith's intense nostalgia for such "primitive" societies, which he compares with the early stages of European culture, and the evident though implicit parallels to traditional Highland Scottish society, we catch a glimpse of the intense interest in historical process and the debates about what is gained *and* lost in historical "progress" in late eighteenth-century

---

1 For example: "I am apt to suspect the negroes and in general all other species of men (for there are four or five different kinds) to be naturally inferior to the whites. There never was a civilized nation of any other complexion than white, nor even any individual eminent either in action or speculation ... " David Hume, "Of National Characters" (excerpt), in Emmanuel Chukwudi Eze, ed., *Race and the Enlightenment: A Reader* (Oxford: Blackwell, 1997) 33.

Scotland.[1] Mackenzie's first two novels show a similar willingness to see certain indigenous peoples as representing the lost virtues and grandeur of pre-modern European life. But brotherhood with African slaves appears to have been beyond his imaginative reach.

Conclusion

Mackenzie, then, undercuts Harley as social critic, in part because he has not yet resolved the problem of his own relation to the British imperialism Harley condemns. There is also one further way in which Harley's uncertain status as social critic is significant: it articulates a more general concern felt by Mackenzie and many other critical readers of sentimental texts about the limited power of literary representations of distress or injustice to effect any kind of practical social change. Seen in this light, Harley's ineffectual tirades collectively appear as a displacement of Mackenzie's sense of the powerlessness of literary texts as social interventions. This anxiety takes a very concrete form in *The Man of Feeling*, that of the mutilated, fragile, abandoned text, an object which is encountered over and over again in Mackenzie's pages: we see the manuscript of the novel itself used as gun wadding by the curate in the Introduction, the poem to "Lavinia" (Miss Walton) left behind as insulation for the handle of a tea-kettle (Chapter XL), the treatise on Common Law reduced to a mere weight for pressing linens (Chapter XII), and poems scratched into the "brittle tenure" of windowpanes and drinking-glasses (Chapter XXXIII). The sense of text that these episodes produce—merely a vulnerable, fragile physical object always likely to be lost, or to fail to reach its intended audience—is a remarkably modest, even self-defeating one.

Mackenzie airs some of his concerns about the social agency or effectiveness of literature within the novel, in the discussion he has Harley and Ben Silton conduct on literature and society in Chap-

---

1 See Adam Smith, *The Theory of Moral Sentiments*, ed. D.D. Raphael and A.L. Macfie (note 2, p. 21), 282-88. On Adam Smith and his contributions to the Scottish Historical School see Ronald Meek, "The Scottish Contribution to Marxist Sociology" in his *Economics and Ideology and Other Essays* (London: Chapman and Hall, 1967) 34-50; and Maureen Harkin, "Natives and Nostalgia: The Problem of the 'North American Savage' in Adam Smith's Historiography" in *Scottish Studies Review* 3:1 (2002): 21-32.

ter XXXIII. The general conclusion of their exchange is that a personal taste for literature is simply part of an unprofitable orientation to curiosity, pleasure and sympathy rather than to the practical requirements of business. The claim that literature does not educate or elevate, but instead is simply part of a tendency, a syndrome of unworldliness, of course goes against the grain of the sentimental project as we have described it, and Mackenzie's sense of conflict about what he is accomplishing with *The Man of Feeling* is palpable. The conflict about what he is doing and what fiction in general *can* do in social life was a topic Mackenzie also raised repeatedly in letters he wrote to various correspondents in the course of finishing the novel. There he alternates between expressing the hope that the new novel would serve "the cause of Virtue"[1] in educating a large readership, and the (contrary) suggestion that the work was composed for and addressed only to a small group of like-minded readers.[2] In light of the intensity of the struggle in Mackenzie between these incompatible positions on what fiction means, and does, in the social world, his abandonment of the novel form after 1777 for a journalism of social observation comes as little surprise.

These profound and unresolved conflicts heighten the novel's distinctive atmosphere of melancholy, nostalgia, powerlessness, and the futility of effort. In grappling with the problems of the functions served by fiction and the representation of distress, Mackenzie gives memorable substance to the catalogue of the quintessential situations and responses of sentimental fiction offered in *The Man of Feeling*.

---

1 See letters of 23 July 1770 and 23 November 1771 to James Elphinston in Appendix B.
2 See correspondence with Elizabeth Rose of Kilravock in Appendix B.

Henry Mackenzie: A Brief Chronology

1745   Henry Mackenzie born 6 August (new style) in Edin-
        burgh, firstborn child of Dr. Joshua Mackenzie, a pros-
        perous physician, and Margaret (née Rose) of Kilrav-
        ock, daughter of the sixteenth baron of Kilravock. On
        the same day, Charles Edward Stuart, the "Young Pre-
        tender" lands in Scotland, beginning the Jacobite
        rebellion of 1745-46.
1747   Publication of first two volumes of Samuel Richardson's
        Clarissa. Concluding five volumes published in 1748.
1749   Publication of Henry Fielding's *Tom Jones*.
1751   Mackenzie enters Edinburgh High School.
1756   First performance of John Home's popular tragedy,
        Douglas, in Edinburgh in December.
1758   Mackenzie enters Edinburgh University. Publication
        of David Hume's *Enquiry Concerning Human
        Understanding*.
1759   Death of Mackenzie's mother. Adam Smith publishes
        The Theory of Moral Sentiments. First two volumes of
        Laurence Sterne's *Tristram Shandy* (-1767) published.
1760   Hugh Blair made Professor of Rhetoric at Edinburgh
        University. James Macpherson publishes his first
        Ossianic text, *Fragments of Ancient Poetry*.
1761   Mackenzie articles as law clerk for five years to George
        Inglis, King's Attorney in Exchequer. Jean-Jacques
        Rousseau's *La Nouvelle Heloise* published.
1763   Mackenzie's first publication, a poem, "Happiness," in
        the *Scots Magazine*.
1764   Mackenzie publishes "Duncan," a ballad, in the *Scots
        Magazine*.
1765   Mackenzie publishes "Kenneth," a ballad, in the *Scots
        Magazine*. Mackenzie admitted attorney in Court of
        Exchequer in Scotland in November and proceeds to
        London to study English law.
1765-68 In London studying English law.
1766   Publication of Oliver Goldsmith's *The Vicar of Wakefield*.
1768   Publication of Laurence Sterne's *A Sentimental Jour-
        ney*. Mackenzie returns to Edinburgh and becomes law
        partner of George Inglis. First mention of *The Man of
        Feeling* in Mackenzie's correspondence.

1769	Mackenzie completes tragedy, *Virginia, or the Roman Father*. Unpublished.
1771	April: *The Man of Feeling* published, London. First edition quickly sells out; second edition published in August. May: Mackenzie publishes *The Pursuits of Happiness*, semi-satirical poem. Tobias Smollett's *Humphry Clinker* and James Beattie's *The Minstrel* published.
1773	February: Mackenzie publishes second novel, *The Man of the World*. March: First performance of Mackenzie's tragedy, *The Prince of Tunis*, in Edinburgh. Mackenzie purchases legal practice in Court of Exchequer from his partner, George Inglis.
1774	Publication of Goethe's *Die Leiden des Jungen Werthers* (*The Sorrows of Young Werther*).
1776	Mackenzie marries Penuel Grant, daughter of a baronet. Adam Smith publishes *The Wealth of Nations*. Death of David Hume.
1777	*Julia de Roubigné*, Mackenzie's third and final (epistolary) novel, published. Mackenzie joins the Mirror Club, an Edinburgh literary society.
1779	23 January, *The Mirror*, a twice-weekly journal (modelled on Addison and Steele's *Tatler*, 1709-11, and *Spectator*, 1711-12), edited and largely written by Mackenzie, begins publication in Edinburgh.
1780	*The Mirror* ceases publication 27 May. Society of Antiquaries of Scotland founded.
1783	Mackenzie a founding member of the Royal Society of Edinburgh.
1784	February, Mackenzie's play *The Shipwreck*, an adaptation of George Lillo's *Fatal Curiosity*, is given one performance at Covent Garden Theatre, London. Mackenzie helps form the Highland Society of Scotland.
1785	5 February, *The Lounger*, a twice weekly journal edited and largely written by Mackenzie, begins publication.
1786	Robert Burns's *Poems in the Scottish Dialect* published. *The Lounger* no. 97 (9 December) carries an enthusiastic review of the collection, helping to establish his reputation. Boswell publishes *Journal of A Tour to the Hebrides*.
1787	6 January, *The Lounger* ceases publication.

1788	April, "Account of the German Theatre" read before the Royal Society of Edinburgh.
1789	December, Mackenzie's comedy *The Force of Fashion*, given one performance at Covent Garden.
1790	April, Mackenzie's *Letters of Brutus* begins publication in the *Edinburgh Herald*. Death of Adam Smith.
1791	*Letters of Brutus to Certain Celebrated Political Characters*, first series, published in collected form. Second series begins publication in May.
1792	Mackenzie publishes *Review of the Principal Proceedings of Parliament of 1784*.
1793	*Letters of Brutus*, second series, published in collected form. "Some Account of the Life and Writings of Dr. Blacklock" prefixed to a new edition of the works of Thomas Blacklock, poet (1721-91).
1798	December, death of John Mackenzie, his youngest son, at the age of six.
1799	Appointed Comptroller of Taxes for Scotland.
1800	Death of Mackenzie's father, Dr. Joshua Mackenzie, at the age of eighty-six.
1805	Publication of *Report of the Committee of the Highland Society of Scotland, appointed to inquire into the nature and authenticity of the poems of Ossian. Drawn up by Henry Mackenzie, Esq., its convener or chairman.*
1808	Authorized Edition of *Works* (8 volumes) published under Mackenzie's supervision.
1809	Mackenzie and Walter Scott become directors of the Edinburgh Theatre.
1814	Sir Walter Scott dedicates his first novel, *Waverley*, to Mackenzie, identified as "Our Scottish Addison."
1822	Mackenzie publishes *Account of the Life and Writings of John Home*.
1823	Scott publishes his essay on Mackenzie (see Appendix D).
1824	Mackenzie begins to write his *Anecdotes and Egotisms*, reminiscences not published until 1927.
1831	Mackenzie dies 14 January. Buried in Greyfriars Cemetery, Edinburgh.

A Note on the Text

The Man of Feeling was published, anonymously, by Thomas Cadell in London, April 1771.

This edition follows the second (corrected) edition of August 1771, which differs from the first in several hundred variants. Most of the alterations Mackenzie made to the second edition are fairly minor, changing individual words or word order, possibly in response to reviewers' criticisms of the first edition's style. Occasionally, however, the changes are more significant. The Introduction's original list of the text's acknowledged literary predecessors (Marmontel, Rousseau, Richardson), for example, is restricted to Marmontel and Richardson alone in the second edition.

Mackenzie's spelling and original notes have been retained. The latter are identified in the text by asterisks. Mackenzie's punctuation has been kept, except in some passages of reported speech. In many of these passages Mackenzie incorporates the tags identifying speakers within their quoted speeches. These passages have been changed to conform with standard modern punctuation (that is, with the identifying tags outside quotation marks).

THE

M A N

OF

F E E L I N G.

THE SECOND EDITION, CORRECTED.

LONDON:

PRINTED FOR T. CADELL, IN THE STRAND.

MDCCLXXI.

INTRODUCTION.

MY dog had made a point[1] on a piece of fallow-ground, and led the curate and me two or three hundred yards over that and some stubble adjoining, in a breathless state of expectation, on a burning first of September.

It was a false point, and our labour was vain: yet, to do Rover justice, (for he's an excellent dog, though I have lost his pedigree) the fault was none of his, the birds were gone; the curate shewed me the spot where they had lain basking, at the root of an old hedge.

I stopped and cried Hem! The curate is fatter than I; he wiped the sweat from his brow.

There is no state where one is apter to pause and look round one, than after such a disappointment. It is even so in life. When we have been hurrying on, impelled by some warm wish or other, looking neither to the right hand nor to the left—we find, of a sudden that all our gay hopes are flown; and the only slender consolation that some friend can give us, is to point where they were once to be found. And lo! if we are not of that combustible race, who will rather beat their heads in spite, than wipe their brows with the curate, we look round and say, with the nauseated listlessness of the king of Israel, "All is vanity and vexation of spirit."[2]

I looked round with some such grave apothegm in my mind, when I discovered, for the first time, a venerable pile, to which the inclosure belonged.[3] An air of melancholy hung about it. There was a languid stillness in the day, and a single crow, that perched on an old tree by the side of the gate, seemed to delight in the echo of its own croaking.

I leaned on my gun and looked; but I had not breath enough to ask the curate a question. I observed carving on the bark of some of the trees: 'twas indeed the only mark of human art about

---

1 "The rigid attitude assumed [by a hunting dog] on finding game, with the head and gaze directed towards it" (OED).

2 Ecclesiastes 1.14: "I have seen all the works that are done under the sun; and behold, all is vanity and vexation of spirit." The opening lines of Ecclesiastes identify the author as "the son of David," and traditionally the book has been ascribed to King Solomon of Israel. Its themes of fruitless effort and exhausted energies set the scene for the losses and disappointments of the narrative to follow.

3 A pile is a "large building or edifice" (OED).

the place, except that some branches appeared to have been lopped, to give a view of the cascade, which was formed by a little rill at some distance.

Just at that instant I saw pass between the trees, a young lady with a book in her hand. I stood upon a stone to observe her; but the curate sat him down on the grass, and, leaning his back where I stood, told me, "That was the daughter of a neighbouring gentleman of the name of WALTON, whom he had seen walking there more than once.

"Some time ago," said he, "one HARLEY lived there, a whimsical sort of a man I am told, but I was not then in the cure; though, if I had a turn for those things, I might know a good deal of his history, for the greatest part of it is still in my possession."

"His history!" said I. "Nay, you may call it what you please," said the curate; "for indeed it is no more a history than it is a sermon. The way I came by it was this: Some time ago, a grave, oddish kind of man, boarded at a farmer's in this parish: The country people called him The Ghost, and he was known by the slouch in his gait, and the length of his stride. I was but little acquainted with him, for he never frequented any of the clubs hereabouts. Yet for all he used to walk a-nights, he was as gentle as a lamb at times; for I have seen him playing at te-totum[1] with the children, on the great stone at the door of our church-yard.

"Soon after I was made curate, he left the parish, and went nobody knows whither; and in his room was found a bundle of papers, which was brought to me by his landlord. I began to read them, but I soon grew weary of the task; for, besides that the hand is intolerably bad, I could never find the author in one strain for two chapters together: and I don't believe there's a single syllogism from beginning to end."

"I should be glad to see this medley," said I. "You shall see it now," answered the curate, "for I always take it along with me a-shooting." "How came it so torn?" "'Tis excellent wadding," said the curate.—This was a plea of expediency I was not in condition to answer; for I had actually in my pocket great part of an edition

---

1 More commonly "teetotum." A game of chance played with a four-sided die or disk, most often, though not exclusively, by children. Players twirled the die like a top by means of a spindle which passed through it. Each side was inscribed with a letter which determined the fortune of the player when it fell (e.g., "T" for "take all," "P" for "put down [a stake]" etc.).

of one of the German Illustrissimi,[1] for the very same purpose. We exchanged books; and by that means (for the curate was a strenuous logician) we probably saved both.

When I returned to town, I had leisure to peruse the acquisition I had made: I found it a bundle of little episodes, put together without art, and of no importance on the whole, with something of nature, and little else in them. I was a good deal affected with some very trifling passages in it; and had the name of a Marmontel, or a Richardson, been on the title-page[2]——'tis odds that I should have wept: But

One is ashamed to be pleased with the works of one knows not whom.

---

1 A title of courtesy originally used in addressing or speaking of Italian nobles, here applied to German and Dutch legal and philosophical thinkers such as Samuel Pufendorf (1632-94) and Hugo Grotius (1583-1645). In this exchange of texts Mackenzie is using the convention of the "found manuscript" typical of the novel of sentiment.

2 Samuel Richardson (1689-1761), author of *Pamela* (1739-40) and *Clarissa* (1748), enormously popular novels in the decades after their publication. *Clarissa* especially was praised widely for its representations of psychological depth and its moving account of the heroine's suffering. This latter novel helped inaugurate the sub-genre of sentimentalism of which *The Man of Feeling* is one of the best exemplars. Jean-François Marmontel (1723-99), a French writer active across many genres, was especially well-known for his *Contes Moraux* published in the *Mercure de France* in the 1760s, part of the contemporaneous French eighteenth-century tradition of sentimentalism which fed into and responded to British sentimental literature.

CHAPTER XI.*

Of bashfulness.—A character.—His opinion on that subject.

THERE is some rust about every man at the beginning; though in some nations (among the French, for instance) the ideas of the inhabitants from climate, or what other cause you will, are so vivacious, so eternally on the wing, that they must, even in small societies, have a frequent collision; the rust therefore will wear off sooner: but in Britain it often goes with a man to his grave; nay, he dares not even pen a *hic jacet*[1] to speak out for him after his death.

"Let them rub it off by travel," said the baronet's brother, who was a striking instance of excellent metal, shamefully rusted. I had drawn my chair near his. Let me paint the honest old man: 'tis but one passing sentence to preserve his image in my mind.

He sat in his usual attitude, with his elbow rested on his knee, and his fingers pressed on his cheek. His face was shaded by his hand; yet it was a face that might once have been well accounted handsome; its features were manly and striking, and a certain dignity resided on his eyebrows, which were the largest I remember to have seen. His person was tall and well-made; but the indolence of his nature had now inclined it to corpulency.

His remarks were few, and made only to his familiar friends; but they were such as the world might have heard with veneration: and his heart, uncorrupted by its ways, was ever warm in the cause of virtue and his friends.

He is now forgotten and gone! The last time I was at Silton hall, I saw his chair stand in its corner by the fire-side; there was an additional cushion on it, and it was occupied by my young lady's favourite lap-dog. I drew near unperceived, and pinched its ear in the bitterness of my soul; the creature howled, and ran to its mistress. She did not suspect the author of its misfortune, but she bewailed it in the most pathetic terms; and kissing its lips, laid it gently on her lap, and covered it with a cambric handkerchief.

---

* The Reader will remember, that the Editor is accountable only for scattered chapters, and fragments of chapters; the curate must answer for the rest. The number at the top, when the chapter was entire, he has given as it originally stood, with the title which its author had affixed to it.

---

1 *Hic jacet* is Latin for "here lies"; a tombstone inscription.

I sat in my old friend's seat; I heard the roar of mirth and gaiety around me: poor Ben Silton! I gave thee a tear then: accept of one cordial drop that falls to thy memory now.

"They should wear it off by travel."—"Why, it is true," said I, "that will go far; but then it will often happen, that in the velocity of a modern tour, and amidst the materials through which it is commonly made, the friction is so violent, that not only the rust, but the metal too is lost in the progress."

"Give me leave to correct the expression of your metaphor," said Mr. Silton: "that is not always rust which is acquired by the inactivity of the body on which it preys; such, perhaps, is the case with me, though indeed I was never cleared from my youth; but (taking it in its first stage) it is rather an encrustation, which nature has given for purposes of the greatest wisdom."

"You are right," I returned, "and sometimes, like certain precious fossils, there may be hid under it gems of the purest brilliancy."

"Nay, farther," continued Mr. Silton, "there are two distinct sorts of what we call bashfulness; this, the aukwardness of a booby, which a few steps into the world will convert into the pertness of a coxcomb;[1] that, a consciousness, which the most delicate feelings produce, and the most extensive knowledge cannot always remove."

From the incidents I have already related, I imagine it will be concluded, that Harley was of the latter species of bashful animals; at least, if Mr. Silton's principle be just, it may be argued on this side: for the gradation of the first mentioned sort, it is certain, he never attained. Some part of his external appearance was modelled from the company of those gentlemen, whom the antiquity of a family, now possessed of bare 250 l. a year,[2] entitled its representative to approach; these, indeed, were not many; great

---

1 A booby is a "dull, heavy, stupid fellow" according to Johnson's *Dictionary* (1755); also "the last boy in a school class, the dunce" (OED); a coxcomb is "a superficial pretender to knowledge or accomplishments" (Johnson).

2 Roy Porter estimates the minimum income necessary for a gentleman living in eighteenth-century England at £300 per annum (*English Society in the Eighteenth Century*, rev. edition. London: Penguin, 1990: xv); though single and living in rural retirement, his income thus puts Harley at the extreme lower limit of the landed social class of which his family has so long been a part. Again Mackenzie sounds the note of long slow decline.

part of the property in his neighbourhood being in the hands of merchants, who had got rich by their lawful calling abroad, and the sons of stewards, who had got rich by their lawful calling at home: persons so perfectly versed in the ceremonial of thousands, tens of thousands, and hundreds of thousands (whose degrees of precedency are plainly demonstrable from the first page of the Compleat Acomptant, or Young Man's Best Pocket Companion) that a bow at church from them to such a man as Harley,—would have made the parson look back into his sermon for some precept of Christian humility.

CHAPTER XII.

Of worldly interests.

THERE are certain interests which the world supposes every man to have, and which therefore are properly enough termed worldly; but the world is apt to make an erroneous estimate: ignorant of the dispositions which constitute our happiness or misery, they bring to an undistinguished scale, the means of the one, as connected with power, wealth, or grandeur, and of the other with their contraries. Philosophers and poets have often protested against this decision; but their arguments have been despised as declamatory, or ridiculed as romantic.

There are never wanting to a young man some grave and prudent friends to set him right in this particular, if he need it: to watch his ideas as they arise, and point them to those objects which a wise man should never forget.

Harley did not want for some monitors of this sort. He was frequently told of men, whose fortunes enabled them to command all the luxuries of life, whose fortunes were of their own acquirement: his envy was excited by a description of their happiness, and his emulation by a recital of the means which had procured it.

Harley was apt to hear those lectures with indifference; nay, sometimes they got the better of his temper; and as the instances were not always amiable, provoked, on his part, some reflections, which I am persuaded his good-nature would else have avoided.

Indeed I have observed one ingredient, somewhat necessary in a man's composition towards happiness, which people of feeling would do well to acquire; a certain respect for the follies of mankind: for there are so many fools whom the opinion of the world entitles to regard, whom accident has placed in heights of which they are unworthy, that he who cannot restrain his contempt or indignation at the sight, will be too often quarrelling with the disposal of things, to relish that share which is allotted to himself. I do not mean, however, to insinuate this to have been the case with Harley; on the contrary, if we might rely on his own testimony, the conceptions he had of pomp and grandeur, served to endear the state which Providence had assigned him.

He lost his father, the last surviving of his parents, as I have already related, when he was a boy. The good man, from a fear of offending, as well as a regard to his son, had named him a variety of guardians; one consequence of which was, that they seldom met at all to consider the affairs of their ward; and when they did meet, their opinions were so opposite, that the only possible method of conciliation, was the mediatory power of a dinner and a bottle, which commonly interrupted, not ended, the dispute; and after that interruption ceased, left the consulting parties in a condition not very proper for adjusting it. His education therefore had been but indifferently attended to; and after being taken from a country school, at which he had been boarded, the young gentleman was suffered to be his own master in the subsequent branches of literature, with some assistance from the parson of the parish in languages and philosophy, and from the exciseman in arithmetic and book-keeping. One of his guardians indeed, who, in his youth, had been an inhabitant of the Temple,[1] set him to read Coke upon Lyttelton;[2] a book which is very properly put into the hands of beginners in that science, as its simplicity is accommodated to their understandings, and its size to their inclination. He profited but little by the perusal; but it was not without its use in the family: for his maiden aunt applied it commonly to the laudable purpose of pressing her rebellious linens to the folds she had allotted them.

---

1 That is, Harley's guardian had studied law in London (as Mackenzie himself did from 1765 to 1768). Law students in London collectively studied at a small number of Inns (Colleges) of Court, among which were the Middle Temple and Inner Temple.

2 Sir Edward Coke (1552-1634) wrote a commentary on English Common Law in his *Institutes of the Lawes of England*, published in four parts between 1624 and 1644. The most famous of these is *The First Part of the Institutes of the Lawes of England; or a Commentary upon Littleton, not the name of the Author only, but of the Law it selfe*, commonly known as *Coke upon Littleton*. The text remained a fundamental part of legal education well into the eighteenth century and beyond, though Mackenzie's ironic asides here allude to its status as byword for a massive tome of impenetrable legalese.

There were particularly two ways of increasing his fortune, which might have occurred to people of less foresight than the counsellors we have mentioned. One of these was the prospect of his succeeding to an old lady, a distant relation, who was known to be possessed of a very large sum in the stocks: but in this their hopes were disappointed; for the young man was so untoward in his disposition, that, notwithstanding the instructions he daily received, his visits rather tended to alienate than gain the good-will of his kinswoman. He sometimes looked grave when the old lady told the jokes of her youth; he often refused to eat when she pressed him, and was seldom or never provided with sugar-candy or liquorice when she was seized with a fit of coughing: nay, he had once the rudeness to fall asleep, while she was describing the composition and virtues of her favourite cholic-water.[1] In short, he accommodated himself so ill to her humour, that she died, and did not leave him a farthing.

The other method pointed out to him was, an endeavour to get a lease of some crown-lands, which lay contiguous to his little paternal estate. This, it was imagined, might be easily procured, as the crown did not draw so much rent as Harley could afford to give, with very considerable profit to himself; and the then lessee had rendered himself so obnoxious to the ministry, by the disposal of his vote at an election, that he could not expect a renewal.[2] This, however, needed some interest with the great, which Harley or his father never possessed.

His neighbour, Mr. Walton, having heard of this affair, generously offered his assistance to accomplish it. He told him, that though he had long been a stranger to courtiers, yet he believed, there were some of them who might pay regard to his recommendation; and that, if he thought it worth the while to take a London journey upon the business, he would furnish him with a letter of introduction to a baronet of his acquaintance, who had a great deal to say with the first lord of the treasury.

When his friends heard of this offer, they pressed him with the utmost earnestness to accept of it. They did not fail to enumer-

---

1 A remedy for digestive or intestinal pain or discomfort. The term
   "cholic" was used to refer to a wide range of abdominal complaints and
   symptoms in the period.
2 The suggestion is that Harley might profit by promising his vote—a very
   valuable commodity in an era when the franchise was restricted to possessors of substantial land or other wealth—to a government minister in
   return for being granted the lease to land owned by the state.

ate the many advantages which a certain degree of spirit and assurance gives a man who would make a figure in the world: they repeated their instances of good fortune in others, ascribed them all to a happy forwardness of disposition; and made so copious a recital of the disadvantages which attend the opposite weakness, that a stranger, who had heard them, would have been led to imagine, that in the British code there was some disqualifying statute against any citizen who should be convicted of—— modesty.

Harley, though he had no great relish for the attempt, yet could not resist the torrent of motives that assaulted him; and as he needed but little preparation for his journey, a day, not very distant, was fixed for his departure.

CHAPTER XIII.

The Man of Feeling in love.

THE day before that on which he set out, he went to take leave of Mr. Walton.——We would conceal nothing;—there was another person of the family to whom also the visit was intended, on whose account, perhaps, there were some tenderer feelings in the bosom of Harley, than his gratitude for the friendly notice of that gentleman (though he was seldom deficient in that virtue) could inspire. Mr. Walton had a daughter; and such a daughter! we will attempt some description of her by and by.

Harley's notions of the καλον, or beautiful,[1] were not always to be defined, nor indeed such as the world would always assent to, though we could define them. A blush, a phrase of affability to an

---

1 καλον is the Greek term for beauty. The use of the Greek phrase suggests an allusion to the works of Anthony Ashley Cooper, third Earl of Shaftesbury (1671-1713), whose discussion of beauty in his collected works, *Characteristics of Men, Manners, Opinions, Times* (1711) links Aristotelian accounts of beauty with moral order. In *Sensus Communis, an Essay on the Freedom of Wit and Humour,* Shaftesbury writes, for example: "the most natural beauty in the world is honesty and moral truth. For all beauty is truth ... (see Shaftesbury, *Characteristics of Men, Manners, Opinions, Times,* ed. John M. Robertson. Bristol, Thoemmes Press, 1997, I:94 and fn.3, 94). Shaftesbury's attempt to fuse the ethical and the aesthetic attracted strong interest for several decades after the publication of his treatise, and forms an important intellectual context for sentimental fiction.

inferior, a tear at a moving tale, were to him, like the Cestus of Cytherea,[1] unequalled in conferring beauty. For all these, Miss Walton was remarkable; but as these, like the above-mentioned Cestus, are perhaps still more powerful, when the wearer is possessed of some degree of beauty, commonly so called; it happened, that, from this cause, they had more than usual power in the person of that young lady.

She was now arrived at that period of life which takes, or is supposed to take, from the flippancy of girlhood those sprightlinesses with which some good-natured old maids oblige the world at three-score. She had been ushered into life (as that word is used in the dialect of St. Jameses)[2] at seventeen, her father being then in parliament, and living in London: at seventeen, therefore, she had been a universal toast; her health, now she was four and twenty was only drank by those who knew her face at least. Her complexion was mellowed into a paleness, which certainly took from her beauty; but agreed, at least Harley used to say so, with the pensive softness of her mind. Her eyes were of that gentle hazel-colour, which is rather mild than piercing; and, except when they were lighted up by good-humour, which was frequently the case, were supposed by the fine gentlemen to want fire. Her air and manner were elegant in the highest degree, and were as sure of commanding respect, as their mistress was far from demanding it. Her voice was inexpressibly soft; it was, according to that incomparable simile of Otway's,

——"like the shepherd's pipe upon the mountains,
"When all his little flock's at feed before him."[3]

The effect it had upon Harley, himself used to paint ridiculously enough; and ascribed to it powers, which few believed, and nobody cared for.

Her conversation was always cheerful, but rarely witty; and without the smallest affectation of learning, had as much senti-

---

1 The Cestus of Cytherea is the girdle or belt of Venus, supposed to endow the woman who wore it with beauty, and to inspire love in the beholder.

2 St. James Palace was and is a Royal residence in London. The phrase refers to her official début, or entry into adult society.

3 Thomas Otway (1652-85) was a popular seventeenth-century dramatist whose plays were still frequently produced well into the eighteenth century. Mackenzie quotes from the deathbed speech of Monimia in *The Orphan*:
   Methought I heard a voice,
   Sweet as the Shepherd's Pipe upon the Mountains,
   When all his little Flock's at feed before him (V.i.415-17).

ment in it as would have puzzled a Turk, upon his principles of female materialism,[1] to account for. Her beneficence was unbounded; indeed the natural tenderness of her heart might have been argued, by the frigidity of a casuist, as detracting from her virtue in this respect, for her humanity was a feeling, not a principle: but minds like Harley's are not very apt to make this distinction, and generally give our virtue credit for all that benevolence which is instinctive in our nature.[2]

As her father had some years retired to the country, Harley had frequent opportunities of seeing her. He looked on her for some time merely with that respect and admiration which her appearance seemed to demand, and the opinion of others conferred upon her: from this cause, perhaps, and from that extreme sensibility of which we have taken frequent notice, Harley was remarkably silent in her presence. He heard her sentiments with peculiar attention, sometimes with looks very expressive of approbation; but seldom declared his opinion on the subject, much less made compliments to the lady on the justness of her remarks.

From this very reason it was, that Miss Walton frequently took more particular notice of him than of other visitors, who, by the laws of precedency, were better entitled to it: it was a mode of politeness she had peculiarly studied, to bring to the line of that equality, which is ever necessary for the ease of our guests, those whose sensibility had placed them below it.

Harley saw this; for though he was a child in the drama of the world, yet was it not altogether owing to a want of knowledge in his part; on the contrary, the most delicate consciousness of

---

1 Popular British travel accounts of Turkey and the Ottoman Empire in the seventeenth and eighteenth centuries, in comparing the condition of women there and in Britain, often erroneously suggest that the Turks (or Muslims in general) believed that women had no souls.

2 Perhaps a (gently) joking reference to Adam Smith's system of virtue in *The Theory of Moral Sentiments*. According to Smith's account of virtues, women tend to sympathize easily and spontaneously, a response to others that Smith classifies as involuntary and hence lower than those coded as male, such as self-denial and generosity: "Humanity is the virtue of a woman, generosity of a man. The fair-sex ... have commonly much more tenderness than ours ... . Humanity consists merely in the exquisite fellow-feeling which the spectator entertains with the sentiments of the persons principally concerned, so as to grieve for their sufferings, to resent their injuries, and to rejoice at their good fortune" (Adam Smith, *The Theory of Moral Sentiments*, ed. D.D. Raphael and A.L. Macfie. Oxford: Oxford UP, 1979 190-91).

propriety often kindled that blush which marred the performance of it: this raised his esteem something above what the most sanguine descriptions of her goodness had been able to do; for certain it is, that notwithstanding the laboured definitions which very wise men have given us of the inherent beauty of virtue, we are always inclined to think her handsomest when she condescends to smile upon ourselves.

It would be trite to observe the easy gradation from esteem to love; in the bosom of Harley there scarce needed a transition; for there were certain seasons when his ideas were flushed to a degree much above their common complexion. In times not credulous of inspiration, we should account for this from some natural cause; but we do not mean to account for it at all; it were sufficient to describe its effects; but they were sometimes so ludicrous, as might derogate from the dignity of the sensations which produced them to describe. They were treated indeed as such by most of Harley's sober friends, who often laughed very heartily at the aukward blunders of the real Harley, when the different faculties, which should have prevented them, were entirely occupied by the ideal. In some of these paroxisms of fancy, Miss Walton did not fail to be introduced; and the picture which had been drawn amidst the surrounding objects of unnoticed levity, was now singled out to be viewed through the medium of romantic imagination: it was improved of course, and esteem was a word inexpressive of the feelings which it excited.

CHAPTER XIV.

He sets out on his journey.—The beggar and his dog.

HE had taken leave of his aunt on the eve of his intended departure; but the good lady's affection for her nephew interrupted her sleep, and early as it was next morning when Harley came down stairs to set out, he found her in the parlour with a tear on her cheek, and her caudle-cup[1] in her hand. She knew enough of physic to prescribe against going abroad of a morning with an empty stomach. She gave her blessing with the draught; her instructions she had delivered the night before. They consisted mostly of negatives; for London, in her idea, was so replete with

---

1   Caudle was "A warm drink consisting of thin gruel, mixed with wine or ale, sweetened and spiced, given chiefly to sick people" (OED).

temptations, that it needed the whole armour of her friendly cautions to repel their attacks.

Peter stood at the door. We have mentioned this faithful fellow formerly: Harley's father had taken him up an orphan, and saved him from being cast on the parish; and he had ever since remained in the service of him and of his son. Harley shook him by the hand as he passed, smiling, as if he had said, "I will not weep." He sprung hastily into the chaise that waited for him: Peter folded up the step. "My dear master," said he, (shaking the solitary lock that hung on either side of his head) "I have been told as how London is a sad place."——He was choaked with the thought, and his benediction could not be heard: but it shall be heard, honest Peter! where these tears will add to its energy.

In a few hours Harley reached the inn where he proposed breakfasting; but the fulness of his heart would not suffer him to eat a morsel. He walked out on the road, and gaining a little height, stood gazing on the quarter he had left. He looked for his wonted prospect, his fields, his woods, and his hills: they were lost in the distant clouds! He pencilled them on the clouds, and bade them farewell with a sigh!

He sat down on a large stone to take out a little pebble from his shoe, when he saw, at some distance, a beggar approaching him. He had on a loose sort of coat, mended with different-coloured rags, amongst which the blue and the russet were predominant. He had a short knotty stick in his hand, and on the top of it was stuck a ram's horn; his knees (though he was no pilgrim) had worn the stuff of his breeches; he wore no shoes, and his stockings had entirely lost that part of them which should have covered his feet and ancles: in his face, however, was the plump appearance of good-humour; he walked a good round pace, and a crook-legged dog trotted at his heels.

"Our delicacies," said Harley to himself, "are fantastic; they are not in nature! that beggar walks over the sharpest of these stones barefooted, whilst I have lost the most delightful dream in the world, from the smallest of them happening to get into my shoe."—The beggar had by this time come up, and pulling off a piece of hat, asked charity of Harley; the dog began to beg too:— it was impossible to resist both; and in truth, the want of shoes and stockings had made both unnecessary, for Harley had destined sixpence for him before. The beggar, on receiving it, poured forth blessings without number; and, with a sort of smile on his countenance, said to Harley, "that, if he wanted to have his fortune told"—Harley turned his eye briskly on the beggar: it was an unpromising look for the subject of a prediction, and silenced the prophet immediately. "I would much rather learn," said Harley, "what it is in your power to tell me: your trade must be an entertaining one: sit down on this stone, and let me know something of your profession; I have often thought of turning fortune-teller for a week or two myself."

"Master," replied the beggar, "I like your frankness much; God knows I had the humour of plain-dealing in me from a child; but there is no doing with it in this world; we must live as we can, and lying is, as you call it, my profession: but I was in some sort forced to the trade, for I dealt once in telling truth.

"I was a labourer, Sir, and gained as much as to make me live: I never laid by indeed; for I was reckoned a piece of a wag, and your wags, I take it, are seldom rich, Mr. Harley." "So," said Harley, "you seem to know me." "Ay, there are few folks in the county that I don't know something of: how should I tell fortunes else?" "True; but to go on with your story: you were a labourer, you say, and a wag; your industry, I suppose, you left with your old trade; but your humour you preserve to be of use to you in your new."

"What signifies sadness, Sir? a man grows lean on't: but I was brought to my idleness by degrees; first I could not work, and it went against my stomach to work ever after. I was seized with a jail-fever at the time of the assizes being in the county where I lived; for I was always curious to get acquainted with the felons, because they are commonly fellows of much mirth and little thought, qualities I had ever an esteem for. In the height of this fever, Mr. Harley, the house where I lay took fire, and burnt to the ground: I was carried out in that condition, and lay all the rest of my illness in a barn. I got the better of my disease however, but I was so weak that I spit blood whenever I attempted to work. I had no relation living that I knew of, and I never kept a friend above a week, when I was able to joke;[1] I seldom remained above six months in a parish, so that I might have died before I had found a settlement in any: thus I was forced to beg my bread, and a

---

1 One of a number of details which evoke the model of Sterne. The fate of Mackenzie's beggar echoes that of Yorick in Sterne's *Tristram Shandy* (1759-67) whose joking costs him friends, professional advancement, and ultimately his spirit (Bk I, ch xii).

sorry trade I found it, Mr. Harley. I told all my misfortunes truly, but they were seldom believed; and the few who gave me a half-penny as they passed, did it with a shake of the head, and an injunction not to trouble them with a long story. In short, I found that people don't care to give alms without some security for their money; a wooden leg or a withered arm, is a sort of draught upon heaven for those who chuse to have their money placed to account there; so I changed my plan, and, instead of telling my own misfortunes, began to prophesy happiness to others. This I found by much the better way: folks will always listen when the tale is their own; and of many who say they do not believe in fortune telling, I have known few on whom it had not a very sensible effect. I pick up the names of their acquaintance; amours and little squabbles are easily gleaned among servants and neighbours; and indeed people themselves are the best intelligencers in the world for our purpose: they dare not puzzle us for their own sakes, for every one is anxious to hear what they wish to believe; and they who repeat it to laugh at it when they have done, are generally more serious than their hearers are apt to imagine. With a tolerable good memory, and some share of cunning, with the help of walking a-nights over heaths and church-yards, with this, and shewing the tricks of that there dog, whom I stole from the serjeant of a marching regiment (and by the way he can steal too upon occasion) I make shift to pick up a livelihood. My trade, indeed, is none of the honestest; yet people are not much cheated neither, who give a few halfpence for a prospect of happiness, which I have heard some persons say is all a man can arrive at in this world.—But I must bid you good-day, Sir; for I have three miles to walk before noon, to inform some boarding-school young ladies, whether their husbands are to be peers of the realm, or captains in the army: a question which I promised to answer them by that time."

Harley had drawn a shilling from his pocket; but virtue bade him consider on whom he was going to bestow it.—Virtue held back his arm:—but a milder form, a younger sister of virtue's, not so severe as virtue, nor so serious as pity, smiled upon him: His fingers lost their compression;—nor did virtue offer to catch the money as it fell. It had no sooner reached the ground than the watchful cur (a trick he had been taught) snapped it up; and, contrary to the most approved method of stewardship, delivered it immediately into the hands of his master.

★ ★ ★ ★ ★

CHAPTER XIX.

He makes a second expedition to the Baronet's.
The laudable ambition of a young man to be thought something
by the world.

WE have related, in a former chapter, the little success of his first visit to the great man, for whom he had the introductory letter from Mr. Walton. To people of equal sensibility, the influence of those trifles we mentioned on his deportment will not appear surprising; but to his friends in the country, they could not be stated, nor would they have allowed them any place in the account. In some of their letters, therefore, which he received soon after, they expressed their surprise at his not having been more urgent in his application, and again recommended the blushless assiduity of successful merit.

He resolved to make another attempt at the baronet's; fortified with higher notions of his own dignity, and with less apprehension of repulse. In his way to Grosvenor-square he began to ruminate on the folly of mankind, who affix those ideas of superiority to riches, which reduced the minds of men, by nature equal with the more fortunate, to that sort of servility which he felt in his own. By the time he had reached the Square, and was walking along the pavement which led to the baronet's, he had brought his reasoning on the subject to such a point, that the conclusion, by every rule of logic, should have led him to a thorough indifference in his approaches to a fellow-mortal, whether that fellow-mortal was possessed of six, or six thousand pounds a year. It is probable, however, that the premises had been improperly formed; for it is certain, that when he approached the great man's door, he felt his heart agitated by an unusual pulsation.

He had almost reached it, when he observed a young gentleman coming out, dressed in a white frock, and a red laced waistcoat, with a small switch in his hand, which he seemed to manage with a particular good grace. As he passed him on the steps, the stranger very politely made him a bow, which Harley returned, though he could not remember ever having seen him before. He asked Harley, in the same civil manner, if he was going to wait on his friend the Baronet? "For I was just calling," said he, "and am sorry to find that he is gone for some days into the country." Harley thanked him for his information; and was turning from the door, when the other observed, that it would be proper to leave his name, and very obligingly knocked for that purpose. "Here is a gentleman, Tom, who meant to have waited on your master." "Your name, if you please, Sir?" "Harley."—"You'll remember, Tom, Harley."—The door was shut. "Since we are here," said he, "we shall not lose our walk, if we add a little to it by a turn or two in Hyde-park." He accompanied this proposal with a second bow, and Harley accepted of it by another in return.

The conversation, as they walked, was brilliant on the side of his companion. The playhouse, the opera, with every occurrence in high life, he seemed perfectly master of; and talked of some reigning beauties of quality, in a manner the most feeling in the world. Harley admired the happiness of his vivacity; and, opposite as it was to the reserve of his own nature, began to be much pleased with its effects.

Though I am not of opinion with some wise men, that the existence of objects depends on idea;[1] yet, I am convinced, that their appearance is not a little influenced by it. The optics of some minds are in so unlucky a perspective, as to throw a certain shade on every picture that is presented to them; while those of others (of which number was Harley) like the mirrors of the ladies, have a wonderful effect in bettering their complexions. Through such a medium perhaps he was looking on his present companion.

When they had finished their walk, and were returning by the corner of the Park, they observed a board hung out of a window, signifying, "an excellent ORDINARY[2] on Saturdays and Sundays." It happened to be Saturday, and the table was covered for the purpose. "What if we should go in and dine here, if you happen not to be engaged, Sir?" said the young gentleman. "It is not impossible but we shall meet with some original or other; it is a sort of humour I like hugely." Harley made no objection; and the stranger showed him the way in to the parlour.

He was placed, by the courtesy of his introductor, in an armchair that stood at one side of the fire. Over-against him was seated a man of a grave considering aspect, with that look of sober

---

1 A reference to philosophical idealism, especially that of George Berkeley (1685-1753), who argued that physical objects exist only insofar as they are perceived.

2 An ordinary is "a public meal regularly provided at a fixed price in an eating-house or tavern" (OED).

prudence which indicates what is commonly called a warm man. He wore a pretty large wig, which had once been white, but was now of a brownish yellow; his coat was one of those modest-coloured drabs which mock the injuries of dust and dirt; two jack-boots concealed, in part, the well-mended knees of an old pair of buckskin breeches, while the spotted handkerchief round his neck, preserved at once its owner from catching cold, and his neckcloth from being dirtied. Next him sat another man, with a tankard in his hand, and a quid of tobacco in his cheek, whose eye was rather more vivacious, and whose dress was something smarter.

The first-mentioned gentleman took notice, that the room had been so lately washed, as not to have had time to dry; and remarked, that wet lodging was unwholesome for man or beast. He looked round at the same time, for a poker to stir the fire with, which, he at last observed to the company, the people of the house had removed, in order to save their coals. This difficulty, however, he overcame, by the help of Harley's stick, saying, "that as they should, no doubt, pay for their fire in some shape or other, he saw no reason why they should not have the use of it while they sat."

The door was now opened for the admission of dinner. "I don't know how it is with you, gentlemen," said Harley's new acquaintance; "but I am afraid I shall not be able to get down a morsel at this horrid mechanical hour of dining." He sat down, however, and did not show any want of appetite by his eating. He took upon him the carving of the meat, and criticised on the goodness of the pudding.

When the table-cloth was removed, he proposed calling for some punch, which was readily agreed to; he seemed at first inclined to make it himself, but afterwards changed his mind, and left that province to the waiter, telling him to have it pure West-Indian, or he could not taste a drop of it.[1]

When the punch was brought, he undertook to fill the glasses, and call the toasts.—"The king."—The toast naturally produced politics. It is the privilege of Englishmen to drink the king's health, and to talk of his conduct. The man who sat opposite to Harley (and who by this time, partly from himself, and partly

---

1 Rum punch. Rum was distilled from sugar-cane raised mostly on West Indian plantations.

from his acquaintance on his left hand, was discovered to be a grazier) observed, "That it was a shame for so many pensioners to be allowed to take the bread out of the mouth of the poor." "Ay, and provisions," said his friend, "were never so dear in the memory of man; I wish the king, and his counsellors, would look to that." "As for the matter of provisions, neighbour Wrightson," he replied, "I am sure the prices of cattle—" A dispute would have probably ensued, but it was prevented by the spruce toast-master, who gave a Sentiment: and turning to the two politicians, "Pray, gentlemen," said he, "let us have done with these musty politics: I would always leave them to the beer-suckers in Butcher-row.[1] Come, let us have something of the fine arts. That was a damn'd hard match betwixt the Nailor and Tim Bucket.[2] The knowing ones were cursedly taken in there! I lost a cool hundred myself, faith."

At mention of the cool hundred, the grazier threw his eyes aslant, with a mingled look of doubt and surprise; while the man at his elbow looked arch, and gave a short emphatical sort of cough.

Both seemed to be silenced, however, by this intelligence; and, while the remainder of the punch lasted, the conversation was wholly engrossed by the gentleman with the fine waistcoat, who told a great many "immense comical stories," and "confounded smart things," as he termed them, acted and spoken by lords, ladies, and young bucks of quality, of his acquaintance. At last, the grazier, pulling out a watch, of a very unusual size, and telling the hour, said, that he had an appointment. "Is it so late?" said the young gentleman; "then I am afraid I have missed an appointment already; but the truth is, I am cursedly given to missing of appointments."

When the grazier and he were gone, Harley turned to the remaining personage, and asked him, If he knew that young

---

1 There were several "Butcher-row"s in mid-eighteenth-century London (in Smithfield, Temple Bar, and Ratcliff), though the social status of the locale is clearly indicated by the name; Harley's new acquaintance here crudely dismisses the discussion of political differences as an activity for tradesmen rather than gentlemen. Mackenzie adds a footnote here to the 1808 text in his Collected Works, stating "It may be necessary to inform readers of the present day, that the noted political debating Society, called the *Robinhood*, was held at a house in Butcher-row."
2 Probably a reference to a boxing match.

gentleman? "A gentleman!" said he; "ay, he is one of your gentle-men at the top of an affidavit.[1] I knew him, some years ago, in the quality of a footman; and, I believe, he had sometimes the hon-our to be a pimp. At last, some of the great folks, to whom he had been serviceable in both capacities, had him made a gauger;[2] in which station he remains, and has the assurance to pretend an acquaintance with men of quality. The impudent dog! with a few shillings in his pocket, he will talk you three times as much as my friend Mundy there, who is worth nine thousand, if he's worth a farthing. But I know the rascal, and despise him, as he deserves."

Harley began to despise him too, and to conceive some indig-nation at having sat with patience to hear such a fellow speak nonsense. But he corrected himself, by reflecting, that he was per-haps as well entertained, and instructed too, by this same modest gauger, as he should have been by such a man as he had thought proper to personate. And surely the fault may more properly be imputed to that rank where the futility is real, than where it is feigned; to that rank, whose opportunities for nobler accomplish-ments have only served to rear a fabric of folly, which the untu-tored hand of affectation, even among the meanest of mankind, can imitate with success.

CHAPTER XX.

He visits Bedlam.[3]———*The distresses of a daughter.*

OF those things called Sights in London, which every stranger is supposed desirous to see, Bedlam is one. To that place, therefore, an acquaintance of Harley's, after having accompanied him to several other shows, proposed a visit. Harley objected to it, "because," said he, "I think it an inhuman practice to expose the

1 A person named in a legal proceeding, suggesting someone of dubious integrity.
2 A gauger is a tax assessor or exciseman. This government-appointed post was considered a lowly sinecure obtained through influence, not merit.
3 The Hospital of St. Mary of Bethlehem, generally called Bedlam, had long been the primary place in London for the confinement of the insane. Visiting the hospital for a view of the disturbed inmates was a common item on the eighteenth-century London tourist's itinerary. For a visual representation of the spectacle provided by the inmates for well-to-do visitors, see William Hogarth's print series, *Rake's Progress* (1735), Plate VIII.

greatest misery with which our nature is afflicted, to every idle visitant who can afford a trifling perquisite to the keeper; especially as it is a distress which the humane must see with the painful reflection, that it is not in their power to alleviate it." He was overpowered, however, by the solicitations of his friend, and the other persons of the party (amongst whom were several ladies); and they went in a body to Moorfields.

Their conductor led them first to the dismal mansions of those who are in the most horrid state of incurable madness. The clanking of chains, the wildness of their cries, and the imprecations which some of them uttered, formed a scene inexpressibly shocking. Harley and his companions, especially the female part of them, begged their guide to return: he seemed surprised at their uneasiness, and was with difficulty prevailed on to leave that part of the house without showing them some others; who, as he expressed it in the phrase of those that keep wild beasts for a shew, were much better worth seeing than any they had passed, being ten times more fierce and unmanageable.

He led them next to that quarter where those reside, who, as they are not dangerous to themselves or others, enjoy a certain degree of freedom, according to the state of their distemper.

Harley had fallen behind his companions, looking at a man who was making pendulums with bits of thread, and little balls of clay. He had delineated a segment of a circle on the wall with chalk, and marked their different vibrations, by intersecting it with cross lines. A decent-looking man came up, and smiling at the maniac, turned to Harley, and told him, that gentleman had once been a very celebrated mathematician. "He fell a sacrifice," said he, "to the theory of comets; for, having, with infinite labour, formed a table on the conjectures of Sir Isaac Newton,[1] he was disappointed in the return of one of those luminaries, and was very soon after obliged to be placed here by his friends. If you please to follow me, Sir," continued the stranger, "I believe I shall be able to give a more satisfactory account of the unfortunate

---

1 Sir Isaac Newton (1642-1727) was an English mathematician, physicist and tremendously influential scientific thinker. His *Philosophiae Naturalis Principia Mathematica* (*Mathematical Principles of Natural Philosophy*), commonly known as the *Principia*, published in Latin in 1687, with a second, extensively revised edition appearing in 1713, established theories of mechanics and gravitation unchallenged for two hundred years. His calculations on the paths of comets are in Book III of the *Principia*.

people you see here, than the man who attends your compan-ions." Harley bowed, and accepted his offer.

The next person they came up to had scrawled a variety of fig-ures on a piece of slate. Harley had the curiosity to take a nearer view of them. They consisted of different columns, on the top of which were marked South-sea annuities, India-stock, and Three per cent. annuities consol.[1] "This," said Harley's instructor, "was a gentleman well known in Change-alley.[2] He was once worth fifty thousand pounds, and had actually agreed for the purchase of an estate in the west, in order to realize his money; but he quar-relled with the proprietor about the repairs of the garden-wall, and so returned to town to follow his old trade of stock-jobbing a little longer; when an unlucky fluctuation of stock, in which he was engaged to an immense extent, reduced him at once to pover-ty and to madness. Poor wretch! he told me t'other day, that against the next payment of differences, he should be some hun-dreds above a plum."[3]—

"It is a spondee,[4] and I will maintain it," interrupted a voice on his left hand. This assertion was followed by a very rapid recital of some verses from Homer. "That figure," said the gentleman, "whose clothes are so bedaubed with snuff, was a schoolmaster of some reputation: he came hither to be resolved of some doubts he entertained concerning the genuine pronunciation of the Greek vowels. In his highest fits, he makes frequent mention of one Mr. Bentley.[5]

"But delusive ideas, Sir, are the motives of the greatest part of mankind, and a heated imagination the power by which their

---

1   The sudden collapse of overvalued stocks in the South Sea Company in 1720 and the East India Company in the 1760s caused enormous finan-cial damage, the first "crashes" of the modern stock market. The first in particular became a byword for the instability and often illusory nature of the wealth generated by investment or speculation. The last column ("Three per cent. annuities consol.") refers to interest earned by Con-solidated Annuities, the government securities of Great Britain.
2   Exchange Alley was a street next to the Royal Exchange, the financial heart of the city.
3   A plum was the popular term for £100,000, a satisfyingly huge and round sum of money.
4   In prosody, a spondee is "a metrical foot consisting of two long sylla-bles" (OED).
5   Richard Bentley (1662-1742) was a famous scholar and editor of classi-cal texts.

actions are incited: the world, in the eye of a philosopher, may be said to be a large madhouse." "It is true," answered Harley, "the passions of men are temporary madnesses; and sometimes very fatal in their effects,

From Macedonia's madman to the Swede."[1]

"It was, indeed," said the stranger, "a very mad thing in Charles, to think of adding so vast a country as Russia to his dominions; that would have been fatal indeed; the balance of the North would then have been lost; but the Sultan and I would never have allowed it."——"Sir!" said Harley, with no small surprise on his countenance. "Why, yes," answered the other, "the Sultan and I; do you know me? I am the Chan of Tartary."[2]

Harley was a good deal struck by this discovery; he had prudence enough, however, to conceal his amazement, and, bowing as low to the monarch as his dignity required, left him immediately, and joined his companions.

He found them in a quarter of the house set apart for the insane of the other sex, several of whom had gathered about the female visitors, and were examining, with rather more accuracy than might have been expected, the particulars of their dress.

Separate from the rest stood one, whose appearance had something of superior dignity. Her face, though pale and wasted, was less squalid than those of the others, and showed a dejection of that decent kind, which moves our pity unmixed with horror: upon her, therefore, the eyes of all were immediately turned. The keeper, who accompanied them, observed it: "This," said he, "is a young lady, who was born to ride in her coach and six. She was beloved, if the story I have heard is true, by a young gentleman, her equal in birth, though by no means her match in fortune: but Love, they say, is blind, and so she fancied him as much as he did her. Her father, it seems, would not hear of their marriage, and

---

1 Macedonia's madman is the famed warrior prince Alexander the Great (356-323 BCE) and the Swede is Charles XII of Sweden (1682-1718). The line is from Alexander Pope's poem *An Essay on Man*, IV, ii, 220.

2 The Chan of Tartary is another legendarily powerful soldier king, the fourteenth-century emperor of Cathay (China), known to Anglophone readers from the late-fourteenth-century *Travels of John Mandeville*.

threatened to turn her out of doors, if ever she saw him again. Upon this the young gentleman took a voyage to the West Indies, in hopes of bettering his fortune, and obtaining his mistress; but he was scarce landed, when he was seized with one of the fevers which are common in those islands, and died in a few days, lamented by every one that knew him. This news soon reached his mistress, who was at the same time pressed by her father to marry a rich miserly fellow, who was old enough to be her grandfather. The death of her lover had no effect on her inhuman parent; he was only the more earnest for her marriage with the man he had provided for her; and what between her despair at the death of the one, and her aversion to the other, the poor young lady was reduced to the condition you see her in. But God would not prosper such cruelty; her father's affairs soon after went to wreck, and he died almost a beggar."

Though this story was told in very plain language, it had particularly attracted Harley's notice: he had given it the tribute of some tears. The unfortunate young lady had till now seemed entranced in thought, with her eyes fixed on a little garnet ring she wore on her finger: she turned them now upon Harley. "My Billy is no more!" said she; "do you weep for my Billy? Blessings on your tears! I would weep too, but my brain is dry; and it burns, it burns, it burns!"—She drew nearer to Harley.—"Be comforted, young Lady," said he, "your Billy is in heaven." "Is he, indeed? and shall we meet again? And shall that frightful man (pointing to the keeper) not be there?—Alas! I am grown naughty of late; I have almost forgotten to think of heaven: yet I pray sometimes; when I can, I pray; and sometimes I sing; when I am saddest, I sing.—You shall hear me, hush!

"Light be the earth on Billy's breast,
"And green the sod that wraps his grave!"[1]

There was a plaintive wildness in the air not to be withstood; and, except the keeper's, there was not an unmoistened eye around her.

"Do you weep again?" said she; "I would not have you weep:

---

1 Like the mad Ophelia in Shakespeare's *Hamlet*, one of the sources for this character, the young woman breaks into song to comment on her tale. Here the ballad comes from John Gay's play *The What D'ye Call It*, II.viii.1.

you are like my Billy; you are, believe me; just so he looked when he gave me this ring; poor Billy! 'twas the last time ever we met!——

"'Twas when the seas were roaring—I love you for resembling my Billy; but I shall never love any man like him."——She stretched out her hand to Harley; he pressed it between both of his, and bathed it with his tears.—"Nay, that is Billy's ring," said she, "you cannot have it, indeed; but here is another, look here, which I plaited to-day, of some gold-thread from this bit of stuff; will you keep it for my sake? I am a strange girl;—but my heart is harmless: my poor heart! it will burst some day; feel how it beats."—She press'd his hand to her bosom, then holding her head in the attitude of listening——"Hark! one, two, three! be quiet, thou little trembler; my Billy's is cold!—but I had forgotten the ring."—She put it on his finger.—"Farewel! I must leave you now."—She would have withdrawn her hand; Harley held it to his lips.—"I dare not stay longer; my head throbs sadly: farewel!"——She walked with a hurried step to a little apartment at some distance. Harley stood fixed in astonishment and pity! his friend gave money to the keeper.—Harley looked on his ring.—He put a couple of guineas into the man's hand: "Be kind to that unfortunate"—He burst into tears, and left them.

CHAPTER XXI.

The Misanthropist.

THE friend, who had conducted him to Moorfields, called upon him again the next evening. After some talk on the adventures of the preceding day; "I carried you yesterday," said he to Harley, "to visit the mad; let me introduce you to-night, at supper, to one of the wise: but you must not look for any thing of the Socratic pleasantry about him; on the contrary, I warn you to expect the spirit of a Diogenes.[1] That you may be a little prepared for his extraordinary manner, I will let you into some particulars of his history:

---

1 Diogenes of Sinope (c. 400-325 BCE) was one of the best-known Cynics, a classical Greek philosophical school characterized by asceticism, bold disregard for convention, and emphasis on the pursuit of virtue rather than pleasure. Diogenes was famous as a rigorous, or harsh, analyst of human life and needs.

"He is the elder of the two sons of a gentleman of considerable estate in the country. Their father died when they were young: both were remarkable at school for quickness of parts, and extent of genius; this had been bred to no profession, because his father's fortune, which descended to him, was thought sufficient to set him above it; the other was put apprentice to an eminent attorney. In this the expectations of his friends were more consulted than his own inclination; for both his brother and he had feelings of that warm kind, that could ill brook a study so dry as the law, especially in that department of it which was allotted to him. But the difference of their tempers made the characteristical distinction between them. The younger, from the gentleness of his nature, bore with patience a situation entirely discordant to his genius and disposition. At times, indeed, his pride would suggest, of how little importance those talents were, which the partiality of his friends had often extolled: they were now incumbrances in a walk of life where the dull and the ignorant passed him at every turn; his fancy and his feeling, were invincible obstacles to eminence in a situation, where his fancy had no room for exertion, and his feeling experienced perpetual disgust. But these murmurings he never suffered to be heard; and that he might not offend the prudence of those who had been concerned in the choice of his profession, he continued to labour in it several years, 'till, by the death of a relation, he succeeded to an estate of little better than 100 l. a year, with which, and the small patrimony left him, he retired into the country, and made a love-match with a young lady of a temper similar to his own, with whom the sagacious world pitied him for finding happiness.

"But his elder brother, whom you are to see at supper, if you will do us the favour of your company, was naturally impetuous, decisive, and overbearing. He entered into life with those ardent expectations by which young men are commonly deluded: in his friendships, warm to excess; and equally violent in his dislikes. He was on the brink of marriage with a young lady, when one of those friends, for whose honour he would have pawned his life, made an elopement with that very goddess, and left him besides deeply engaged for sums which that good friend's extravagance had squandered.

"The dreams he had formerly enjoyed were now changed for ideas of a very different nature. He abjured all confidence in any thing of human form; sold his lands, which still produced him a very large reversion, came to town, and immured himself with a woman who had been his nurse, in little better than a garret; and has ever since applied his talents to the vilifying of his species. In one thing I must take the liberty to instruct you: however different your sentiments may be (and different they must be) you will suffer him to go on without contradiction; otherwise he will be silent immediately, and we shall not get a word from him all the night after." Harley promised to remember this injunction, and accepted the invitation of his friend.

When they arrived at the house, they were informed that the gentleman was come, and had been shown into the parlour. They found him sitting with a daughter of his friend's, about three years old, on his knee, whom he was teaching the alphabet from a horn-book:[1] at a little distance stood a sister of hers, some years older. "Get you away, Miss," said he to this last, "you are a pert gossip, and I will have nothing to do with you." "Nay," answered she, "Nancy is your favourite, you are quite in love with Nancy." "Take away that girl," said he to her father, whom he now observed to have entered the room, "she has woman about her already." The children were accordingly dismissed.

Betwixt that and supper-time he did not utter a syllable. When supper came, he quarrelled with every dish at table, but eat of them all; only exempting from his censures a sallad, "which you have not spoiled," said he, "because you have not attempted to cook it."

When the wine was set upon the table, he took from his pocket a particular smoking apparatus, and filled his pipe, without taking any more notice of Harley or his friend, than if no such persons had been in the room.

Harley could not help stealing a look of surprize at him, but his friend, who knew his humour, returned it, by annihilating his presence in the like manner, and, leaving him to his own meditations, addressed himself entirely to Harley.

In their discourse, some mention happened to be made of an

---

1   A horn-book is a device for teaching young children and other beginners to read, comprising "a leaf of paper containing the alphabet (often with the addition of the ten digits, some elements of spelling, and the Lord's Prayer) protected by a thin plate of transparent horn, and mounted on a tablet of wood with a projecting piece for a handle" (OED).

amiable character, and the words *honour* and *politeness* were applied to it. Upon this the gentleman, laying down his pipe, and changing the tone of his countenance, from an ironical grin to something more intently contemptuous: "Honour," said he, "Honour and Politeness! this is the coin of the world, and passes current with the fools of it. You have substituted the shadow Honour, instead of the substance Virtue; and have banished the reality of Friendship for the fictitious semblance, which you have termed Politeness: politeness, which consists in a certain ceremonious jargon, more ridiculous to the ear of reason than the voice of a puppet. You have invented sounds, which you worship, though they tyrannize over your peace: and are surrounded with empty forms, which take from the honest emotions of joy, and add to the poignancy of misfortune."——"Sir," said Harley—His friend winked to him, to remind him of the caution he had received. He was silenced by the thought—The philosopher turned his eye upon him: he examined him from top to toe, with a sort of triumphant contempt. Harley's coat happened to be a new one; the other's was as shabby as could possibly be supposed to be on the back of a gentleman: there was much significance in his look with regard to this coat: it spoke of the sleekness of folly, and the threadbareness of wisdom.

"Truth," continued he, "the most amiable, as well as the most natural of virtues, you are at pains to eradicate. Your very nurseries are seminaries of falsehood; and what is called Fashion in manhood completes the system of avowed insincerity. Mankind, in the gross, is a gaping monster, that loves to be deceived, and has seldom been disappointed: nor is their vanity less fallacious to your philosophers, who adopt modes of truth to follow them through the paths of error, and defend paradoxes merely to be singular in defending them. These are they whom ye term Ingenious; 'tis a phrase of commendation I detest; it implies an attempt to impose on my judgment, by flattering my imagination: yet these are they whose works are read by the old with delight, which the young are taught to look upon as the codes of knowledge and philosophy.

"Indeed, the education of your youth is every way preposterous; you waste at school years in improving talents, without having ever spent an hour in discovering them; one promiscuous line of instruction is followed, without regard to genius, capacity, or probable situation in the commonwealth. From this beargarden of the pedagogue, a raw unprincipled boy is turned loose upon the world to travel; without any ideas but those of improving his dress at Paris, or starting into taste by gazing on some paintings at Rome. Ask him of the manners of the people, and he will tell you, That the skirt is worn much shorter in France, and that every body eats macaroni in Italy. When he returns home, he buys a seat in parliament, and studies the constitution at Arthur's.[1]

"Nor are your females trained to any more useful purpose: they are taught, by the very rewards which their nurses propose for good behaviour, by the first thing like a jest which they hear from every male visitor of the family, that a young woman is a creature to be married; and when they are grown somewhat older, are instructed, that it is the purpose of marriage to have the enjoyment of pin money, and the expectation of a jointure."

*"These indeed are the effects of luxury, which is perhaps inseparable from a certain degree of power and grandeur in a nation. But it is not simply of the progress of luxury that we have to complain: did its votaries keep in their own sphere of thoughtless dissipation, we might despise them without emotion; but the frivolous pursuits of pleasure are mingled with the most important concerns of the state; and public enterprise shall sleep till he who should guide its operation has decided his bets at Newmar-

---

* Though the Curate could not remember having shown this chapter to any body, I strongly suspect that these political observations are the work of a later pen than the rest of this performance. There seems to have been, by some accident, a gap in the manuscript, from the words, "Expectation of a jointure," to these, "In short, man is an animal," where the present blank ends; and some other person (for the hand is different, and the ink whiter) has filled part of it with sentiments of his own. Whoever he was, he seems to have caught some portion of the spirit of the man he personates.

---

1 Arthur's Chocolate House, a well-known London gathering place, was established in 1755. The first coffee and chocolate houses opened in London in the second half of the seventeenth century and by the early eighteenth century there were hundreds of such establishments. A major part of their attraction was the newspapers kept there for the use of their (mostly male) patrons and they offered an important new space for political debate, though Mackenzie's characterization suggests a certain skepticism about the depth of such discussions. See details in Bryant Lillywhite, *London Coffee Houses* (London: 1963), item 54.

ket,[1] or fulfilled his engagement with a favourite mistress in the country. We want some man of acknowledged eminence to point our counsels with that firmness which the counsels of a great people require. We have hundreds of ministers, who press forward into office, without having ever learned that art which is necessary for every business, the art of thinking; and mistake the petulance, which could give inspiration to smart sarcasms on an obnoxious measure in a popular assembly, for the ability which is to balance the interest of kingdoms, and investigate the latent sources of national superiority. With the administration of such men the people can never be satisfied; for, besides that their confidence is gained only by the view of superior talents, there needs that depth of knowledge, which is not only acquainted with the just extent of power, but can also trace its connection with the expedient, to preserve its possessors from the contempt which attends irresolution, or the resentment which follows temerity."

★ ★ ★ ★ ★

[Here a considerable part is wanting.]

★ ★ "In short, man is an animal equally selfish and vain. Vanity, indeed, is but a modification of selfishness. From the latter, there are some who pretend to be free: they are generally such as declaim against the lust of wealth and power, because they have never been able to attain any high degree in either: they boast of generosity and feeling. They tell us (perhaps they tell us in rhime) that the sensations of an honest heart, of a mind universally benevolent, make up the quiet bliss which they enjoy; but they will not, by this, be exempted from the charge of selfishness. Whence the luxurious happiness they describe in their little family-circles? Whence the pleasure which they feel, when they trim their evening-fires, and listen to the howl of winter's wind? whence, but from the secret reflection of what houseless wretches feel from it? Or do you administer comfort in affliction—the motive is at hand; I have had it preached to me in nineteen out of twenty of your consolatory discourses——the comparative littleness of our own misfortunes.

"With vanity your best virtues are grossly tainted: your benev-

---

1 Newmarket was a horse-racing venue north of London, in Cambridgeshire, whose meetings were significant events in fashionable English life.

olence, which ye deduce immediately from the natural impulse of the heart, squints to it for its reward. There are some, indeed, who tell us of the satisfaction which flows from a secret consciousness of good actions: this secret satisfaction is truly excellent—when we have some friend to whom we may discover its excellence."

He now paus'd a moment to relight his pipe, when a clock, that stood at his back, struck eleven; he started up at the sound, took his hat and his cane, and, nodding good night with his head, walked out of the room. The gentleman of the house called a servant to bring the stranger's surtout.[1] "What sort of a night is it, fellow?" said he. "It rains, Sir," answered the servant, "with an easterly wind."—"Easterly for ever!"——He made no other reply; but shrugging up his shoulders till they almost touched his ears, wrapped himself tight in his great coat, and disappeared.

"This is a strange creature," said his friend to Harley. "I cannot say," answered he, "that his remarks are of the pleasant kind: it is curious to observe, how the nature of truth may be changed by the garb it wears; softened to the admonition of friendship, or soured into the severity of reproof: yet this severity may be useful to some tempers; it somewhat resembles a file; disagreeable in its operation, but hard metals may be the brighter for it.

★ ★ ★ ★ ★

CHAPTER XXV.

His skill in physiognomy.[2]

THE company at the baronet's removed to the playhouse accordingly, and Harley took his usual route into the Park. He observed, as he entered, a fresh-looking elderly gentleman, in conversation with a beggar, who, leaning on his crutch, was recounting the hardships he had undergone, and explaining the wretchedness of his present condition. This was a very interesting dialogue to Harley; he was rude enough therefore to slacken his pace as he approached, and at last, to make a full stop at the gentleman's back, who was just then expressing his compassion for the beggar, and regretting that he had not a farthing of change about

---

1 A surtout is "a man's great-coat or overcoat" (OED).
2 A number of eighteenth-century thinkers, most famously the Swiss theologian and scientist Johann Casper Lavater (1741-1801), had theorized and popularized the once-marginal study of physiognomy, the interpretation of facial features as signs of character or type.

him. At saying this, he looked piteously on the fellow: there was something in his physiognomy which caught Harley's notice: indeed physiognomy was one of Harley's foibles, for which he had been often rebuked by his aunt in the country; who used to tell him, that when he was come to her years and experience, he would know that all's not gold that glisters: and it must be owned, that his aunt was a very sensible, harsh-looking, maiden-lady of threescore and upwards. But he was too apt to forget this caution; and now, it seems, it had not occurred to him: stepping up, therefore, to the gentleman, who was lamenting the want of silver, "Your intentions, Sir," said he, "are so good, that I cannot help lending you my assistance to carry them into execution," and gave the beggar a shilling. The other returned a suitable compliment, and extolled the benevolence of Harley. They kept walking together, and benevolence grew the topic of discourse.

The stranger was fluent on the subject. "There is no use of money," said he, "equal to that of beneficence: with the profuse, it is lost; and even with those who lay it out according to the prudence of the world, the objects acquired by it pall on the sense, and have scarce become our own till they lose their value with the power of pleasing; but here the enjoyment grows on reflection, and our money is most truly ours, when it ceases being in our possession."

"Yet I agree in some measure," answered Harley, "with those who think, that charity to our common beggars is often misplaced; there are objects less obtrusive, whose title is a better one."

"We cannot easily distinguish," said the stranger; "and even of the worthless, are there not many whose impudence, or whose vice, may have been one dreadful consequence of misfortune?"

Harley looked again in his face, and blessed himself for his skill in physiognomy.

By this time they had reached the end of the walk: the old gentleman leaned on the rails to take breath, and in the mean time they were joined by a younger man, whose figure was much above the appearance of his dress, which was poor and shabby: Harley's former companion addressed him as an acquaintance, and they turned on the walk together.

The elder of the strangers complained of the closeness of the evening, and asked the other, if he would go with him into a house hard by, and take one draught of excellent cyder. "The man who keeps this house," said he to Harley, "was once a servant of mine: I could not think of turning loose upon the world a faithful old fellow, for no other reason but that his age had incapacitated him; so I gave him an annuity of ten pounds, with the help of which he has set up this little place here, and his daughter goes and sells milk in the city, while her father manages his taproom, as he calls it, at home. I can't well ask a gentleman of your appearance to accompany me to so paltry a place."—"Sir," replied Harley, interrupting him, "I would much rather enter it than the most celebrated tavern in town: to give to the necessitous, may sometimes be a weakness in the man; to encourage industry, is a duty in the citizen." They entered the house accordingly.

On a table, at the corner of the room, lay a pack of cards, loosely thrown together. The old gentleman reproved the man of the house for encouraging so idle an amusement: Harley attempted to defend him from the necessity of accommodating himself to the humour of his guests, and taking up the cards, began to shuffle them backwards and forwards in his hand. "Nay, I don't think cards so unpardonable an amusement as some do," replied the other; "and now and then, about this time of the evening, when my eyes begin to fail me for my book, I divert myself with a game at piquet,[1] without finding my morals a bit relaxed by it. Do you play piquet, Sir?" (to Harley.) Harley answered in the affirmative; upon which the other proposed playing a pool at a shilling the game, doubling the stakes: adding, that he never played higher with any body.

Harley's good nature could not refuse the benevolent old man; and the younger stranger, though he at first pleaded prior engagement, yet being earnestly solicited by his friend, at last yielded to solicitation.

When they began to play, the old gentleman, somewhat to the surprise of Harley, produced ten shillings to serve for markers of his score. "He had no change for the beggar," said Harley to himself; "but I can easily account for it: it is curious to observe the affection that inanimate things will create in us by a long acquaintance: if I may judge from my own feelings, the old man would not part with one of these counters for ten times its intrinsic value; it even got the better of his benevolence! I myself have a

---

1 Piquet is a card game, popular from the seventeenth to nineteenth centuries, "played by two persons with a pack of 32 cards (the low cards from the two to the six being excluded) in which points are scored on various groups or combinations of cards, and on tricks" (OED).

pair of old brass sleeve-buttons"—Here he was interrupted by being told, that the old gentleman had beat the younger, and that it was his turn to take up the conqueror. "Your game has been short;" said Harley. "I repiqued him," answered the old man, with joy sparkling in his countenance. Harley wished to be repiqued too, but he was disappointed; for he had the same good fortune against his opponent. Indeed, never did fortune, mutable as she is, delight in mutability so much as at that moment; the victory was so quick, and so constantly alternate, that the stake, in a short time, amounted to no less a sum than 12 1. Harley's proportion of which was within half a guinea of the money he had in his pocket. He had before proposed a division, but the old gentleman opposed it with such a pleasant warmth in his manner, that it was always over-ruled. Now, however, he told them, that he had an appointment with some gentlemen, and it was within a few minutes of his hour. The young stranger had gained one game, and was engaged in the second with the other: they agreed therefore that the stake should be divided, if the old gentleman won that; which was more than probable, as his score was 90 to 35, and he was elder hand; but a momentous repique decided it in favour of his adversary, who seemed to enjoy his victory mingled with regret, for having won too much, while his friend, with great ebullience of passion, many praises of his own good play, and many maledictions on the power of chance, took up the cards, and threw them into the fire.

CHAPTER XXVI.

The Man of Feeling in a brothel.

THE company he was engaged to meet were assembled in Fleet-street. He had walked some time along the Strand, amidst a crowd of those wretches who wait the uncertain wages of prostitution, with ideas of pity suitable to the scene around him, and the feelings he possessed, and had got as far as Somerset-house, when one of them laid hold of his arm, and, with a voice tremulous and faint, asked him for a pint of wine, in a manner more supplicatory than is usual with those whom the infamy of their profession has deprived of shame: he turned round at the demand, and looked stedfastly on the person who made it.

She was above the common size, and elegantly formed; her face was thin and hollow, and showed the remains of tarnished beauty. Her eyes were black, but had little of their lustre left: her cheeks had some paint laid on without art, and productive of no advantage to her complexion, which exhibited a deadly paleness on the other parts of her face.

Harley stood in the attitude of hesitation; which she interpreting to her advantage, repeated her request, and endeavoured to force a leer of invitation into her countenance. He took her arm, and they walked on to one of those obsequious taverns in the neighbourhood, where the dearness of the wine is a discharge in full for the character of the house. From what impulse he did this, we do not mean to inquire; as it has ever been against our nature to search for motives where bad ones are to be found.—They entered, and a waiter shewed them a room, and placed a bottle of claret on the table.

Harley filled the lady's glass; which she had no sooner tasted, than dropping it on the floor, and eagerly catching his arm, her eye grew fixed, her lip assumed a clayey whiteness, and she fell back lifeless in her chair.

Harley started from his seat, and, catching her in his arms, supported her from falling to the ground, looking wildly at the door, as if he wanted to run for assistance, but durst not leave the miserable creature. It was not till some minutes after, that it occurred to him to ring the bell, which at last however he thought of, and rung with repeated violence even after the waiter appeared. Luckily the waiter had his senses somewhat more about him; and snatching up a bottle of water, which stood on a buffet at the end of the room, he sprinkled it over the hands and face of the dying figure before him. She began to revive; and with the assistance of some hartshorn drops,[1] which Harley now for the first time drew from his pocket, was able to desire the waiter to bring her a crust of bread; of which she swallowed some mouthfuls with the appearance of the keenest hunger. The waiter withdrew: when turning to Harley, sobbing at the same time, and shedding tears, "I am sorry, Sir," said she, "that I should have given you so much trouble; but you will pity me when I tell you, that till now I have not tasted a morsel these two days past."— He fixed his eyes on hers—every circumstance but the last was forgotten; and he took her hand with as much respect as if she

---

1 Hartshorn drops are an aqueous solution of ammonia used to revive the faint, the chief source for which, in the seventeenth and eighteenth centuries, was harts' "horns" or antlers.

had been a dutchess. It was ever the privilege of misfortune to be revered by him.—"Two days!"—said he; "and I have fared sumptuously every day!"—He was reaching to the bell; she understood his meaning, and prevented him. "I beg, Sir," said she, "that you would give yourself no more trouble about a wretch who does not wish to live; but, at present, I could not eat a bit; my stomach even rose at the last mouthful of that crust." He offered to call a chair, saying, that he hoped a little rest would relieve her. He had one half-guinea left: "I am sorry," he said, "that at present I should be able to make you an offer of no more than this paltry sum." She burst into tears: "Your generosity, Sir, is abused; to bestow it on me is to take it from the virtuous: I have no title but misery to plead; misery of my own procuring." "No more of that," answered Harley; "there is virtue in these tears; let the fruit of them be virtue."—He rung, and ordered a chair.—"Though I am the vilest of beings," said she, "I have not forgotten every virtue; gratitude, I hope, I shall still have left, did I but know who is my benefactor."—"My name is Harley"—"Could I ever have an opportunity"—"You shall, and a glorious one too! your future conduct—but I do not mean to reproach you—if, I say—it will be the noblest reward—I will do myself the pleasure of seeing you again."—Here the waiter entered, and told them the chair was at the door: the lady informed Harley of her lodgings, and he promised to wait on her at ten next morning.

He led her to the chair, and returned to clear with the waiter, without ever once reflecting that he had no money in his pocket. He was ashamed to make an excuse; yet an excuse must be made: he was beginning to frame one, when the waiter cut him short, by telling him, that he could not run scores; but that, if he would leave his watch, or any other pledge, it would be as safe as if it lay in his pocket. Harley jumped at the proposal, and pulling out his watch, delivered it into his hands immediately; and having, for once, had the precaution to take a note of the lodging he intended to visit next morning, sallied forth with a flush of triumph on his face, without taking notice of the sneer of the waiter, who, twirling the watch in his hand, made him a profound bow at the door, and whispered to a girl, who stood in the passage, something, in which the word CULLY[1] was honoured with a particular emphasis.

---

1 A cully is "a man deceived or imposed upon; as, by sharpers or a strumpet" (Johnson's *Dictionary*).

CHAPTER XXVII.

His skill in physiognomy is doubted.

AFTER he had been some time with the company he had appointed to meet, and the last bottle was called for, he first recollected that he should be again at a loss how to discharge his share of the reckoning. He applied therefore to one of them, with whom he was most intimate, acknowledging that he had not a farthing of money about him; and, upon being jocularly asked the reason, acquainted them with the two adventures we have just now related. One of the company asked him, if the old man in Hyde-park did not wear a brownish coat, with a narrow gold-edging, and his companion an old green frock, with a buff-coloured waistcoat? Upon Harley's recollecting that they did; "Then," said he, "you may be thankful you have come off so well; they are two as noted sharpers, in their way, as any in town, and but t'other night took me in for a much larger sum: I had some thoughts of applying to a justice, but one does not like to be seen in those matters."

Harley answered, "That he could not but fancy the gentleman was mistaken, as he never saw a face promise more honesty than that of the old man he had met with."—"His face!" said a grave-looking man, who sat opposite to him, squirting the juice of his tobacco obliquely into the grate. There was something very emphatical in the action; for it was followed by a burst of laughter round the table. "Gentlemen," said Harley, "you are disposed to be merry; it may be as you imagine, for I confess myself ignorant of the town: but there is one thing which makes me bear the loss of my money with temper; the young fellow who won it, must have been miserably poor; I observed him borrow money for the stake from his friend; he had distress and hunger in his countenance: be his character what it may, his necessities at least plead for him."——At this there was a louder laugh than before. "Gentlemen," said the lawyer, (one of whose conversations with Harley we have already recorded) "here's a very pretty fellow for you: to have heard him talk some nights ago, as I did, you might have sworn he was a saint; yet now he games with sharpers, and loses his money; and is bubbled[1] by a fine story invented by a whore,

---

1 "To bubble. To cheat: a cant word" (Johnson's *Dictionary*).

and pawns his watch: here are sanctified doings with a witness!"

"Young gentleman," said his friend on the other side of the table, "let me advise you to be a little more cautious for the future; and as for faces——you may look into them to know, whether a man's nose be a long or a short one."

CHAPTER XXVIII.

He keeps his appointment.

THE last night's rallery of his companions was recalled to his remembrance when he awoke, and the colder homilies of prudence began to suggest some things which were nowise favourable for a performance of his promise to the unfortunate female he had met with before. He rose uncertain of his purpose; but the torpor of such considerations was seldom prevalent over the warmth of his nature. He walked some turns backwards and forwards in his room; he recalled the languid form of the fainting wretch to his mind; he wept at the recollection of her tears. "Though I am the vilest of beings, I have not forgotten every virtue; gratitude, I hope, I shall still have left."—He took a larger stride——"Powers of mercy that surround me!" cried he, "do ye not smile upon deeds like these? to calculate the chances of deception is too tedious a business for the life of man!"—The clock struck ten!—When he was got down stairs, he found that he had forgot the note of her lodgings; he gnawed his lips at the delay; he was fairly on the pavement, when he recollected having left his purse; he did but just prevent himself from articulating an imprecation. He rushed a second time up into his chamber. "What a wretch I am," said he; "ere this time perhaps—" 'Twas a perhaps not to be born:—two vibrations of a pendulum would have served him to lock his bureau;—but they could not be spared.

When he reached the house, and inquired for Miss Atkins, (for that was the lady's name) he was shown up three pair of stairs into a small room lighted by one narrow lattice, and patched round with shreds of different-coloured paper. In the darkest corner stood something like a bed, before which a tattered coverlet hung by way of curtain. He had not waited long when she appeared. Her face had the glister of new-washed tears on it. "I am ashamed, Sir," said she, "that you should have taken this fresh piece of trouble about one so little worthy of it; but, to the humane, I know there is a pleasure in goodness for its own sake:

if you have patience for the recital of my story, it may palliate, though it cannot excuse, my faults." Harley bowed, as a sign of assent, and she began as follows:

"I am the daughter of an officer, whom a service of forty years had advanced no higher than to the rank of captain. I have had hints from himself, and been informed by others, that it was in some measure owing to those principles of rigid honour, which it was his boast to possess, and which he early inculcated on me, that he had been able to arrive at no better station. My mother died when I was a child; old enough to grieve for her death, but incapable of remembering her precepts. Though my father was doatingly fond of her, yet there were some sentiments in which they materially differed: She had been bred from her infancy in the strictest principles of religion, and took the morality of her conduct from the motives which an adherence to those principles suggested. My father, who had been in the army from his youth, affixed an idea of pusillanimity to that virtue, which was formed by the doctrines, excited by the rewards, or guarded by the terrors of revelation; his darling idol was the honour of a soldier; a term which he held in such reverence, that he used it for his most sacred asseveration. When my mother died, I was for some time suffered to continue in those sentiments which her instructions had produced; but soon after, though, from respect to her memory, my father did not absolutely ridicule them, yet he shewed, in his discourse to others, so little regard to them, and, at times, suggested to me motives of action so different, that I was soon weaned from opinions, which I began to consider as the dreams of superstition, or the artful inventions of designing hypocrisy. My mother's books were left behind at the different quarters we removed to, and my reading was principally confined to plays, novels, and those poetical descriptions of the beauty of virtue and honour, which the circulating libraries easily afforded.[1]

---

1   The young person—especially the young girl—seduced by a course of novel-reading into lax morals and potential disaster had become a stock figure in literary texts by mid-century; Samuel Johnson's *Rambler* no.4 (31 March 1750) is the most well-known instance of the voluminous literature on the subject. Circulating libraries, from which books could be borrowed by subscribers, were widely regarded as promoting young women's novel-reading habits. First established in the 1720s, they were a flourishing national network by the second half of the century. Richard Brinsley Sheridan famously summarized (and satirized) concerns about such libraries and their novels in his play *The Rivals* (1775): "A circulating library ... is an evergreen tree of diabolical knowledge" (I.ii).

"As I was generally reckoned handsome, and the quickness of my parts extolled by all our visitors, my father had a pride in showing me to the world. I was young, giddy, open to adulation, and vain of those talents which acquired it.

"After the last war, my father was reduced to half-pay; with which we retired to a village in the country, which the acquaintance of some genteel families who resided in it, and the cheapness of living, particularly recommended. My father rented a small house, with a piece of ground sufficient to keep a horse for him, and a cow for the benefit of his family. An old man-servant managed his ground; while a maid, who had formerly been my mother's, and had since been mine, undertook the care of our little dairy: they were assisted in each of their provinces by my father and me; and we passed our time in a state of tranquillity, which he had always talked of with delight, and which my train of reading had taught me to admire.

"Though I had never seen the polite circles of the metropolis, the company my father had introduced me into had given me a degree of good-breeding, which soon discovered a superiority over the young ladies of our village. I was quoted as an example of politeness, and my company courted by most of the considerable families in the neighbourhood.

"Amongst the houses where I was frequently invited, was Sir George Winbrooke's. He had two daughters nearly of my age, with whom, though they had been bred up in those maxims of vulgar doctrine, which my superior understanding could not but despise, yet as their good-nature led them to an imitation of my manners in every thing else, I cultivated a particular friendship.

"Some months after our first acquaintance, Sir George's eldest son came home from his travels. His figure, his address, and conversation, were not unlike those warm ideas of an accomplished man which my favourite novels had taught me to form; and his sentiments, on the article of religion, were as liberal as my own: when any of these happened to be the topic of our discourse, I, who before had been silent, from a fear of being single in opposition, now kindled at the fire he raised, and defended our mutual opinions with all the eloquence I was mistress of. He would be respectfully attentive all the while; and when I had ended, would raise his eyes from the ground, look at me with a gaze of admiration, and express his applause in the highest strain of encomium. This was an incense the more pleasing, as I seldom or never had met with it before; for the young gentlemen who visited Sir

George were for the most part of that athletic order, the pleasure of whose lives is derived from fox-hunting: these are seldom solicitous to please the women at all; or if they were, would never think of applying their flattery to the mind.

"Mr. Winbrooke observed the weakness of my soul, and took every occasion of improving the esteem he had gained. He asked my opinion of every author, of every sentiment, with that submissive diffidence, which shewed an unlimited confidence in my understanding. I saw myself revered, as a superior being, by one whose judgment my vanity told me was not likely to err; preferred by him to all the other visitors of my sex, whose fortunes and rank should have entitled them to a much higher degree of notice: I saw their little jealousies at the distinguished attention he paid me; it was gratitude, it was pride, it was love! Love which had made too fatal a progress in my heart, before any declaration on his part should have warranted a return: but I interpreted every look of attention, every expression of compliment, to the passion I imagined him inspired with, and imputed to his sensibility that silence which was the effect of art and design. At length, however, he took an opportunity of declaring his love: he now expressed himself in such ardent terms, that prudence might have suspected their sincerity; but prudence is rarely found in the situation I had been unguardedly led into; besides, that the course of reading to which I had been accustomed, did not lead me to conclude, that his expressions could be too warm to be sincere: nor was I even alarmed at the manner in which he talked of marriage, a subjection, he often hinted, to which genuine love should scorn to be confined. The woman, he would often say, who had merit like mine to fix his affection, could easily command it for ever. That honour too which I revered, was often called in to enforce his sentiments. I did not, however, absolutely assent to them; but I found my regard for their opposites diminish by degrees. If it is dangerous to be convinced, it is dangerous to listen; for our reason is so much of a machine, that it will not always be able to resist, when the ear is perpetually assailed.

"In short, Mr. Harley, (for I tire you with a relation, the catastrophe of which you will already have imagined) I fell a prey to his artifices. He had not been able so thoroughly to convert me, that my conscience was silent on the subject; but he was so assiduous to give repeated proofs of unabated affection, that I hushed its suggestions as they rose. The world, however, I knew, was not to be silenced; and therefore I took occasion to express my uneasiness to my seducer, and intreat him, as he valued the peace of one to whom he professed such attachment, to remove it by a marriage. He made excuse from his dependance on the will of his father, but quieted my fears by the promise of endeavouring to win his assent.

"My father had been some days absent on a visit to a dying relation, from whom he had considerable expectations. I was left at home, with no other company than my books: my books I found were not now such companions as they used to be: I was restless, melancholy, unsatisfied with myself. But judge my situation when I received a billet from Mr. Winbrooke, informing me, that he had sounded Sir George on the subject we had talked of, and found him so averse to any match so unequal to his own rank and fortune, that he was obliged, with whatever reluctance, to bid adieu to a place, the remembrance of which should ever be dear to him.

"I read this letter a hundred times over. Alone, helpless, conscious of guilt, and abandoned by every better thought, my mind was one motley scene of terror, confusion, and remorse. A thousand expedients suggested themselves, and a thousand fears told me they would be vain: at last, in an agony of despair, I packed up a few clothes, took what money and trinkets were in the house, and set out for London, whither I understood he was gone; pretending to my maid, that I had received letters from my father requiring my immediate attendance. I had no other companion than a boy, a servant to the man from whom I hired my horses. I arrived in London within an hour of Mr. Winbrooke, and accidentally alighted at the very inn where he was.

"He started and turned pale when he saw me; but recovered himself in time enough to make many new protestations of regard, and beg me to make myself easy under a disappointment which was equally afflicting to him. He procured me lodgings, where I slept, or rather endeavoured to sleep, for that night. Next morning I saw him again; he then mildly observed on the imprudence of my precipitate flight from the country, and proposed my removing to lodgings at another end of the town, to elude the search of my father, till he should fall upon some method of excusing my conduct to him, and reconciling him to my return. We took a hackney-coach, and drove to the house he mentioned.[1]

---

1 A hackney coach is a carriage for public hire.

"It was situated in a dirty lane, furnished with a taudry affectation of finery, with some old family-pictures hanging on walls which their own cobwebs would better have suited. I was struck with a secret dread at entering; nor was it lessened by the appearance of the landlady, who had that look of selfish shrewdness, which, of all others, is the most hateful to those whose feelings are untinctured with the world. A girl, who she told us was her niece, sat by her, playing on a guitar, while herself was at work, with the assistance of spectacles, and had a prayer-book, with the leaves folded down in several places, lying on the table before her. Perhaps, Sir, I tire you with my minuteness; but the place, and every circumstance about it, is so impressed on my mind, that I shall never forget it.

"I dined that day with Mr. Winbrooke alone. He lost by degrees that restraint which I perceived too well to hang about him before, and, with his former gaiety and good-humour, repeated the flattering things, which, though they had once been fatal, I durst not now distrust. At last, taking my hand and kissing it, 'It is thus,' said he, 'that love will last, while freedom is preserved; thus let us ever be blest, without the galling thought that we are tied to a condition where we may cease to be so.' I answered, 'That the world thought otherwise; that it had certain ideas of good fame, which it was impossible not to wish to maintain.' 'The world,' said he, 'is a tyrant; they are slaves who obey it: let us be happy without the pale of the world. To-morrow I shall leave this quarter of it, for one, where the talkers of the world shall be foiled, and lose us. Could not my Emily accompany me? my friend, my companion, the mistress of my soul! Nay, do not look so, Emily! your father may grieve for a while, but your father shall be taken care of; this bank-bill I intend as the comfort for his daughter.'

"I could contain myself no longer: 'Wretch!' I exclaimed, 'dost thou imagine that my father's heart could brook dependance on the destroyer of his child, and tamely accept of a base equivalent for her honour and his own!' 'Honour, my Emily,' said he, 'is the word of fools, or of those wiser men who cheat them. 'Tis a fantastic bauble that does not suit the gravity of your father's age; but, whatever it is, I am afraid it can never be perfectly restored to you: exchange the word then, and let pleasure be your object now.' At these words he clasped me in his arms, and pressed his lips rudely to my bosom. I started from my seat, 'Perfidious villain!' said I, 'who dar'st insult the weakness thou hast undone;

were that father here, thy coward-soul would shrink from the vengeance of his honour! Curst be that wretch who has deprived him of it! oh! doubly curst, who has dragg'd on his hoary head the infamy which should have crushed her own!' I snatched a knife which lay beside me, and would have plunged it in my breast; but the monster prevented my purpose, and smiling with the grin of barbarous insult, 'Madam,' said he, 'I confess you are rather too much in heroics for me: I am sorry we should differ about trifles; but as I seem somehow to have offended you, I would willingly remedy it by taking my leave. You have been put to some foolish expence in this journey on my account; allow me to reimburse you.' So saying, he laid a bank-bill, of what amount I had no patience to see, upon the table. Shame, grief, and indignation, choaked my utterance; unable to speak my wrongs, and unable to bear them in silence, I fell in a swoon at his feet.

"What happened in the interval I cannot tell; but when I came to myself, I was in the arms of the landlady, with her niece chafing my temples, and doing all in her power for my recovery. She had much compassion in her countenance: the old woman assumed the softest look she was capable of, and both endeavoured to bring me comfort. They continued to show me many civilities, and even the aunt began to be less disagreeable in my sight. To the wretched, to the forlorn, as I was, small offices of kindness are endearing.

"Mean time my money was far spent, nor did I attempt to conceal my wants from their knowledge. I had frequent thoughts of returning to my father; but the dread of a life of scorn is insurmountable. I avoided therefore going abroad when I had a chance of being seen by any former acquaintance, nor indeed did my health for a great while permit it; and suffered the old woman, at her own suggestion, to call me niece at home, where we now and then saw (when they could prevail on me to leave my room) one or two other elderly women, and sometimes a grave business-like man, who showed great compassion for my indisposition, and made me very obligingly an offer of a room at his country-house for the recovery of my health. This offer I did not chuse to accept; but told my landlady, 'that I should be glad to be employed in any way of business which my skill in needle-work could recommend me to; confessing, at the same time, that I was afraid I should scarce be able to pay her what I already owed for board and lodging; and that for her other good offices, I had nothing but thanks to give her.'

"'My dear child,' said she, 'do not talk of paying; since I lost my own sweet girl, (here she wept) your very picture she was, Miss Emily, I have no body, except my niece, to whom I should leave any little thing I have been able to save: you shall live with me, my dear; and I have sometimes a little millenery work,[1] in which, when you are inclined to it, you may assist us. By the way, here are a pair of ruffles we have just finished for that gentleman you saw here at tea; a distant relation of mine, and a worthy man he is. 'Twas pity you refused the offer of an apartment at his country-house; my niece, you know, was to have accompanied you, and you might have fancied yourself at home: a most sweet place it is, and but a short mile beyond Hampstead. Who knows, Miss Emily, what effect such a visit might have had: if I had half your beauty, I should not waste it pining after e'er a worthless fellow of them all.' I felt my heart swell at her words; I would have been angry if I could; but I was in that stupid state which is not easily awakened to anger: when I would have chid her, the reproof stuck in my throat; I could only weep!

"Her want of respect increased, as I had not spirit to assert it; my work was now rather imposed than offered, and I became a drudge for the bread I eat: but my dependance and servility grew in proportion, and I was now in a situation which could not make any extraordinary exertions to disengage itself from either; I found myself with child.

"At last the wretch, who had thus trained me to destruction, hinted the purpose for which those means had been used. I discovered her to be an artful procuress for the pleasures of those, who are men of decency to the world in the midst of debauchery.

"I roused every spark of courage within me at the horrid proposal. She treated my passion at first somewhat mildly; but when I continued to exert it, she resented it with insult, and told me plainly, That if I did not soon comply with her desires, I should pay her every farthing I owed, or rot in a jail for life. I trembled at the thought; still, however, I resisted her importunities, and she put her threats in execution. I was conveyed to prison, weak from my condition, weaker from that struggle of grief and misery which for some time I had suffered. A miscarriage was the consequence.

---

1 Because of low wages, women working in the apparel and millinery trades were often driven into and associated with prostitution. Mackenzie hints here at the real business of the landlady and her "niece."

"Amidst all the horrors of such a state, surrounded with wretches totally callous, lost alike to humanity and to shame, think, Mr. Harley, think what I endured: nor wonder that I at last yielded to the solicitations of that miscreant I had seen at her house, and sunk to the prostitution which he tempted. But that was happiness compared to what I have suffered since. He soon abandoned me to the common use of the town, and I was cast among those miserable beings in whose society I have since remained.

"Oh! did the daughters of virtue know our sufferings! did they see our hearts torn with anguish amidst the affectation of gaiety which our faces are obliged to assume; our bodies tortured by disease, our minds with that consciousness which they cannot lose! Did they know, did they think of this, Mr. Harley!—their censures are just; but their pity perhaps might spare the wretches whom their justice should condemn.

"Last night, but for an exertion of benevolence which the infection of our infamy prevents even in the humane, had I been thrust out from this miserable place which misfortune has yet left me; exposed to the brutal insults of drunkenness, or dragged by that justice which I could not bribe, to the punishment which may correct, but, alas! can never amend, the abandoned objects of its terrors. From that, Mr. Harley, your goodness has relieved me."

He beckoned with his hand: he would have stopped the mention of his favours; but he could not speak, had it been to beg a diadem.

She saw his tears; her fortitude began to fail at the sight, when the voice of some stranger on the stairs awakened her attention. She listened for a moment; then starting up, exclaimed, "Merciful God! my father's voice!"

She had scarce uttered the word, when the door burst open, and a man entered in the garb of an officer. When he discovered his daughter and Harley, he started back a few paces; his look assumed a furious wildness! he laid his hand on his sword. The two objects of his wrath did not utter a syllable. "Villain," he cried, "thou seest a father who had once a daughter's honour to preserve; blasted as it now is, behold him ready to avenge its loss!"

Harley had by this time some power of utterance. "Sir," said he, "if you will be a moment calm"—"Infamous coward!" interrupted the other, "dost thou preach calmness to wrongs like mine?" He drew his sword. "Sir," said Harley, "let me tell you"—

The blood ran quicker to his cheek—his pulse beat one—no more—and regained the temperament of humanity!— "You are deceived, Sir," said he, "you are much deceived; but I forgive suspicions which your misfortunes have justified: I would not wrong you, upon my soul, I would not, for the dearest gratification of a thousand worlds: my heart bleeds for you!"

His daughter was now prostrate at his feet. "Strike," said she, "strike here a wretch, whose misery cannot end but with that death she deserves." Her hair had fallen on her shoulders! her look had the horrid calmness of out-breathed despair! Her father would have spoken; his lip quivered, his cheek grew pale! his eyes lost the lightning of their fury! there was a reproach in them, but with a mingling of pity! he turned them up to heaven—then on his daughter.—He laid his left hand on his heart—the sword dropped from his right——he burst into tears.

CHAPTER XXIX.

The distresses of a father.

HARLEY kneeled also at the side of the unfortunate daughter: "Allow me, Sir," said he, "to entreat your pardon for one whose offences have been already so signally punished. I know, I feel, that those tears, wrung from the heart of a father, are more dreadful to her than all the punishments your sword could have inflicted: accept the contrition of a child, whom heaven has restored to you." "Is she not lost," answered he, "irrecoverably lost? Damnation! a common prostitute to the meanest ruffian!"—"Calmly, my dear Sir," said Harley,—"did you know by what complicated misfortunes she had fallen to that miserable state in which you now behold her, I should have no need of words to excite your compassion. Think, Sir, of what once she was! Would you abandon her to the insults of an unfeeling world, deny her opportunity of penitence, and cut off the little comfort that still remains for your afflictions and her own!" "Speak," said he, addressing himself to his daughter; "speak, I will hear thee."—The desperation that supported her was lost; she fell to the ground, and bathed his feet with her tears!

Harley undertook her cause: he related the treacheries to which she had fallen a sacrifice, and again solicited the forgiveness of her father. He looked on her for some time in silence; the pride of a soldier's honour checked for a while the yearnings of his heart; but nature at last prevailed, he fell on her neck, and mingled his tears with hers.

Harley, who discovered from the dress of the stranger that he was just arrived from a journey, begged that they would both remove to his lodgings, till he could procure others for them. Atkins looked at him with some marks of surprise. His daughter now first recovered the power of speech: "Wretch as I am," said she, "yet there is some gratitude due to the preserver of your child. See him now before you. To him I owe my life, or at least the comfort of imploring your forgiveness before I die." "Pardon me, young gentleman," said Atkins, "I fear my passion wronged you."

"Never, never, Sir," said Harley; "if it had, your reconciliation to your daughter were an atonement a thousand fold." He then repeated his request that he might be allowed to conduct them to his lodgings, to which Mr. Atkins at last consented. He took his daughter's arm, "Come, my Emily," said he, "we can never, never recover that happiness we have lost; but time may teach us to remember our misfortunes with patience."

When they arrived at the house where Harley lodged, he was informed, that the first floor was then vacant, and that the gentleman and his daughter might be accommodated there. While he was upon this inquiry, Miss Atkins informed her father more particularly what she owed to his benevolence. When he returned into the room where they were, Atkins ran and embraced him; begged him again to forgive the offence he had given him, and made the warmest protestations of gratitude for his favours. We would attempt to describe the joy which Harley felt on this occasion, did it not occur to us, that one half of the world could not understand it though we did; and the other half will, by this time, have understood it without any description at all.

Miss Atkins now retired to her chamber, to take some rest from the violence of the emotions she had suffered. When she was gone, her father, addressing himself to Harley, said, "You have a right, Sir, to be informed of the present situation of one who owes so much to your compassion for his misfortunes. My daughter I find has informed you what that was at the fatal juncture when they began. Her distresses you have heard, you have pitied as they deserved; with mine perhaps I cannot so easily make you acquainted. You have a feeling heart, Mr. Harley; I bless it that it has saved my child; but you never were a father; a father torn by that most dreadful of calamities, the dishonour of a child he doated on! You have been already informed of some of the circumstances of her elopement. I was then from home, called by the death of a relation, who, though he would never advance me a shilling on the utmost exigency in his lifetime, left me all the gleanings of his frugality at his death. I would not write this intelligence to my daughter, because I intended to be the bearer myself; and, as soon as my business would allow me, I set out on my return, winged with all the haste of paternal affection. I fondly built those schemes of future happiness, which present prosperity is ever busy to suggest: my Emily was concerned in them all. As I approached our little dwelling, my heart throbbed with the anticipation of joy and welcome. I imagined the cheering fire, the blissful contentment of a frugal meal, made luxurious by a daughter's smile: I painted to myself her surprize at the tidings of our new-acquired riches, our fond disputes about the disposal of them.

"The road was shortened by the dreams of happiness I enjoyed, and it began to be dark as I reached the house: I alighted from my horse, and walked softly up stairs to the room we commonly sat in. I was somewhat disappointed at not finding my daughter there. I rung the bell; her maid appeared, and showed no small signs of wonder at the summons. She blessed herself as she entered the room: I smiled at her surprize. 'Where is Miss Emily, Sir?' said she. 'Emily!' 'Yes, Sir; she has been gone hence some days, upon receipt of those letters you sent her.' 'Letters!' said I.—'Yes, Sir; so she told me, and went off in all haste that very night.'

"I stood aghast as she spoke; but was able so far to recollect myself, as to put on the affectation of calmness, and telling her there was certainly some mistake in the affair, desired her to leave me.

"When she was gone, I threw myself into a chair in that state of uncertainty which is of all others the most dreadful. The gay visions with which I had delighted myself, vanished in an instant: I was tortured with tracing back the same circle of doubt and disappointment. My head grew dizzy as I thought: I called the servant again, and asked her a hundred questions to no purpose; there was not room even for conjecture.

"Something at last arose in my mind, which we call Hope, without knowing what it is. I wished myself deluded by it; but it could not prevail over my returning fears. I rose and walked through the room. My Emily's spinet stood at the end of it, open, with a book of music folded down at some of my favourite lessons. I touched the keys; there was a vibration in the sound that froze my blood: I looked around, and methought the family-pictures on the walls gazed on me with compassion in their faces. I sat down again with an attempt at more composure; I started at every creaking of the door, and my ears rung with imaginary noises!

"I had not remained long in this situation, when the arrival of a friend, who had accidentally heard of my return, put an end to my doubts, by the recital of my daughter's dishonour. He told me he had his information from a young gentleman, to whom Winbrooke had boasted of having seduced her.

"I started from my seat, with broken curses on my lips, and, without knowing whither I should pursue them, ordered my servant to load my pistols, and saddle my horses. My friend, however, with great difficulty, persuaded me to compose myself for that night, promising to accompany me on the morrow to Sir George Winbrooke's in quest of his son.

"The morrow came, after a night spent in a state little distant from madness. We went as early as decency would allow to Sir George's; He received me with politeness, and indeed compassion; protested his abhorrence of his son's conduct, and told me that he had set out some days before for London, on which place he had procured a draught for a large sum, on pretence of finishing his travels; but that he had not heard from him since his departure.

"I did not wait for any more, either of information or comfort; but, against the united remonstrances of Sir George and my friend, set out instantly for London with a frantic uncertainty of purpose; but there all manner of search was in vain. I could trace neither of them any farther than the inn where they first put up on their arrival; and after some days fruitless inquiry, returned home destitute of every little hope that had hitherto supported me. The journeys I had made, the restless nights I had spent, above all, the perturbation of my mind, had the effect which naturally might be expected; a very dangerous fever was the consequence. From this, however, contrary to the expectation of my physicians, I recovered. It was now that I first felt something like calmness of mind; probably from being reduced to a state which could not produce the exertions of anguish or despair. A stupid melancholy settled on my soul: I could endure to live with an apathy of life; at times I forgot my resentment, and wept at the remembrance of my child.

"Such has been the tenor of my days since that fatal moment when these misfortunes began, till yesterday, that I received a letter from a friend in town, acquainting me of her present situation. Could such tales as mine, Mr. Harley, be sometimes suggested to the daughters of levity, did they but know with what anxiety the heart of a parent flutters round the child he loves, they would be less apt to construe into harshness that delicate concern for their conduct, which they often complain of as laying restraint upon things, to the young, the gay, and the thoughtless, seemingly harmless and indifferent. Alas! I fondly imagined that I needed not even these common cautions! my Emily was the joy of my age, and the pride of my soul!—Those things are now no more! they are lost for ever! Her death I could have born! but the death of her honour has added obloquy and shame to that sorrow which bends my gray hairs to the dust!"

As he spoke these last words, his voice trembled in his throat; it was now lost in his tears! He sat with his face half-turned from Harley, as if he would have hid the sorrow which he felt. Harley was in the same attitude himself; he durst not meet Atkins' eye with a tear; but gathering his stifled breath, "Let me intreat you, Sir," said he, "to hope better things. The world is ever tyrannical; it warps our sorrows to edge them with keener affliction: let us not be slaves to the names it affixes to motive or to action. I know an ingenuous mind cannot help feeling when they sting: but there are considerations by which it may be overcome; its fantastic ideas vanish as they rise; they teach us—to look beyond it."

★ ★ ★ ★ ★

A FRAGMENT.

Showing his success with the baronet.

* * * THE card he received was in the politest style in which disappointment could be communicated; the baronet "was under a necessity of giving up his application for Mr. Harley, as he was informed, that the lease was engaged for a gentleman who had long served his majesty in another capacity, and whose merit had entitled him to the first lucrative thing that should be vacant." Even Harley could not murmur at such a disposal.—"Perhaps," said he to himself, "some war-worn officer, who, like poor Atkins, had been neglected from reasons which merited the highest

advancement; whose honour could not stoop to solicit the preferment he deserved; perhaps, with a family, taught the principles of delicacy, without the means of supporting it; a wife and children—gracious heaven! whom my wishes would have deprived of bread."—

He was interrupted in his reverie by some one tapping him on the shoulder, and, on turning round, he discovered it to be the very man who had explained to him the condition of his gay companion at Hydepark-corner. "I am glad to see you, Sir," said he; "I believe we are fellows in disappointment." Harley stared, and said that he was at a loss to understand him. "Poh! you need not be so shy," answered the other; "every one for himself is but fair, and I had much rather you had got it than the rascally gauger." Harley still protested his ignorance of what he meant. "Why, the lease of Bancroft-manor; had not you been applying for it?" "I confess I was," replied Harley; "but I cannot conceive how you should be interested in the matter."—"Why, I was making interest for it myself," said he, "and I think I had some title: I voted for this same baronet at the last election, and made some of my friends do so too; though I would not have you imagine that I sold my vote; no, I scorn it, let me tell you, I scorn it; but I thought as how this man was staunch and true, and I find he's but a double-faced fellow after all, and speechifies in the house for any side he hopes to make most by. Oh! how many fine speeches and squeezings by the hand we had of him on the canvass!—'And if I shall ever be so happy as to have an opportunity of serving you'——A murrain[1] on the smooth-tongu'd knave; and after all to get it for this pimp of a gauger."—"The gauger! there must be some mistake," said Harley; "he writes me, that it was engaged for one whose long services"— "Services!" interrupted the other; "you shall hear: Services! Yes, his sister arrived in town a few days ago, and is now sempstress to the baronet. A plague on all rogues! says honest Sam Wrightson: I shall but just drink damnation to them to-night, in a crown's worth of Ashley's, and leave London to-morrow by sunrise."—"I shall leave it too," said Harley; and so he accordingly did.

In passing through Piccadilly, he had observed on the window of an inn a notification of the departure of a stage-coach for a place in his road homewards; in the way back to his lodgings he took a seat in it for his return.

---

1 "Plague, pestilence" (OED).

CHAPTER XXXIII

He leaves London.—Characters in a stage-coach.[1]

THE company in the stage-coach consisted of a grocer and his wife, who were going to pay a visit to some of their country friends; a young officer, who took this way of marching to quarters; a middle-aged gentlewoman, who had been hired as housekeeper to some family in the country; and an elderly well-looking man, with a remarkable old-fashioned periwig.

Harley, upon entering, discovered but one vacant seat, next the grocer's wife, which, from his natural shyness of temper, he made no scruple to occupy, however aware that being driven backwards always disagreed with him.

Though his inclination to physiognomy had met with some rubs in the metropolis, he had not yet lost his attachment to that science: he set himself therefore to examine, as usual, the countenances of his companions. Here indeed he was not long in doubt as to the preference; for besides that the elderly gentleman, who sat opposite to him, had features by nature more expressive of good dispositions, there was something in that periwig we mentioned peculiarly attractive of Harley's regard.

He had not been long employed in these speculations, when he found himself attacked with that faintish sickness, which was the natural consequence of his situation in the coach. The paleness of his countenance was first observed by the housekeeper, who immediately made offer of her smelling-bottle, which Harley however declined, telling at the same time the cause of his uneasiness. The gentleman on the opposite side of the coach now first turned his eye from the side-direction in which it had been fixed, and begged Harley to exchange places with him, expressing his regret that he had not made the proposal before. Harley thanked him; and, upon being assured that both seats were alike to him,

---

1   The use of the stage-coach as an important locus for social interaction, here and in other eighteenth-century novels—most famously in Book One of Henry Fielding's *Joseph Andrews* (1742)—reflects the enormous increase and improvement of transport networks including toll-roads and stage-coach lines across England and Scotland in the period. The drawn-out encounter of socially diverse and otherwise unacquainted types in long-distance coach trips functions as a self-consciously modern set-piece.

was about to accept of his offer, when the young gentleman of the sword, putting on an arch look, laid hold of the other's arm, "So, my old boy," said he, "I find you have still some youthful blood about you; but, with your leave, I will do myself the honour of sitting by this lady;" and took his place accordingly. The grocer stared him as full in the face as his own short neck would allow; and his wife, who was a little round-fac'd woman, with a great deal of colour in her cheeks, drew up at the compliment that was paid her, looking first at the officer, and then at the housekeeper.

This incident was productive of some discourse; for before, though there was sometimes a cough or a hem from the grocer, and the officer now and then humm'd a few notes of a song, there had not a single word passed the lips of any of the company.

Mrs. Grocer observed, how ill-convenient it was for people, who could not be drove backwards, to travel in a stage. This brought on a dissertation on stage-coaches in general, and the pleasure of keeping a chay[1] of one's own; which led to another, on the great riches of Mr. Deputy Bearskin, who, according to her, had once been of that industrious order of youths who sweep the crossings of the streets for the conveniency of passengers, but, by various fortunate accidents, had now acquired an immense fortune, and kept his coach and a dozen livery servants. All this afforded ample fund for conversation, if conversation it might be called, that was carried on solely by the before-mentioned lady, nobody offering to interrupt her, except that the officer sometimes signified his approbation by a variety of oaths, a sort of phraseology in which he seemed extremely versant. She appealed indeed frequently to her husband for the authenticity of certain facts, of which the good man as often protested his total ignorance; but as he was always called fool, or something very like it, for his pains, he at last contrived to support the credit of his wife without prejudice to his conscience, and signified his assent by a noise not unlike the grunting of that animal which in shape and fatness he somewhat resembled.

The housekeeper, and the old gentleman who sat next to Harley, were now observed to be fast asleep; at which the lady,

---

1 Chay is a "vulgar corruption of CHAISE" (OED); "Mrs. Grocer"'s comments on keeping one's own coach as a sign of wealth are accurate: the costs of feeding, housing, and caring for the horses alone amounted to several hundred pounds a year.

who had been at such pains to entertain them, muttered some words of displeasure, and, upon the officer's whispering to smoke the old put,[1] both she and her husband purs'd up their mouths into a contemptuous smile. Harley looked sternly on the grocer: "You are come, Sir," said he, "to those years when you might have learned some reverence for age: as for this young man, who has so lately escaped from the nursery, he may be allowed to divert himself." "Dam'-me, Sir," said the officer, "do you call me young?" striking up the front of his hat, and stretching forward on his seat, till his face almost touched Harley's. It is probable, however, that he discovered something there which tended to pacify him; for, on the lady's intreating them not to quarrel, he very soon resumed his posture and calmness together, and was rather less profuse of his oaths during the rest of the journey.

It is possible the old gentleman had waked time enough to hear the last part of this discourse; at least (whether from that cause, or that he too was a physiognomist) he wore a look remarkably complacent[2] to Harley, who, on his part, shewed a particular observance of him: indeed they had soon a better opportunity of making their acquaintance, as the coach arrived that night at the town where the officer's regiment lay, and the places of destination of their other fellow-travellers, it seems, were at no great distance; for next morning the old gentleman and Harley were the only passengers remaining.

When they left the inn in the morning, Harley, pulling out a little pocket-book, began to examine the contents, and make some corrections with a pencil. "This," said he, turning to his companion, "is an amusement with which I sometimes pass idle hours at an inn: these are quotations from those humble poets, who trust their fame to the brittle tenure of windows and drinking-glasses."[3] "From our inns," returned the gentleman, "a stranger might imagine that we were a nation of poets; machines at least con-

---

1   To smoke is "to sneer; to ridicule to the face" (Johnson's *Dictionary*); a put is "a stupid man, silly fellow, blockhead, 'duffer'" (OED).

2   Complacent is used here in the older sense of "showing a disposition to please, obliging in manner, complaisant" (OED).

3   The habit of inscribing verse or commentary on windows and drinking glasses with a diamond ring, as in the proposal scene between Moll and her Virginian husband in Daniel Defoe's *Moll Flanders* (1722), was observed to be an especially popular custom in inns along the road to Scotland.

taining poetry, which the motion of a journey emptied of their contents: is it from the vanity of being thought geniuses, or a mere mechanical imitation of the custom of others, that we are tempted to scrawl rhime upon such places?"

"Whether vanity is the cause of our becoming rhimesters or not," answered Harley, "it is a pretty certain effect of it. An old man of my acquaintance, who deals in apothegms, used to say, That he had known few men without envy, few wits without ill-nature, and no poet without vanity; and I believe his remark is a pretty just one: vanity has been immemorially the charter of poets. In this the ancients were more honest than we are; the old poets frequently make boastful predictions of the immortality their works shall acquire them; ours, in their dedications and prefatory discourses, employ much eloquence to praise their patrons, and much seeming honesty to condemn themselves, or at least to apologize for their productions to the world: but this, in my opinion, is the more assuming manner of the two; for of all the garbs I ever saw pride put on, that of her humility is to me the most disgusting."

"It is natural enough for a poet to be vain," said the stranger: "the little worlds which he raises, the inspiration which he claims, may easily be productive of self-importance; though that inspiration is fabulous, it brings on egotism, which is always the parent of vanity."

"It may be supposed," answered Harley, "that inspiration of old was an article of religious faith; in modern times it may be translated a propensity to compose; and I believe it is not always most readily found where the poets have fixed its residence, amidst groves and plains, and the scenes of pastoral retirement. The mind may be there unbent from the cares of the world; but it will frequently, at the same time, be unnerved from any great exertion: it will feel imperfect ideas which it cannot express, and wander without effort over the regions of reflection."

"There is at least," said the stranger, "one advantage in the poetical inclination, that it is an incentive to philanthropy. There is a certain poetic ground, on which a man cannot tread without feelings that enlarge the heart: the causes of human depravity vanish before the romantic enthusiasm he professes; and many who are not able to reach the Parnassian[1] heights,

---

1 Poetic. Mount Parnassus "is the name of a mountain in central Greece, anciently sacred to Apollo and the muses. Hence used allusively in reference to literature, especially poetry" (OED).

may yet approach so near as to be bettered by the air of the climate."

"I have always thought so," replied Harley; "but this is an argument with the prudent against it: they urge the danger of unfitness for the world."

"I allow it," returned the other; "but I believe it is not always rightfully imputed to the bent for poetry: that is only one effect of the common cause.—Jack, says his father, is indeed no scholar; nor could all the drubbings from his master ever bring him one step forward in his accidence or syntax: but I intend him for a merchant.—Allow the same indulgence to Tom.—Tom reads Virgil and Horace when he should be casting accounts; and but t'other day he pawned his great-coat for an edition of Shakespeare.—But Tom would have been as he is, though Virgil and Horace had never been born, though Shakespeare had died a link-boy;[1] for his nurse will tell you, that when he was a child, he broke his rattle, to discover what it was that sounded within it; and burnt the sticks of his go-cart, because he liked to see the sparkling of timber in the fire.—'Tis a sad case; but what is to be done?—Why, Jack shall make a fortune, dine on venison, and drink claret.—Ay, but Tom—Tom shall dine with his brother, when his pride will let him; at other times, he shall bless God over a half-pint of ale and a Welsh-rabbit;[2] and both shall go to heaven as they may.—That's a poor prospect for Tom, says the father.—To go to heaven! I cannot agree with him."

"Perhaps," said Harley, "we now-a-days discourage the romantic turn a little too much. Our boys are prudent too soon. Mistake me not, I do not mean to blame them for want of levity or dissipation; but their pleasures are those of hackneyed vice, blunted to every finer emotion by the repetition of debauch; and their desire of pleasure is warped to the desire of wealth, as the means of procuring it. The immense riches acquired by individuals have erected a standard of ambition, destructive of private morals, and of public virtue. The weaknesses of vice are left us; but the most

---

1 A link-boy is "a boy employed to carry a link [torch] to light passengers along the streets" (OED).

2 Welsh-rabbit is a poor man's meal of melted cheese mixed with beer or ale, salt, and pepper, poured over toasted bread.

allowable of our failings we are taught to despise. Love, the passion most natural to the sensibility of youth, has lost the plaintive dignity he once possessed, for the unmeaning simper of a dangling coxcomb; and the only serious concern, that of a dowry, is settled, even amongst the beardless leaders of the dancing-school. The Frivolous and the Interested (might a satyrist say) are the characteristical features of the age; they are visible even in the essays of our philosophers. They laugh at the pedantry of our fathers, who complained of the times in which they lived; they are at pains to persuade us how much those were deceived; they pride themselves in defending things as they find them, and in exploring the barren sounds which had been reared into motives for action. To this their style is suited; and the manly tone of reason is exchanged for perpetual efforts at sneer and ridicule. This I hold to be an alarming crisis in the corruption of a state; when not only is virtue declined, and vice prevailing, but when the praises of virtue are forgotten, and the infamy of vice unfelt."

They soon after arrived at the next inn upon the route of the stage-coach, when the stranger told Harley, that his brother's house, to which he was returning, lay at no great distance, and he must therefore unwillingly bid him adieu.

"I should like," said Harley, taking his hand, "to have some word to remember so much seeming worth by: my name is Harley."—"I shall remember it," answered the old gentleman, "in my prayers; mine is Silton."

And Silton indeed it was; Ben Silton himself! Once more, my honoured friend, farewel!——Born to be happy without the world, to that peaceful happiness which the world has not to bestow! Envy never scowled on thy life, nor hatred smiled on thy grave.

CHAPTER. XXXIV.

He meets an old acquaintance.

WHEN the stage-coach arrived at the place of its destination, Harley began to consider how he should proceed the remaining part of his journey. He was very civilly accosted by the master of the inn, who offered to accommodate him either with a post-chaise[1] or horses, to any distance he had a mind: but as he did

---

1   "A travelling carriage, either hired from stage to stage, or drawn by horses so hired" (OED).

things frequently in a way different from what other people call natural, he refused these offers, and set out immediately a-foot, having first put a spare shirt in his pocket, and given directions for the forwarding of his portmanteau. This was a method of travelling which he was accustomed to take; it saved the trouble of provision for any animal but himself, and left him at liberty to chuse his quarters, either at an inn, or at the first cottage in which he saw a face he liked: nay, when he was not peculiarly attracted by the reasonable creation, he would sometimes consort with a species of inferior rank, and lay himself down to sleep by the side of a rock, or on the banks of a rivulet. He did few things without a motive, but his motives were rather eccentric; and the usual and expedient were terms which he held to be very indefinite, and which therefore he did not always apply to the sense in which they are commonly understood.

The sun was now in his decline, and the evening remarkably serene, when he entered a hollow part of the road, which winded between the surrounding banks, and seamed the sward in different lines, as the choice of travellers had directed them to tread it. It seemed to be little frequented now, for some of those had partly recovered their former verdure. The scene was such as induced Harley to stand and enjoy it; when, turning round, his notice was attracted by an object, which the fixture of his eye on the spot he walked had before prevented him from observing.

An old man, who from his dress seemed to have been a soldier, lay fast asleep on the ground; a knapsack rested on a stone at his right hand, while his staff and brass-hilted sword were crossed at his left.

Harley looked on him with the most earnest attention. He was one of those figures which Salvator[1] would have drawn; nor was the surrounding scenery unlike the wildness of that painter's backgrounds. The banks on each side were covered with fantastic shrub-wood, and at a little distance, on the top of one of them, stood a finger-post, to mark the directions of two roads which diverged from the point where it was placed. A rock, with some

---

1 Salvatore Rosa (1615-73) was an Italian painter of wild and sublime landscapes and their inhabitants (seamen, soldiers, shepherds, and bandits) whose work was widely known and extremely popular in eighteenth-century Britain. Here Mackenzie displays his familiarity with the dominant conventions of eighteenth-century visual art and landscape aesthetics.

dangling wild flowers, jutted out above where the soldier lay; on which grew the stump of a large tree, white with age, and a single twisted branch shaded his face as he slept. His face had the marks of manly comeliness impaired by time; his forehead was not altogether bald, but its hairs might have been numbered; while a few white locks behind crossed the brown of his neck with a contrast the most venerable to a mind like Harley's. "Thou art old," said he to himself; "but age has not brought thee rest for its infirmities; I fear those silver hairs have not found shelter from thy country, though that neck has been bronzed in its service." The stranger waked. He looked at Harley with the appearance of some confusion: it was a pain the latter knew too well to think of causing in another; he turned and went on. The old man readjusted his knapsack, and followed in one of the tracks on the opposite side of the road.

When Harley heard the tread of his feet behind him, he could not help stealing back a glance at his fellow-traveller. He seemed to bend under the weight of his knapsack; he halted on his walk, and one of his arms was supported by a sling, and lay motionless across his breast. He had that steady look of sorrow, which indicates that its owner has gazed upon his griefs till he has forgotten to lament them; yet not without those streaks of complacency, which a good mind will sometimes throw into the countenance, through all the incumbent load of its depression.

He had now advanced nearer to Harley, and, with an uncertain sort of voice, begged to know what it was o'clock; "I fear," said he, "sleep has beguiled me of my time, and I shall hardly have light enough left to carry me to the end of my journey." "Father!" said Harley, (who by this time found the romantic enthusiasm rising within him) "how far do you mean to go?" "But a little way, Sir," returned the other; "and indeed it is but a little way I can manage now: 'tis just four miles from the height to the village, thither I am going." "I am going thither too," said Harley; "we may make the road shorter to each other. You seem to have served your country, Sir, to have served it hardly too; 'tis a character I have the highest esteem for.—I would not be impertinently inquisitive; but there is that in your appearance which excites my curiosity to know something more of you: in the mean time suffer me to carry that knapsack."

The old man gazed on him; a tear stood in his eye! "Young gentleman," said he, "you are too good: may Heaven bless you for an old man's sake, who has nothing but his blessing to give! but my knapsack is so familiar to my shoulders, that I should walk the worse for wanting it; and it would be troublesome to you, who have not been used to its weight." "Far from it," answered Harley, "I should tread the lighter; it would be the most honourable badge I ever wore."

"Sir," said the stranger, who had looked earnestly in Harley's face during the last part of his discourse, "is not your name Harley?" "It is," replied he; "I am ashamed to say I have forgotten yours." "You may well have forgotten my face," said the stranger, "'tis a long time since you saw it; but possibly you may remember something of old Edwards."—"Edwards!" cried Harley, "Oh! heavens!" and sprung to embrace him; "let me clasp those knees on which I have sat so often: Edwards!——I shall never forget that fire-side, round which I have been so happy! But where, where have you been? where is Jack? where is your daughter? How has it fared with them when fortune, I fear, has been so unkind to you?"—"'Tis a long tale," replied Edwards, "but I will try to tell it you as we walk.

"When you were at school in the neighbourhood, you remember me at South-hill: that farm had been possessed by my father, grandfather, and great-grandfather, which last was a younger brother of that very man's ancestor who is now lord of the manor. I thought I managed it, as they had done, with prudence; I paid my rent regularly as it became due, and had always as much behind as gave bread to me and my children. But my last lease was out soon after you left that part of the country; and the squire, who had lately got a London-attorney for his steward, would not renew it, because, he said, he did not chuse to have any farm under 300 l. a year value on his estate; but offered to give me the preference on the same terms with another, if I chose to take the one he had marked out, of which mine was a part.

"What could I do, Mr. Harley? I feared the undertaking was too great for me; yet to leave, at my age, the house I had lived in from my cradle! I could not, Mr. Harley, I could not; there was not a tree about it that I did not look on as my father, my brother, or my child: so I even ran the risk, and took the squire's offer of the whole. But I had soon reason to repent of my bargain: the steward had taken care that my former farm should be the best land of the division: I was obliged to hire more servants, and I could not have my eye over them all; some unfavourable seasons followed one another, and I found my affairs entangling on my hands. To add to my distress, a considerable corn-factor turned bankrupt with a sum of mine in his possession: I failed paying my rent so punctually as I was wont to do, and the same steward had my stock taken in execution in a few days after. So, Mr. Harley, there was an end of my prosperity. However, there was as much produced from the sale of my effects as paid my debts and saved me from a jail: I thank God I wronged no man, and the world could never charge me with dishonesty.

"Had you seen us, Mr. Harley, when we were turned out of South-hill, I am sure you would have wept at the sight. You remember old Trusty, my shag house-dog; I shall never forget it while I live; the poor creature was blind with age, and could scarce crawl after us to the door; he went however as far as the gooseberry-bush; that you may remember stood on the left side of the yard; he was wont to bask in the sun there: when he had reached that spot, he stopped; we went on: I called to him; he wagged his tail, but did not stir: I called again; he lay down: I whistled, and cried Trusty; he gave a short howl, and died! I could have lain down and died too; but God gave me strength to live for my children."

The old man now paused a moment to take breath. He eyed Harley's face; it was bathed in tears: the story was grown familiar to himself; he dropped one tear and no more.

"Though I was poor," continued he, "I was not altogether without credit. A gentleman in the neighbourhood, who had a small farm unoccupied at the time, offered to let me have it, on giving security for the rent, which I made shift to procure. It was a piece of ground which required management to make any thing of; but it was nearly within the compass of my son's labour and my own. We exerted all our industry to bring it into some heart. We began to succeed tolerably, and lived content on its produce, when an unlucky accident brought us under the displeasure of a neighbouring justice of the peace, and broke all our family-happiness again.

"My son was a remarkable good shooter; he had always kept a pointer on our former farm, and thought no harm in doing so now; when one day, having sprung a covey[1] on our own ground, the dog, of his own accord, followed them into the justice's. My son laid down his gun, and went after his dog to bring him back:

---

1 A covey is "a brood or hatch of partridges" or sometimes other game birds such as grouse (OED).

the game-keeper, who had marked the birds, came up, and seeing the pointer, shot him just as my son approached. The creature fell; my son ran up to him: he died with a complaining sort of cry at his master's feet. Jack could bear it no longer; but flying at the game-keeper, wrenched his gun out of his hand, and with the butt-end of it felled him to the ground.

"He had scarce got home, when a constable came with a warrant, and dragged him to prison; there he lay, for the justices would not take bail, till he was tried at the quarter-sessions[1] for the assault and battery. His fine was hard upon us to pay; we contrived however to live the worse for it, and make up the loss by our frugality: but the justice was not content with that punishment, and soon after had an opportunity of punishing us indeed.

"An officer with press-orders[2] came down to our county, and having met with the justices, agreed that they should pitch on a certain number, who could most easily be spared from the county, of whom he would take care to clear it: my son's name was in the justices' list.

"'Twas on a Christmas eve, and the birth-day too of my son's little boy. The night was piercing cold, and it blew a storm, with showers of hail and snow. We had made up a cheering fire in an inner room; I sat before it in my wicker-chair, blessing Providence, that had still left a shelter for me and my children. My son's two little ones were holding their gambols around us; my heart warmed at the sight; I brought a bottle of my best ale, and all our misfortunes were forgotten.

"It had long been our custom to play a game at blind-man's-buff on that night, and it was not omitted now; so to it we fell, I, and my son, and his wife, the daughter of a neighbouring farmer, who happened to be with us at the time, the two children, and an old maid-servant, that had lived with me from a child. The lot fell on my son to be blindfolded: we had continued some time in our game, when he groped his way into an outer-room in pursuit of some of us, who, he imagined, had taken shelter there; we kept

---

1 "A court of limited criminal and civil jurisdiction, and of appeal, held quarterly" (OED).
2 A reference to the notorious practice of press-ganging men, or drafting them by use of force, into the navy, a practice which continued in Britain into the nineteenth century. The navy found difficulty in recruiting sailors by regular means because of high mortality rates and brutal treatment and conditions.

snug in our places, and enjoyed his mistake. He had not been long there, when he was suddenly seized from behind; 'I shall have you now,' said he, and turned about. 'Shall you so, master?' answered the ruffian, who had laid hold of him; 'we shall make you play at another sort of game by and by.'"—At these words Harley started with a convulsive sort of motion, and grasping Edwards's sword, drew it half out of the scabbard, with a look of the most frantic wildness. Edwards gently replaced it in its sheath, and went on with his relation.

"On hearing these words in a strange voice, we all rushed out to discover the cause; the room by this time was almost full of the gang. My daughter-in-law fainted at the sight; the maid and I ran to assist her, while my poor son remained motionless, gazing by turns on his children and their mother. We soon recovered her to life, and begged her to retire and wait the issue of the affair; but she flew to her husband, and clung round him in an agony of terror and grief.

"In the gang was one of a smoother aspect, whom, by his dress, we discovered to be a serjeant of foot: he came up to me, and told me, that my son had his choice of the sea or land service, whispering at the same time, that if he chose the land, he might get off, on procuring him another man, and paying a certain sum for his freedom. The money we could just muster up in the house, by the assistance of the maid, who produced, in a green bag, all the little savings of her service; but the man we could not expect to find. My daughter-in-law gazed upon her children with a look of the wildest despair: 'My poor infants!' said she, 'your father is forced from you; who shall now labour for your bread; or must your mother beg for herself and you?' I prayed her to be patient; but comfort I had none to give her. At last, calling the serjeant aside, I asked him, 'If I was too old to be accepted in place of my son?' 'Why, I don't know,' said he; 'you are rather old to be sure, but yet the money may do much.' I put the money in his hand; and coming back to my children, 'Jack,' said I, 'you are free; live to give your wife and these little ones bread; I will go, my child, in your stead: I have but little life to lose, and if I staid, should add one to the wretches you left behind.'—'No,' replied my son, 'I am not that coward you imagine me; heaven forbid, that my father's grey hairs should be so exposed, while I sat idle at home; I am young, and able to endure much, and God will take care of you and my family.' 'Jack,' said I, 'I will put an end to this matter; you have never hitherto disobeyed me; I will not be contradicted in this; stay at home, I charge you, and, for my sake, be kind to my children.'

"Our parting, Mr. Harley, I cannot describe to you; it was the first time we ever had parted: the very press-gang could scarce keep from tears; but the serjeant, who had seemed the softest before, was now the least moved of them all. He conducted me to a party of new-raised recruits, who lay at a village in the neighbourhood; and we soon after joined the regiment. I had not been long with it, when we were ordered to the East Indies,[1] where I was soon made a serjeant, and might have picked up some money, if my heart had been as hard as some others were; but my nature was never of that kind, that could think of getting rich at the expence of my conscience.

"Amongst our prisoners was an old Indian, whom some of our officers supposed to have a treasure hidden somewhere; which is no uncommon practice in that country. They pressed him to discover it. He declared he had none; but that would not satisfy them: so they ordered him to be tied to a stake, and suffer fifty lashes every morning, till he should learn to speak out, as they said. Oh! Mr. Harley, had you seen him, as I did, with his hands bound behind him, suffering in silence, while the big drops trickled down his shrivelled cheeks, and wet his gray beard, which some of the inhuman soldiers plucked in scorn! I could not bear it, I could not for my soul; and one morning, when the rest of the guard were out of the way, I found means to let him escape. I was tried by a court-martial for negligence of my post, and ordered, in compassion of my age, and having got this wound in my arm, and that in my leg, in the service, only to suffer 300 lashes, and be turned out of the regiment; but my sentence was mitigated as to the lashes, and I had only 200.[2] When

---

1 The term "East Indies" refers to Southeast Asia, including India, Indonesia, and Malaysia; as "opposed to the West Indies, or Central American islands" (OED). Here Mackenzie begins a critique of colonialism and its extortionary practices continued in ch. xxxvi, though he seems to conflate the West and East Indies here in a somewhat generically imagined colonial site: the hidden trove of gold and unearthly stoicism of the captive Indian in particular seem to recall European accounts of North and South American native inhabitants.

2 The severity of the punishment far exceeds standard naval practice. Even notoriously harsh disciplinarians such as Captain William Bligh of the *Bounty* punished serious infractions such as desertion with floggings of 24 or 48 lashes. See Greg Dening, *Mr Bligh's Bad Language* (Cambridge: Cambridge UP, 1992).

I had suffered these, I was turned out of the camp, and had betwixt three and four hundred miles to travel before I could reach a sea-port, without guide to conduct me, or money to buy me provisions by the way. I set out however, resolved to walk as far as I could, and then to lay myself down and die. But I had scarce gone a mile, when I was met by the Indian whom I had delivered. He pressed me in his arms, and kissed the marks of the lashes on my back a thousand times: he led me to a little hut, where some friend of his dwelt; and after I was recovered of my wounds, conducted me so far on my journey himself, and sent another Indian to guide me through the rest. When we parted, he pulled out a purse with two hundred pieces of gold in it: 'Take this,' said he, 'my dear preserver, it is all I have been able to procure.' I begged him not to bring himself to poverty for my sake, who should probably have no need of it long; but he insisted on my accepting it. He embraced me:—'You are an Englishman,' said he, 'but the Great Spirit has given you an Indian heart; may he bear up the weight of your old age, and blunt the arrow that brings it rest!' We parted; and not long after I made shift to get my passage to England. 'Tis but about a week since I landed, and I am going to end my days in the arms of my son. This sum may be of use to him and his children; 'tis all the value I put upon it. I thank heaven, I never was covetous of wealth; I never had much, but was always so happy as to be content with my little."

When Edwards had ended his relation Harley stood a while looking at him in silence; at last he pressed him in his arms, and when he had given vent to the fullness of his heart by a shower of tears, "Edwards," said he, "let me hold thee to my bosom; let me imprint the virtue of thy sufferings on my soul. Come, my hon-oured veteran! let me endeavour to soften the last days of a life, worn out in the service of humanity: call me also thy son, and let me cherish thee as a father." Edwards, from whom the recollec-tion of his own sufferings had scarce forced a tear, now blubbered like a boy; he could not speak his gratitude, but by some short exclamations of blessings upon Harley.

CHAPTER XXXV.

He misses an old acquaintance.—
An adventure consequent upon it.

WHEN they had arrived within a little way of the village they journeyed to, Harley stopped short, and looked stedfastly on the mouldering walls of a ruined house that stood on the road-side. "Oh heavens!" he cried, "what do I see! silent, unroofed, and desolate! Are all thy gay tenants gone? do I hear their hum no more? Edwards, look there, look there! the scene of my infant joys, my earliest friendships, laid waste and ruinous! That was the very school where I was boarded when you were at South-hill; 'tis but a twelvemonth since I saw it standing, and its benches filled with cherubs: that opposite side of the road was the green on which they sported; see it now ploughed up! I would have given fifty times its value to have saved it from the sacrilege of that plough."

"Dear Sir," replied Edwards, "perhaps they have left it from choice, and may have got another spot as good." "They cannot," said Harley, "they cannot! I shall never see the sward covered with its daisies, nor pressed by the dance of the dear innocents: I shall never see that stump decked with the garlands which their little hands had gathered. These two long stones which now lie at the foot of it, were once the supports of a hut I myself assisted to rear: I have sat on the sods within it, when we had spread our banquet of apples before us, and been more blest—Oh! Edwards! infinitely more blest than ever I shall be again."

Just then a woman passed them on the road, and discovered some signs of wonder at the attitude of Harley, who stood, with his hands folded together, looking with a moistened eye on the fallen pillars of the hut. He was too much entranced in thought to observe her at all; but Edwards civilly accosting her, desired to know, if that had not been the school-house, and how it came into the condition in which they now saw it? "Alack a-day!" said she, "it was the school-house indeed; but to be sure, Sir, the squire has pulled it down, because it stood in the way of his prospects."—"What! how! prospects! pulled down!" cried Harley.[1]—"Yes, to be sure, Sir; and the green, where the children used to play, he has ploughed up, because, he said, they hurt his fence on the other side of it."—"Curses on his narrow heart," cried Harley, "that could violate a right so sacred! Heaven blast the wretch!

---

1   A critique of the destruction of the older social fabric of country life by landlords eager to "improve" their estates by pulling down cottages and structures impeding their views. Mackenzie here directly echoes Oliver Goldsmith's famous complaint in "The Deserted Village," a poem which he praised to correspondents, just after its publication in May 1770, while working on his novel.

'And from his derogate body never spring
'A babe to honour him!'[1]

But I need not, Edwards, I need not, (recovering himself a little) he is cursed enough already: to him the noblest source of happiness is denied; and the cares of his sordid soul shall gnaw it, while thou sittest over a brown crust, smiling on those mangled limbs that have saved thy son and his children!" "If you want any thing with the school-mistress, Sir," said the woman, "I can show you the way to her house." He followed her without knowing whither he went.

They stopped at the door of a snug habitation, where sat an elderly woman with a boy and a girl before her, each of whom held a supper of bread and milk in their hands. "There, Sir, is the school-mistress."—"Madam," said Harley, "was not an old venerable man school-master here some time ago?" "Yes, Sir, he was; poor man! the loss of his former school-house, I believe, broke his heart, for he died soon after it was taken down; and as another has not yet been found, I have that charge in the mean time."—"And this boy and girl, I presume, are your pupils?"— "Ay, Sir, they are poor orphans, put under my care by the parish; and more promising children I never saw." "Orphans!" said Harley. "Yes, Sir, of honest creditable parents as any in the parish; and it is a shame for some folks to forget their relations, at a time when they have most need to remember them."—— "Madam," said Harley, "let us never forget that we are all relations." He kissed the children.

"Their father, Sir," continued she, "was a farmer here in the neighbourhood, and a sober industrious man he was; but nobody can help misfortunes: what with bad crops, and bad debts, which are worse, his affairs went to wreck, and both he and his wife died of broken hearts. And a sweet couple they were, Sir; there was not a properer man to look on in the country than John Edwards, and so indeed were all the Edwardses." "What Edwardses?" cried the old soldier hastily. "The Edwardses of South-hill; and a worthy family they were."——"South-hill!" said he, in a languid voice, and fell back into the arms of the astonished Harley. The school-mistress ran for some water, and a smelling-bottle, with the assis-

---

1   A slightly altered quotation from Shakespeare's *King Lear*, I. iv, where Lear curses his daughter Goneril: "And from her derogate body never spring / A babe to honour her!"

tance of which they soon recovered the unfortunate Edwards. He stared wildly for some time, then folding his orphan grand-children in his arms, "Oh! my children, my children!" he cried, "have I found you thus? My poor Jack! art thou gone? I thought thou shouldst have carried thy father's grey hairs to the grave! And these little ones"—his tears choaked his utterance, and he fell again on the necks of the children.

"My dear old man!" said Harley, "Providence has sent you to relieve them; it will bless me, if I can be the means of assisting you."—"Yes indeed, Sir," answered the boy, "father, when he was a dying, bade God bless us; and prayed, that if grandfather lived, he might send him to support us."—"Where did they lay my boy?" said Edwards. "In the Old Church-yard," replied the woman, "hard by his mother."—"I will show it you," answered the boy; "for I have wept over it many a time, when first I came amongst strange folks." He took the old man's hand, Harley laid hold of his sister's, and they walked in silence to the church-yard.

There was an old stone, with the corner broken off, and some letters, half-covered with moss, to denote the names of the dead: there was a cyphered R.E. plainer than the rest: it was the tomb they sought. "Here it is, grandfather," said the boy. Edwards gazed upon it without uttering a word: the girl, who had only sighed before, now wept outright; her brother sobbed, but he stifled his sobbing. "I have told sister," said he, "that she should not take it so to heart; she can knit already, and I shall soon be able to dig: we shall not starve, sister, indeed we shall not, nor shall grandfather neither."—The girl cried afresh; Harley kissed off her tears as they flowed, and wept between every kiss.

CHAPTER XXXVI.

He returns home.——A description of his retinue.

IT was with some difficulty that Harley prevailed on the old man to leave the spot where the remains of his son were laid. At last, with the assistance of the school-mistress, he prevailed; and she accommodated Edwards and him with beds in her house, there being nothing like an inn nearer than the distance of some miles.

In the morning, Harley persuaded Edwards to come, with the children, to his house, which was distant but a short day's journey. The boy walked in his grandfather's hand; and the name of

Edwards procured him a neighbouring farmer's horse, on which a servant mounted, with the girl on a pillow before him.

With this train Harley returned to the abode of his fathers: and we cannot but think, that his enjoyment was as great as if he had arrived from the tour of Europe, with a Swiss valet for his companion, and half a dozen snuff-boxes, with invisible hinges, in his pocket. But we take our ideas from sounds which folly has invented; Fashion, Bon-ton, and Virtu, are the names of certain idols, to which we sacrifice the genuine pleasures of the soul:[1] in this world of semblance, we are contented with personating happiness; to feel it, is an art beyond us.

It was otherwise with Harley: he ran up stairs to his aunt, with the history of his fellow-travellers glowing on his lips. His aunt was an economist; but she knew the pleasure of doing charitable things, and withal was fond of her nephew, and solicitous to oblige him. She received old Edwards therefore with a look of more complacency than is perhaps natural to maiden-ladies of threescore, and was remarkably attentive to his grand-children: she roasted apples with her own hands for their supper, and made up a little bed beside her own for the girl. Edwards made some attempts towards an acknowledgment for these favours; but his young friend stopped them in their beginnings. "Whosoever receiveth any of these children"—said his aunt,[2] for her acquaintance with her Bible was habitual.

Early next morning, Harley stole into the room where Edwards lay: he expected to have found him a-bed; but in this he was mistaken: the old man had risen, and was leaning over his sleeping grand-son, with the tears flowing down his cheeks. At first he did not perceive Harley; when he did, he endeavoured to hide his grief, and crossing his eyes with his hand, expressed his surprise at seeing him so early astir. "I was thinking of you," said Harley,

---

1 Mackenzie mockingly contrasts Harley's trip with the 'Grand Tour' of Europe, customary among upper-class young men at this time. The goal was to arrive home with a greater level of cultural sophistication and a knowledge of modern European languages and societies. However, Mackenzie suggests, the young gentleman more often returned only with trifling souvenirs, an obsession with modishness, and mere pretensions to erudition: sprinkling his conversation with foreign phrases such as "virtu" (a taste for and knowledge of the fine arts), for example.
2 Quoting Jesus' injunction to his disciples to seek humility: "Whosoever ... shall receive one such little child in my name receiveth me" Matthew 18.5 (also recorded in Mark 9.37 and Luke 9.48).

"and your children: I learned last night that a small farm of mine in the neighbourhood is now vacant; if you will occupy it, I shall gain a good neighbour, and be able in some measure to repay the notice you took of me when a boy; and as the furniture of the house is mine, it will be so much trouble saved." Edwards's tears gushed afresh, and Harley led him to see the place he intended for him.

The house upon this farm was indeed little better than a hut; its situation, however, was pleasant, and Edwards, assisted by the beneficence of Harley, set about improving its neatness and convenience. He staked out a piece of the green before for a garden, and Peter, who acted in Harley's family as valet, butler, and gardener, had orders to furnish him with parcels of the different seeds he chose to sow in it. I have seen his master at work in this little spot, with his coat off, and his dibble[1] in his hand: it was a scene of tranquil virtue to have stopped an angel on his errands of mercy! Harley had contrived to lead a little bubbling brook through a green walk in the middle of the ground, upon which he had erected a mill in miniature for the diversion of Edwards's infant-grandson, and made shift in its construction to introduce a pliant bit of wood, that answered with its fairy clack to the murmuring of the rill that turned it. I have seen him stand, listening to these mingled sounds, with his eye fixed on the boy, and the smile of conscious satisfaction on his cheek; while the old man, with a look half turned to Harley, and half to Heaven, breathed an ejaculation of gratitude and piety.

Father of mercies! I also would thank thee, that not only hast thou assigned eternal rewards to virtue, but that, even in this bad world, the lines of our duty, and our happiness, are so frequently woven together.

A FRAGMENT.

The Man of Feeling talks of what he does not understand.—
An incident.

* * * * "EDWARDS," said he, "I have a proper regard for the prosperity of my country: every native of it appropriates to him-

---

1 "An instrument used to make holes in the ground for seeds, bulbs, or young plants. In its simplest form, a stout pointed cylindrical stick, with or without a handle" (OED).

self some share of the power, or the fame, which, as a nation, it acquires; but I cannot throw off the man so much, as to rejoice at our conquests in India.[1] You tell me of immense territories subject to the English: I cannot think of their possessions, without being led to enquire, by what right they possess them. They came there as traders, bartering the commodities they brought for others which their purchasers could spare; and however great their profits were, they were then equitable. But what title have the subjects of another kingdom to establish an empire in India? to give laws to a country where the inhabitants received them on the terms of friendly commerce? You say they are happier under our regulations than the tyranny of their own petty princes. I must doubt it, from the conduct of those by whom these regulations have been made. They have drained the treasuries of Nabobs,[2] who must fill them by oppressing the industry of their subjects. Nor is this to be wondered at, when we consider the motive upon which those gentlemen do not deny their going to India. The fame of conquest, barbarous as that motive is, is but a secondary consideration: there are certain stations in wealth to which the warriors of the East aspire. It is there indeed where the wishes of their friends assign them eminence, where the question of their country is pointed at their return. When shall I see a commander return from India in the pride of honourable poverty?—You describe the victories they have gained; they are sullied by the cause in which they fought: you enumerate the spoils of

---

1 The British moved from being trading partners with India in the seventeenth century, through the British East India Company, to taking control of most of the country by the early nineteenth century. The decisive event in the shift from trade to rule is usually considered to be the defeat of the army of the Nawab of Bengal by Robert Clive (leading the armed forces of the East India Company) in the 1757 Battle of Plassey. Public concern about the role and conduct of the British in India, especially in connection with unscrupulous profiteering and cruel treatment of the native Indian population, was intense in the decades following 1757, with famous trials of prominent British leaders in India for corruption and other crimes, such as Clive himself after his return from India in 1767, and Warren Hastings, the first Governor-General of India, in 1788-95.

2 Mackenzie uses the word "nabobs" in its original sense of provincial rulers and governors under the Mughal empire in India. The term was also commonly used to refer to Europeans returned from India with large fortunes acquired there.

those victories; they are covered with the blood of the van-quished!

"Could you tell me of some conqueror giving peace and happiness to the conquered? did he accept the gifts of their princes to use them for the comfort of those whose fathers, sons, or husbands, fell in battle? did he use his power to gain security and freedom to the regions of oppression and slavery? did he endear the British name by examples of generosity, which the most barbarous or most depraved are rarely able to resist? did he return with the consciousness of duty discharged to his country, and humanity to his fellow-creatures? did he return with no lace on his coat, no slaves in his retinue, no chariot at his door, and no Burgundy at his table?—these were laurels which princes might envy—which an honest man would not condemn!"

"Your maxims, Mr. Harley, are certainly right," said Edwards. "I am not capable of arguing with you; but I imagine there are great temptations in a great degree of riches, which it is no easy matter to resist: those a poor man like me cannot describe, because he never knew them; and perhaps I have reason to bless God that I never did; for then, it is likely, I should have withstood them no better than my neighbours. For you know, Sir, that it is not the fashion now, as it was in former times, that I have read of in books, when your great generals died so poor, that they did not leave wherewithal to buy them a coffin; and people thought the better of their memories for it:[1] if they did so now-a-days, I question if any body, except yourself, and some few like you, would thank them."

"I am sorry," replied Harley, "that there is so much truth in what you say; but, however the general current of opinion may point, the feelings are not yet lost that applaud benevolence, and censure inhumanity. Let us endeavour to strengthen them in ourselves; and we, who live sequestered from the noise of the multitude, have better opportunities of listening undisturbed to their voice."

---

1 Mackenzie here makes a standard contrast between British and Roman imperial greed and the virtuous austerity of the early Roman republic, when famous soldiers and statesmen such as Publius Valerius and Menenius Agrippa, after a lifetime of public service, died in honorable poverty and were buried at public expense. See Livy, *The Early History of Rome*, books I-V of *The History of Rome From its Foundation*, trans. Aubrey de Selincount with an introduction by R.M. Ogilvie (London: Penguin, 1971) 123, 143.

They now approached the little dwelling of Edwards. A maid-servant, whom he had hired to assist him in the care of his grand-children, met them a little way from the house: "There is a young lady within with the children," said she. Edwards expressed his surprise at the visit: it was, however, not the less true; and we mean to account for it.

This young lady then was no other than Miss Walton. She had heard the old man's history from Harley, as we have already relat-ed it. Curiosity, or some other motive, made her desirous to see his grandchildren: this she had an opportunity of gratifying soon, the children, in some of their walks, having strolled as far as her father's avenue. She put several questions to both; she was delighted with the simplicity of their answers, and promised, that if they continued to be good children, and do as their grandfather bid them, she would soon see them again, and bring some present or other for their reward. This promise she had performed now: she came attended only by her maid, and brought with her a com-plete suit of green for the boy, and a chintz gown, a cap, and a suit of ribbands, for his sister. She had time enough, with her maid's assistance, to equip them in their new habiliments before Harley and Edwards returned. The boy heard his grandfather's voice, and, with that silent joy which his present finery inspired, ran to the door to meet him: putting one hand in his, with the other pointed to his sister, "See," said he, "what Miss Walton has brought us."——Edwards gazed on them. Harley fixed his eyes on Miss Walton: hers were turned to the ground;—in Edwards's was a beamy moisture.—He folded his hands together—"I can-not speak, young lady," said he, "to thank you." Neither could Harley. There were a thousand sentiments;—but they gushed so impetuously on his heart, that he could not utter a syllable.

★ ★ ★ ★ ★

CHAPTER XL.

The Man of Feeling jealous.

THE desire of communicating knowledge or intelligence, is an argument with those who hold that man is naturally a social ani-mal. It is indeed one of the earliest propensities we discover; but it may be doubted whether the pleasure (for pleasure there cer-tainly is) arising from it be not often more selfish than social: for we frequently observe the tidings of Ill communicated as eagerly as the annunciation of Good. Is it that we delight in observing the effects of the stronger passions? for we are all philosophers in this respect; and it is perhaps amongst the spectators at Tyburn[1] that the most genuine are to be found.

Was it from this motive that Peter came one morning into his master's room with a meaning face of recital? His master indeed did not at first observe it; for he was sitting, with one shoe buckled, delineating portraits in the fire. "I have brushed those clothes, Sir, as you ordered me."—Harley nodded his head; but Peter observed that his hat wanted brushing too: his master nodded again. At last Peter bethought him, that the fire needed stirring; and, taking up the poker, demolished the turban'd-head of a Saracen, while his master was seeking out a body for it. "The morning is main cold, Sir," said Peter. "Is it?" said Harley. "Yes, Sir; I have been as far as Tom Dowson's to fetch some barberries he had picked for Mrs. Margery. There was a rare junketting last night at Thomas's among Sir Harry Benson's servants: he lay at Squire Walton's, but he would not suffer his servants to trouble the family; so, to be sure, they were all at Tom's, and had a fiddle and a hot supper in the big room where the justices meet about the destroying of hares and partridges, and them things; and Tom's eyes looked so red and so bleared when I called him to get the barberries:—And I hear as how Sir Harry is going to be married to Miss Walton."——"How! Miss Walton married!" said Harley. "Why, it mayn't be true, Sir; for all that; but Tom's wife told it me, and to be sure the servants told her, and their master told them, as I guess, Sir; but it mayn't be true for all that, as I said before."—"Have done with your idle information," said Harley:—"Is my aunt come down into the parlour to breakfast?"——"Yes, Sir."—"Tell her I'll be with her immediately."——

When Peter was gone, he stood with his eyes fixed on the ground, and the last words of his intelligence vibrating in his ears. "Miss Walton married!" he sighed—and walked down stairs, with his shoe as it was, and the buckle in his hand. His aunt, however, was pretty well accustomed to those appearances of absence; besides that the natural gravity of her temper, which was commonly called into exertion by the care of her household concerns, was such, as not easily to be discomposed by any circumstance of

1 Tyburn was the main site of public executions by hanging in London from 1571 to 1783.

accidental impropriety. She too had been informed of the intended match between Sir Harry Benson and Miss Walton. "I have been thinking," said she, "that they are distant relations; for the great-grandfather of this Sir Harry Benson, who was knight of the shire in the reign of Charles the First and one of the cavaliers of those times, was married to a daughter of the Walton family." Harley answered drily, that it might be so; but that he never troubled himself about those matters. "Indeed," said she, "you are to blame, nephew, for not knowing a little more of them: before I was near your age, I had sewed the pedigree of our family in a set of chair-bottoms, that were made a present of to my grandmother, who was a very notable woman, and had a proper regard for gentility, I'll assure you; but now-a-days, it is money, not birth, that makes people respected; the more shame for the times."

Harley was in no very good humour for entering into a discussion of this question; but he always entertained so much filial respect for his aunt, as to attend to her discourse.

"We blame the pride of the rich," said he, "but are not we ashamed of our poverty?"

"Why, one would not chuse," replied his aunt, "to make a much worse figure than one's neighbours; but, as I was saying before, the times (as my friend Mrs. Dorothy Walton observes) are shamefully degenerated in this respect. There was but t'other day, at Mr. Walton's, that fat fellow's daughter, the London Merchant, as he calls himself, though I have heard that he was little better than the keeper of a chandler's shop:—We were leaving the gentlemen to go to tea. She had a hoop forsooth as large and as stiff—and it shewed a pair of bandy legs as thick as two——I was nearer the door by an apron's length, and the pert hussy brushed by me, as who should say, Make way for your betters, and with one of her London-bobs[1]——but Mrs. Dorothy did not let her pass with it; for all the time of drinking tea, she spoke of the precedency of family, and the disparity there is between people who are come of something, and your mushroom-gentry[2] who wear their coats of arms in their purses."

Her indignation was interrupted by the arrival of her maid with a damask table-cloth, and a set of napkins, from the loom, which

---

1 A bob is a curtsy (OED); here apparently in the sense of a rather perfunctory one.
2 "The mushroom is a proverbial type of rapid growth.... A person or family that has suddenly sprung into notice; an upstart"(OED).

had been spun by her mistress's own hand. There was the family-crest in each corner, and in the middle a view of the battle of Worcester, where one of her ancestors had been a captain in the king's forces; and, with a sort of poetical licence in perspective, there was seen the Royal Oak,[1] with more wig than leaves upon it.

On all this the good lady was very copious, and took up the remaining intervals of filling tea, to describe its excellencies to Harley; adding, that she intended this as a present for his wife, when he should get one. He sighed and looked foolish, and commending the serenity of the day, walked out into the garden.

He sat down on a little seat which commanded an extensive prospect round the house. He leaned on his hand, and scored the ground with his stick: "Miss Walton married!" said he; "but what is that to me? May she be happy! her virtues deserve it; to me her marriage is otherwise indifferent:—I had romantic dreams! they are fled!—it is perfectly indifferent."

Just at that moment, he saw a servant, with a knot of ribbands in his hat, go into the house. His cheeks grew flushed at the sight! He kept his eye fixed for some time on the door by which he had entered, then, starting to his feet, hastily followed him.

When he approached the door of the kitchen where he supposed the man had entered, his heart throbbed so violently, that when he would have called Peter, his voice failed in the attempt. He stood a moment listening in this breathless state of palpitation: Peter came out by chance. "Did your honour want any thing?"—"Where is the servant that came just now from Mr. Walton's?"—"From Mr. Walton's, Sir! there is none of his servants here that I know of."—"Nor of Sir Harry Benson's?"—He did not wait for an answer; but having by this time observed the hat with its party-coloured ornament hanging on a peg near the door, he pressed forwards into the kitchen, and addressing himself to a stranger whom he saw there, asked him, with no small tremor in his voice, If he had any commands for him? The man looked silly,

---

1 The Battle of Worcester in 1651 pitted the army of the young King Charles II against that of the Commonwealth Army of Oliver Cromwell. Charles was reputed to have escaped his would-be captors after the defeat of his Royalist forces by concealing himself in an oak tree. The designs on the napkins and table-cloth of Harley's aunt thus signify both the ancientness of her family's prominence and her conservative, Royalist political sympathies.

and said, That he had nothing to trouble his honour with. "Are not you a servant of Sir Harry Benson's?"—"No, Sir."—"You'll pardon me, young man; I judged by the favour in your hat."——"Sir, I'm his majesty's servant, God bless him! and these favours we always wear when we are recruiting." —"Recruiting!" his eyes glistened at the word: he seized the soldier's hand, and shaking it violently, ordered Peter to fetch a bottle of his aunt's best dram. The bottle was brought: "You shall drink the king's health," said Harley, "in a bumper."——"The king and your honour."—"Nay, you shall drink the king's health by itself; you may drink mine in another." Peter looked in his master's face, and filled with some little reluctance. "Now to your mistress," said Harley; "every soldier has a mistress." The man excused himself—"to your mistress! you cannot refuse it." 'Twas Mrs. Margery's best dram! Peter stood with the bottle a little inclined, but not so as to discharge a drop of its contents: "Fill it, Peter," said his master, "fill it to the brim." Peter filled it, and the soldier having named Suky Simpson, dispatched it in a twinkling. "Thou art an honest fellow," said Harley, "and I love thee;" and shaking his hand again, desired Peter to make him his guest at dinner, and walked up into his room with a pace much quicker and more springy than usual.

This agreeable disappointment however, he was not long suffered to enjoy. The curate happened that day to dine with him: his visits indeed were more properly to the aunt than the nephew; and many of the intelligent ladies in the parish, who, like some very great philosophers, have the happy knack at accounting for every thing, gave out, that there was a particular attachment between them, which wanted only to be matured by some more years of courtship to end in the tenderest connection. In this conclusion indeed, supposing the premises to have been true, they were somewhat justified by the known opinion of the lady, who frequently declared herself a friend to the ceremonial of former times, when a lover might have sighed seven years at his mistress's feet, before he was allowed the liberty of kissing her hand. 'Tis true Mrs. Margery was now about her grand climacteric;[1] no matter: that is just the age when we expect to grow younger. But

---

1   "A critical stage in human life; a point at which the person was supposed to be specially liable to change in health or fortune. According to some, all the years denoted by multiples of 7 (7, 14, 21 etc.) were climacterics.... *Grand climacteric*...: the 63rd year of life (63=7x9), supposed to be specially critical" (OED).

I verily believe there was nothing in the report; the curate's connection was only that of a genealogist; for in that character he was no way inferior to Mrs. Margery herself. He dealt also in the present times; for he was a politician and a newsmonger.

He had hardly said grace after dinner, when he told Mrs. Margery, that she might soon expect a pair of white gloves, as Sir Harry Benson, he was very well informed, was just going to be married to Miss Walton. Harley spilt the wine he was carrying to his mouth: he had time however to recollect himself before the curate had finished the different particulars of his intelligence, and summing up all the heroism he was master of, filled a bumper and drank to Miss Walton. "With all my heart," said the curate, "the bride that is to be." Harley would have said bride too; but the word Bride stuck in his throat. His confusion indeed was manifest: but the curate began to enter on some point of descent with Mrs. Margery, and Harley had very soon after an opportunity of leaving them, while they were deeply engaged in a question, whether the name of some great man in the time of Henry the Seventh, was Richard or Humphrey.

He did not see his aunt again till supper; the time between he spent in walking, like some troubled ghost, round the place where his treasure lay. He went as far as a little gate, that led into a copse near Mr. Walton's house, to which that gentleman had been so obliging as to let him have a key. He had just begun to open it, when he saw, on a terrass below, Miss Walton walking with a gentleman in a riding-dress, whom he immediately guessed to be Sir Harry Benson. He stopped of a sudden; his hand shook so much that he could hardly turn the key; he opened the gate however, and advanced a few paces. The lady's lap-dog pricked up its ears, and barked: he stopped again——

———— "The little dogs and all
Tray, Blanch, and Sweetheart, see they bark at me!"[1]

His resolution failed; he slunk back, and locking the gate as softly as he could, stood on tiptoe looking over the wall till they were gone. At that instant a shepherd blew his horn: the romantic

---

1 In Shakespeare's *King Lear*, the title character uses these lines (from III. vi) to emphasize how low his fortunes have fallen; even his own dogs fail to respect him.

melancholy of the sound quite overcame him!—it was the very note that wanted to be touched—he sighed! he dropped a tear!—and returned.

At supper his aunt observed that he was graver than usual; but she did not suspect the cause: indeed it may seem odd that she was the only person in the family who had no suspicion of his attachment to Miss Walton. It was frequently matter of discourse amongst the servants: perhaps her maiden coldness—but for those things we need not account.

In a day or two he was so much master of himself as to be able to rhime upon the subject. The following pastoral he left, some time after, on the handle of a tea-kettle, at a neighbouring house where we were visiting; and as I filled the teapot after him, I happened to put it in my pocket by a similar act of forgetfulness. It is such as might be expected from a man who makes verses for amusement. I am pleased with somewhat of good-nature that runs through it, because I have commonly observed the writers of those complaints to bestow epithets on their lost mistresses rather too harsh for the mere liberty of choice, which led them to prefer another to the poet himself: I do not doubt the vehemence of their passion; but, alas! the sensations of love are something more than the returns of gratitude.

LAVINIA. A PASTORAL.

WHY steals from my bosom the sigh?
   Why fix'd is my gaze on the ground?
Come, give me my pipe, and I'll try
   To banish my cares with the sound.

Erewhile were its notes of accord
   With the smile of the flow'r-footed muse;
Ah! why by its master implor'd
   Shou'd it now the gay carrol refuse?

'Twas taught by LAVINIA's sweet smile
   In the mirth-loving chorus to join:
Ah me! how unweeting the while!
   LAVINIA——can never be mine!

Another, more happy, the maid
   By fortune is destined to bless——

Tho' the hope has forsook that betray'd,
  Yet why shou'd I love her the less?

Her beauties are bright as the morn,
  With rapture I counted them o'er;
Such virtues those beauties adorn,
  I knew her, and prais'd them no more.

I term'd her no goddess of love,
  I call'd not her beauty divine:
These far other passions may prove,
  But they could not be figures of mine.

It ne'er was apparell'd with art,
  On words it could never rely;
It reign'd in the throb of my heart,
  It gleam'd in the glance of my eye.

Oh fool! in the circle to shine
  That fashion's gay daughters approve,
You must speak as the fashions incline;—
  Alas! are there fashions in love?

Yet sure they are simple who prize
  The tongue that is smooth to deceive;
Yet sure she had sense to despise
  The tinsel that folly may weave.

When I talk'd, I have seen her recline
  With an aspect so pensively sweet,——
Tho' I spoke what the shepherds opine,
  A fop were asham'd to repeat.

She is soft as the dew-drops that fall
  From the lip of the sweet-scented pea;
Perhaps when she smil'd upon all,
  I have thought that she smil'd upon me.

But why of her charms should I tell?
  Ah me! whom her charms have undone!
Yet I love the reflection too well,
  The painful reflection to shun.

Ye souls of more delicate kind,
 Who feast not on pleasure alone,
Who wear the soft sense of the mind,
 To the sons of the world still unknown;

Ye know, tho' I cannot express,
 Why I foolishly doat on my pain;
Nor will ye believe it the less
 That I have not the skill to complain.

I lean on my hand with a sigh,
 My friends the soft sadness condemn;
Yet, methinks, tho' I cannot tell why,
 I should hate to be merry like them.

When I walk'd in the pride of the dawn,
 Methought all the region look'd bright:
Has sweetness forsaken the lawn?
 For, methinks, I grow sad at the sight.

When I stood by the stream, I have thought
 There was mirth in the gurgling soft sound;
But now 'tis a sorrowful note,
 And the banks are all gloomy around!

I have laugh'd at the jest of a friend;
 Now they laugh, and I know not the cause,
Tho' I seem with my looks to attend,
 How silly! I ask what it was!

They sing the sweet song of the May,
 They sing it with mirth and with glee;
Sure I once thought the sonnet was gay,
 But now 'tis all sadness to me.

Oh! give me the dubious light
 That gleams thro' the quivering shade;
Oh! give me the horrors of night
 By gloom and by silence array'd!

Let me walk where the soft-rising wave
 Has pictur'd the moon on its breast:

Let me walk where the new-cover'd grave
  Allows the pale lover to rest!

When shall I in its peaceable womb
  Be laid with my sorrows asleep!
Should LAVINIA but chance on my tomb—
  I could die if I thought she would weep.

Perhaps, if the souls of the just
  Revisit these mansions of care,
It may be my favourite trust
  To watch o'er the fate of the fair.

Perhaps the soft thought of her breast
  With rapture more favour'd to warm;
Perhaps, if with sorrow oppress'd,
  Her sorrow with patience to arm.

Then! then! in the tenderest part
  May I whisper, "Poor COLIN was true;"
And mark if a heave of her heart
  The thought of her COLIN pursue.

THE PUPIL. A FRAGMENT.

* * * * "BUT as to the higher part of education, Mr. Harley, the culture of the Mind;—let the feelings be awakened, let the heart be brought forth to its object, placed in the light in which nature would have it stand, and its decisions will ever be just. The world

Will smile, and smile, and be a villain;[1]

and the youth, who does not suspect its deceit, will be content to smile with it.—Men will put on the most forbidding aspect in nature, and tell him of the beauty of virtue.

"I have not, under these grey hairs, forgotten that I was once a young man, warm in the pursuit of pleasure, but meaning to be honest as well as happy. I had ideas of virtue, of honour, of benev-

---

1 Hamlet's "one may smile, and smile, and be a villain!" (from *Hamlet* I.v) refers to his uncle, who has murdered Hamlet's father, married the widowed Queen, and thus become king.

olence, which I had never been at the pains to define; but I felt my bosom heave at the thoughts of them, and I made the most delightful soliloquies——It is impossible, said I, that there can be half so many rogues as are imagined.

"I travelled, because it is the fashion for young men of my fortune to travel: I had a travelling tutor, which is the fashion too; but my tutor was a gentleman, which it is not always the fashion for tutors to be. His gentility indeed was all he had from his father, whose prodigality had not left him a shilling to support it.

"I have a favour to ask of you, my dear Mountford," said my father, "which I will not be refused: You have travelled as became a man; neither France nor Italy have made any thing of Mountford, which Mountford before he left England would have been ashamed of: my son Edward goes abroad, would you take him under your protection?"—He blushed—my father's face was scarlet—he pressed his hand to his bosom, as if he had said,—my heart does not mean to offend you. Mountford sighed twice—"I am a proud fool," said he, "and you will pardon it;—there!" (he sighed again) "I can hear of dependance, since it is dependance on my Sedley."—"Dependance!" answered my father; "there can be no such word between us: what is there in 9000 l. a-year that should make me unworthy of Mountford's friendship?"——They embraced; and soon after I set out on my travels, with Mountford for my guardian.

"We were at Milan, where my father happened to have an Italian friend, to whom he had been of some service in England. The count, for he was of quality, was solicitous to return the obligation, by a particular attention to his son: we lived in his palace, visited with his family, were caressed by his friends, and I began to be so well pleased with my entertainment, that I thought of England as of some foreign country.

"The count had a son not much older than myself. At that age a friend is an easy acquisition: we were friends the first night of our acquaintance.

"He introduced me into the company of a set of young gentlemen, whose fortunes gave them the command of pleasure, and whose inclinations incited them to the purchase. After having spent some joyous evenings in their society, it became a sort of habit which I could not miss without uneasiness; and our meetings, which before were frequent, were now stated and regular.

"Sometimes, in the pauses of our mirth, gaming was introduced as an amusement: it was an art in which I was a novice; I received instruction, as other novices do, by losing pretty largely to my teachers. Nor was this the only evil which Mountford foresaw would arise from the connection I had formed; but a lecture of sour injunctions was not his method of reclaiming. He sometimes asked me questions about the company; but they were such as the curiosity of any indifferent man might have prompted: I told him of their wit, their eloquence, their warmth of friendship, and their sensibility of heart; "And their honour," said I, laying my hand on my breast, "is unquestionable." Mountford seemed to rejoice at my good fortune, and begged that I would introduce him to their acquaintance. At the next meeting I introduced him accordingly.

"The conversation was as animated as usual; they displayed all that sprightliness and good-humour which my praises had led Mountford to expect; subjects too of sentiment occurred, and their speeches, particularly those of our friend the son of count Respino, glowed with the warmth of honour, and softened into the tenderness of feeling. Mountford was charmed with his companions; when we parted he made the highest eulogiums upon them: 'When shall we see them again?' said he. I was delighted with the demand, and promised to reconduct him on the morrow.

"In going to their place of rendezvous, he took me a little out of the road, to see, as he told me, the performances of a young statuary. When we were near the house in which Mountford said he lived, a boy of about seven years old crossed us in the street. At sight of Mountford he stopped, and grasping his hand, 'My dearest Sir,' said he, 'my father is likely to do well; he will live to pray for you, and to bless you: yes, he will bless you, though you are an Englishman, and some other hard word that the monk talked of this morning which I have forgot, but it meant that you should not go to heaven,[1] but he shall go to heaven, said I, for he has saved my father: come and see him, Sir, that we may be happy.'——'My dear, I am engaged at present with this gentleman.'——'But he shall come along with you; he is an Englishman too, I fancy; he shall come and learn how an Englishman

---

1 The hard word is presumably "Protestant." The communion between well-meaning souls in the sentimental novel often smooths over the deep cultural differences between English Protestants and continental Roman Catholics: Sterne makes similar assertions of finding amity between traditional enemies, the French and the English, in *A Sentimental Journey* (1768).

may go to heaven.'—Mountford smiled, and we followed the boy together.

"After crossing the next street, we arrived at the gate of a prison. I seemed surprised at the sight; our little conductor observed it. 'Are you afraid, Sir?' said he; 'I was afraid once too, but my father and mother are here, and I am never afraid when I am with them.' He took my hand, and led me through a dark passage that fronted the gate. When we came to a little door at the end, he tapped; a boy, still younger than himself, opened it to receive us. Mountford entered with a look in which was pictured the benign assurance of a superior being. I followed in silence and amazement.

"On something like a bed lay a man, with a face seemingly emaciated with sickness, and a look of patient dejection; a bundle of dirty shreds served him for a pillow; but he had a better support—the arm of a female who kneeled beside him, beautiful as an angel, but with a fading languor in her countenance, the still life of melancholy, that seemed to borrow its shade from the object on which she gazed. There was a tear in her eye! the sick man kissed it off in its bud, smiling through the dimness of his own!—when she saw Mountford, she crawled forward on the ground and clasped his knees; he raised her from the floor; she threw her arms round his neck, and sobbed out a speech of thankfulness, eloquent beyond the power of language.

"'Compose yourself, my love,' said the man on the bed; 'but he, whose goodness has caused that emotion, will pardon its effects.'——'How is this, Mountford?' said I; 'what do I see? what must I do?'——'You see,' replied the stranger, 'a wretch, sunk in poverty, starving in prison, stretched on a sick bed! but that is little:——there are his wife and children, wanting the bread which he has not to give them! Yet you cannot easily imagine the conscious serenity of his mind; in the gripe of affliction, his heart swells with the pride of virtue! it can even look down with pity on the man whose cruelty has wrung it almost to bursting. You are, I fancy, a friend of Mr. Mountford's; come nearer, and I will tell you; for, short as my story is, I can hardly command breath enough for a recital. The son of count Respino' (I started as if I had trod on a viper) 'has long had a criminal passion for my wife: this her prudence had concealed from me; but he had lately the boldness to declare it to myself. He promised me affluence in exchange for honour; and threatened misery, as its attendant, if I kept it. I treated him with the contempt he deserved: the consequence was, that he hired a couple of bravoes (for I am persuaded they acted under his direction) who attempted to assassinate me in the street; but I made such a defence as obliged them to fly, after having given me two or three stabs, none of which however were mortal. But his revenge was not thus to be disappointed: in the little dealings of my trade I had contracted some debts, of which he had made himself master for my ruin;[1] I was confined here at his suit, when not yet recovered from the wounds I had received ; that dear woman, and these two boys, followed me, that we might starve together; but Providence interposed, and sent Mr. Mountford to our support: he has relieved my family from the gnawings of hunger, and rescued me from death, to which a fever, consequent on my wounds, and increased by the want of every necessary, had almost reduced me.'

"'Inhuman villain!' I exclaimed, lifting up my eyes to heaven. 'Inhuman indeed!' said the lovely woman who stood at my side: 'Alas! Sir, what had we done to offend him? what had these little ones done, that they should perish in the toils of his vengeance?'——I reached a pen which stood in an ink-standish at the bed-side—'May I ask what is the amount of the sum for which you are imprisoned?'—'I was able,' he replied, 'to pay all but 500 crowns.'—I wrote a draught on the banker with whom I had a credit from my father for 2500, and presenting it to the stranger's wife, 'You will receive, Madam, on presenting this note, a sum more than sufficient for your husband's discharge; the remainder I leave for his industry to improve.' I would have left the room: each of them laid hold of one of my hands; the children clung to my coat:—Oh! Mr. Harley, methinks I feel their gentle violence at this moment; it beats here with delight inexpressible!—'Stay, Sir,' said he, 'I do not mean attempting to thank you; (he took a pocket-book from under his pillow) let me but know what name I shall place here next to Mr. Mountford's?'—Sedley——he writ it down—'An Englishman too I presume.'—'He shall go to heaven notwithstanding,' said the boy who had been our guide. It began to be too much for me; I squeezed his hand that was clasped in mine; his wife's I pressed to my lips, and burst from the place to give vent to the feelings that laboured within me.

---

1 The strategy of the son of Count Respino for entrapping and imprisoning his victim echoes that used by Squire Thornfield on Vicar Primrose in Goldsmith's *The Vicar of Wakefield*, 1766.

"'Oh! Mountford!' said I, when he had overtaken me at the door: 'It is time,' replied he, 'that we should think of our appointment; young Respino and his friends are waiting us.'——'Damn him, damn him!' said I; 'let us leave Milan instantly; but soft—— I will be calm; Mountford, your pencil.' I wrote on a slip of paper,

"To Signor RESPINO,

"When you receive this I am at a distance from Milan. Accept of my thanks for the civilities I have received from you and your family. As to the friendship with which you were pleased to honour me, the prison, which I have just left, has exhibited a scene to cancel it for ever. You may possibly be merry with your companions at my weakness, as I suppose you will term it. I give you leave for derision: you may affect a triumph; I shall feel it.

EDWARD SEDLEY."

"'You may send this if you will,' said Mountford coolly; 'but still Respino is *a man of honour*, the world will continue to call him so.'——'It is probable,' I answered, 'they may; I envy not the appellation. If this is the world's honour, if these men are the guides of its manners'—'Tut!' said Mountford, 'do you eat macaroni?'[1]——

* * * * *

[At this place had the greatest depredations of the curate begun. There were so very few connected passages of the subsequent chapters remaining, that even the partiality of an editor could not offer them to the public. I discovered, from some scattered sentences, that they were of much the same tenor with the preceding; recitals of little adventures, in which the dispositions of a man, sensible to judge, and still more warm to feel, had room to unfold themselves. Some instruction, and some example, I make no doubt they contained; but it is likely that many of those,

---

1 A macaroni is a person "of a class which arose in England about 1760 and consisted of young men who had travelled and affected the tastes and fashions prevalent in continental society" (OED). The term connoted absurd excess in dress and mannerism. The Oxford editors note that the term was probably adapted from the Macaroni Club, a name indicating the members' preference for foreign cookery. Mountford's question thus pointedly asks where the young British gentleman's values and cultural loyalties lie: with manly British virtues or continental urbanity?

whom chance has led to a perusal of what I have already presented, may have read it with little pleasure, and will feel no disappointment from the want of those parts which I have been unable to procure: to such as may have expected the intricacies of a novel, a few incidents in a life undistinguished, except by some features of the heart, cannot have afforded much entertainment.

Harley's own story, from the mutilated passages I have mentioned, as well as from some inquiries I was at the trouble of making in the country, I found to have been simple to excess. His mistress I could perceive was not married to Sir Harry Benson: but it would seem, by one of the following chapters, which is still entire, that Harley had not profited on the occasion by making any declaration of his own passion, after those of the other had been unsuccessful. The state of his health for some part of this period, appears to have been such as to forbid any thoughts of that kind: he had been seized with a very dangerous fever, caught by attending old Edwards in one of an infectious kind. From this he had recovered but imperfectly, and though he had no formed complaint, his health was manifestly on the decline.

It appears that the sagacity of some friend had at length pointed out to his aunt a cause from which this might be supposed to proceed, to wit, his hopeless love for Miss Walton; for according to the conceptions of the world, the love of a man of Harley's fortune for the heiress of 4000 l. a-year, is indeed desperate. Whether it was so in this case may be gathered from the next chapter, which, with the two subsequent, concluding the performance, have escaped those accidents that proved fatal to the rest.]

CHAPTER LV.

He sees Miss Walton, and is happy.

HARLEY was one of those few friends whom the malevolence of fortune had yet left me: I could not therefore but be sensibly concerned for his present indisposition; there seldom passed a day on which I did not make inquiry about him.

The physician who attended him had informed me the evening before, that he thought him considerably better than he had been for some time past. I called next morning to be confirmed in a piece of intelligence so welcome to me.

When I entered his apartment, I found him sitting on a couch, leaning on his hand, with his eye turned upwards in the attitude of thoughtful inspiration. His look had always an open benignity, which commanded esteem; there was now something more—a gentle triumph in it.

He rose, and met me with his usual kindness. When I gave him the good accounts I had had from his physician, "I am foolish enough," said he, "to rely but little, in this instance, upon physic: my presentiment may be false; but I think I feel myself approaching to my end, by steps so easy, that they woo me to approach it.

"There is a certain dignity in retiring from life at a time, when the infirmities of age have not sapped our faculties. This world, my dear Charles, was a scene in which I never much delighted. I was not formed for the bustle of the busy, nor the dissipation of the gay: a thousand things occurred where I blushed for the impropriety of my conduct when I thought on the world, though my reason told me I should have blushed to have done otherwise.—It was a scene of dissimulation, of restraint, of disappointment. I leave it to enter on that state, which, I have learned to believe, is replete with the genuine happiness attendant upon virtue. I look back on the tenor of my life, with the consciousness of few great offences to account for. There are blemishes, I confess, which deform in some degree the picture. But I know the benignity of the Supreme Being, and rejoice at the thoughts of its exertion in my favour. My mind expands at the thought I shall enter into the society of the blessed, wise as angels, with the simplicity of children." He had by this time clasped my hand, and found it wet by a tear which had just fallen upon it.—His eye began to moisten too—we sat for some time silent—At last, with an attempt to a look of more composure, "There are some remembrances," (said Harley) "which rise involuntarily on my heart, and make me almost wish to live. I have been blessed with a few friends, who redeem my opinion of mankind. I recollect, with the tenderest emotion, the scenes of pleasure I have passed among them; but we shall meet again, my friend, never to be separated. There are some feelings which perhaps are too tender to be suffered by the world. The world is in general selfish, interested, and unthinking, and throws the imputation of romance or melancholy on every temper more susceptible than its own. I cannot think but in those regions which I contemplate, if there is any thing of mortality left about us, that these feelings will subsist;— they are called,—perhaps they are—weaknesses here;—but there may be some better modifications of them in heaven, which may deserve the name of virtues." He sighed as he spoke these last words. He had scarcely finished them, when the door opened, and his aunt appeared leading in Miss Walton. "My dear," says she, "here is Miss Walton, who has been so kind as to come and inquire for you herself." I could observe a transient glow upon his face. He rose from his seat—"If to know Miss Walton's goodness," said he, "be a title to deserve it, I have some claim." She begged him to resume his seat, and placed herself on the sofa beside him. I took my leave. Mrs. Margery accompanied me to the door. He was left with Miss Walton alone. She inquired anxiously about his health. "I believe," said he, "from the accounts which my physicians unwillingly give me, that they have no great hopes of my recovery."—She started as he spoke; but recollecting herself immediately, endeavoured to flatter him into a belief that his apprehensions were groundless. "I know," said he, "that it is usual with persons at my time of life to have these hopes which your kindness suggests; but I would not wish to be deceived. To meet death as becomes a man, is a privilege bestowed on few.— I would endeavour to make it mine;—nor do I think that I can ever be better prepared for it than now:—It is that chiefly which determines the fitness of its approach."—"Those sentiments," answered Miss Walton, "are just; but your good sense, Mr. Harley, will own, that life has its proper value.—As the province of virtue, life is ennobled; as such, it is to be desired.—To virtue has the Supreme Director of all things assigned rewards enough even here to fix its attachment."

The subject began to overpower her.—Harley lifted his eyes from the ground—"There are," said he, in a very low voice, "there are attachments, Miss Walton"—His glance met hers—They both betrayed a confusion, and were both instantly withdrawn.—He paused some moments—"I am in such a state as calls for sincerity, let that also excuse it—It is perhaps the last time we shall ever meet. I feel something particularly solemn in the acknowledgment, yet my heart swells to make it, awed as it is by a sense of my presumption, by a sense of your perfections"——He paused again—"Let it not offend you to know their power over one so unworthy—It will, I believe, soon cease to beat, even with that feeling which it shall lose the latest.—To love Miss Walton could not be a crime;—if to declare it is one—the expiation will be made."—Her tears were now flowing without controul.—"Let me intreat you," said she, "to have better hopes—Let not life be so indifferent to you; if my wishes can put any value on it—I will not pretend to misunderstand you—I know your worth—I have known it long—I have esteemed it—What would you have me say?—I have loved it as it deserved."——He seized her hand—a languid colour reddened his cheek—a smile brightened faintly in his eye. As he gazed on her, it grew dim, it fixed, it closed—He sighed, and fell back on his seat.—Miss Walton screamed at the sight—His aunt and the servants rushed into the room—They found them lying motionless together.—His physician happened to call at that instant.—Every art was tried to recover them—With Miss Walton they succeeded—But Harley was gone for ever!

CHAPTER LVI.

The emotions of the heart.

I Entered the room where his body lay; I approached it with reverence, not fear: I looked, the recollection of the past crowded upon me. I saw that form, which, but a little before, was animated with a soul which did honour to humanity, stretched without sense or feeling before me. 'Tis a connection we cannot easily forget:—I took his hand in mine; I repeated his name involuntarily:—I felt a pulse in every vein at the sound. I looked earnestly in his face; his eye was closed, his lip pale and motionless. There is an enthusiasm in sorrow that forgets impossibility; I wondered that it was so. The sight drew a prayer from my heart; it was the voice of frailty and of man! the confusion of my mind began to subside into thought; I had time to weep!

I turned, with the last farewel upon my lips, when I observed old Edwards standing behind me. I looked him full in the face; but his eye was fixed on another object: he pressed between me and the bed, and stood gazing on the breathless remains of his benefactor. I spoke to him I know not what; but he took no notice of what I said, and remained in the same attitude as before. He stood some minutes in that posture, then turned and walked towards the door. He paused as he went;—he returned a second time: I could observe his lips move as he looked; but the voice they would have uttered was lost. He attempted going again; and a third time he returned as before.—I saw him wipe his cheek; then covering his face with his hands, his breast heaving with the most convulsive throbs, he flung out of the room.

THE CONCLUSION.

HE had hinted that he should like to be buried in a certain spot near the grave of his mother. This is a weakness; but it is universally incident to humanity: 'tis at least a memorial for those who survive; for some indeed a slender memorial will serve; and the soft affections, when they are busy that way, will build their structures, were it but on the paring of a nail.

He was buried in the place he had desired. It was shaded by an old tree, the only one in the church-yard, in which was a cavity worn by time. I have sat with him in it, and counted the tombs. The last time we passed there, methought he looked wistfully on that tree: there was a branch of it, that bent towards us, waving in the wind; he waved his hand, as if he mimicked its motion. There was something predictive in his look! perhaps it is foolish to remark it; but there are times and places when I am a child at those things.

I sometimes visit his grave; I sit in the hollow of the tree. It is worth a thousand homilies! every nobler feeling rises within me! every beat of my heart awakens a virtue!—but it will make you hate the world——No: there is such an air of gentleness around, that I can hate nothing; but, as to the world——I pity the men of it.

FINIS.

Appendix A: Sympathy and Sentiment

1. From David Hume, *A Treatise of Human Nature* (1739-40)

[Sympathy, in Hume's account of the passions in Book II of his *Treatise of Human Nature*, is the means by which sentiments are communicated from one subject to another. Hume asserts that it is the "soul or animating principle" of all the passions (363). In the first excerpt here, Hume traces the way sympathy permits observers to enter into the pleasurable sensations of the wealthy; in the second, Hume discusses the strength of the sentiments generated by sympathy. The selections are taken from the second edition, edited by L.A. Selby-Bigge and revised by P.H. Nidditch (Oxford: Clarendon, 1978). Hume's original notes have been retained and are identified by asterisks.]

Of Our Esteem for the Rich and Powerful (II.v)

.... Upon the whole, there remains nothing, which can give us an esteem for power and riches, and a contempt for meanness and poverty, except the principle of *sympathy*, by which we enter into the sentiments of the rich and poor, and partake of their pleasure and uneasiness. Riches give satisfaction to their possessor; and this satisfaction is convey'd to the beholder by the imagination, which produces an idea resembling the original impression in force and vivacity. This agreeable idea or impression is connected with love, which is an agreeable passion. It proceeds from a thinking conscious being, which is the very object of love. From this relation of impressions, and identity of ideas, the passion arises, according to my hypothesis.

The best method of reconciling us to this opinion is to take a general survey of the universe, and observe the force of sympathy thro' the whole animal creation, and the easy communication of sentiments from one thinking being to another. In all creatures, that prey not upon others, and are not agitated with violent passions, there appears a remarkable desire of company, which associates them together, without any advantages they can ever propose to reap from their union. This is still more conspicuous in man, as being the creature of the universe, who has the most ardent desire of society, and is fitted for it by the most advantages. We can form no wish, which has not a reference to society. A perfect solitude is, perhaps, the greatest punishment we can suffer. Every pleasure languishes when enjoy'd a-part from company, and every pain becomes more cruel and intolerable. Whatever other passions we may be actuated by; pride, ambition, avarice, curiosity, revenge or lust; the soul or animating principle of them all is sympathy; nor wou'd they have any force, were we to abstract entirely from the thoughts and sentiments of others. Let all the powers and elements of nature conspire to serve and obey one man: Let the sun rise and set at his command: The sea and rivers roll as he pleases, and the earth furnish spontaneously whatever may be useful or agreeable to him: He will still be miserable, till you give him some one person at least, with whom he may share his happiness, and whose esteem and friendship he may enjoy.

This conclusion from a general view of human nature, we may confirm by particular instances, wherein the force of sympathy is very remarkable. Most kinds of beauty are deriv'd from this origin; and tho' our first object be some senseless inanimate piece of matter, 'tis seldom we rest there, and carry not our view to its influence on sensible and rational creatures. A man, who shews us any house or building, takes particular care among other things to point out the convenience of the apartments, the advantages of their situation, and the little room lost in the stairs, anti-chambers and passages; and indeed 'tis evident, the chief part of the beauty consists in these particulars. The observation of convenience gives pleasure, since convenience is a beauty. But after what manner does it give pleasure? 'Tis certain our own interest is not in the least concern'd; and as this is a beauty of interest, not of form, so to speak, it must delight us merely by communication, and by our sympathizing with the proprietor of the lodging. We enter into his interest by the force of imagination, and feel the same satisfaction, that the objects naturally occasion in him.

This observation extends to tables, chairs, scritoires, chimneys, coaches, sadles, ploughs, and indeed to every work of art; it being an universal rule, that their beauty is chiefly deriv'd from their utility, and from their fitness for that purpose, to which they are destin'd. But this is an advantage, that concerns only the owner, nor is there any thing but sympathy, which can interest the spectator.

'Tis evident, that nothing renders a field more agreeable than its fertility, and that scarce any advantages of ornament or situation will be able to equal this beauty. 'Tis the same case with particular trees and plants, as with the field on which they grow. I know not but a plain, overgrown with furze and broom, may be, in itself, as beautiful as a hill cover'd with vines or olive-trees; tho' it will never appear so to one, who is acquainted with the value of each. But this is a beauty merely of imagination, and has no foundation in what appears to the senses. Fertility and value have a plain reference to use; and that to riches, joy, and plenty; in which tho' we have no hope of partaking, yet we enter into them by the vivacity of the fancy, and share them, in some measure, with the proprietor.

There is no rule in painting more reasonable than that of ballancing the figures, and placing them with the greatest exactness on their proper center of gravity. A figure, which is not justly ballanc'd, is disagreeable; and that because it conveys the ideas of its fall, of harm, and of pain: Which ideas are painful, when by sympathy they acquire any degree of force and vivacity.

Add to this, that the principal part of personal beauty is an air of health and vigour, and such a construction of members as promises strength and activity. This idea of beauty cannot be accounted for but by sympathy.

In general we may remark, that the minds of men are mirrors to one another, not only because they reflect each others emotions, but also because those rays of passions, sentiments and opinions may be often reverberated, and may decay away by insensible degrees. Thus the pleasure, which a rich man receives from his possessions, being thrown upon the beholder, causes a pleasure and esteem; which sentiments again, being perceiv'd and sympathiz'd with, encrease the pleasure of the possessor; and being once more reflected, become a new foundation for pleasure and esteem in the beholder. There is certainly an original satisfaction in riches deriv'd from that power, which they bestow, of enjoying all the pleasures of life; and as this is their very nature and essence, it must be the first source of all the passions, which arise from them. One of the most considerable of these passions is that of love or esteem in others, which therefore proceeds from a sympathy with the pleasure of the possessor. But the possessor has also a secondary satisfaction in riches arising from the love and esteem he acquires by them, and this satisfaction is nothing but a second reflexion of that original pleasure, which proceeded from himself. This secondary satisfaction or vanity becomes one of the principal recommendations of riches, and is the chief reason, why we either desire them for ourselves, or esteem them in others. Here then is a third rebound of the original pleasure; after which 'tis difficult to distinguish the images and reflexions, by reason of their faintness and confusion.

Of Compassion (II.vii)

But tho' the desire of the happiness or misery of others, according to the love or hatred we bear them, be an arbitrary and original instinct implanted in our nature, we find it may be counterfeited on many occasions, and may arise from secondary principles. *Pity* is a concern for, and *malice* a joy in the misery of others, without any friendship or enmity to occasion this concern or joy. We pity even strangers, and such as are perfectly indifferent to us: And if our ill-will to another proceed from any harm or injury, it is not, properly speaking, malice, but revenge. But if we examine these affections of pity and malice we shall find them to be secondary ones, arising from original affections, which are varied by some particular turn of thought and imagination.

'Twill be easy to explain the passion of *pity*, from the precedent reasoning concerning *sympathy*. We have a lively idea of every thing related to us. All human creatures are related to us by resemblance. Their persons, therefore, their interests, their passions, their pains and pleasures must strike upon us in a lively manner, and produce an emotion similar to the original one; since a lively idea is easily converted into an impression. If this be true in general, it must be more so of affliction and sorrow. These have always a stronger and more lasting influence than any pleasure or enjoyment.

A spectator of a tragedy passes thro' a long train of grief, terror, indignation, and other affections, which the poet represents in the persons he introduces. As many tragedies end happily, and no excellent one can be compos'd without some reverses of fortune, the spectator must sympathize with all these changes, and receive the fictitious joy as well as every other passion. Unless, therefore, it be asserted, that every distinct passion is communicated by a distinct original quality, and is not deriv'd from the general principle of sympathy above-explain'd, it must be allow'd, that all of them arise from that principle. To except any one in particular must appear highly unreasonable. As they are all first present in the mind of one person, and afterwards appear in the mind of another; and as the manner of their appearance, first as an idea, then as an impression, is in every case the same, the transition must arise from the same principle. I am at least sure, that this method of reasoning wou'd be consider'd as certain, either in natural philosophy or common life.

Add to this, that pity depends, in a great measure, on the contiguity, and even sight of the object; which is a proof, that 'tis deriv'd from the imagination. Not to mention that women and children are most subject to pity, as being most guided by that faculty. The same infirmity, which makes them faint at the sight of a naked sword, tho' in the hands of their best friend, makes them pity extremely those, whom they find in any grief or affliction. Those philosophers, who derive this passion from I know not what subtile reflections on the instability of fortune, and our being liable to the same miseries we behold, will find this observation contrary to them among a great many others, which it were easy to produce.

There remains only to take notice of a pretty remarkable phænomenon of this passion; which is, that the communicated passion of sympathy sometimes acquires strength from the weakness of its original, and even arises by a transition from affections, which have no existence. Thus when a person obtains any honourable office, or inherits a great fortune, we are always the more rejoic'd for his prosperity, the less sense he seems to have of it, and the greater equanimity and indifference he shews in its enjoyment. In like manner a man, who is not dejected by misfortunes, is the more lamented on account of his patience; and if that virtue extends so far as utterly to remove all sense of uneasiness, it still farther encreases our compassion. When a person of merit falls into what is vulgarly esteem'd a great misfortune, we form a notion of his condition; and carrying our fancy from the cause to the usual effect, first conceive a lively idea of his sorrow, and then feel an impression of it, entirely overlooking that greatness of mind, which elevates him above such emotions, or only considering it so far as to encrease our admiration, love and tenderness for him. We find from experience, that such a degree of passion is usually connected with such a misfortune; and tho' there be an exception in the present case, yet the imagination is affected by the *general rule*, and makes us conceive a lively idea of the passion, or rather feel the passion itself, in the same manner, as if the person were really actuated by it. From the same principles we blush for the conduct of those, who behave themselves foolishly before us; and that tho' they shew no sense of shame, nor seem in the least conscious of their folly. All this proceeds from sympathy; but 'tis of a partial kind, and views its objects only on one side, without considering the other, which has a contrary effect, and wou'd entirely destroy that emotion, which arises from the first appearance.

We also have instances, wherein an indifference and insensibility under misfortune encreases our concern for the misfortune, even tho' the indifference proceed not from any virtue and magnanimity. 'Tis an aggravation of a murder, that it was committed upon persons asleep and in perfect security; as historians readily observe of any infant prince, who is captive in the hands of his enemies, that he is more worthy of compassion the less sensible he is of his miserable condition. As we ourselves are here acquainted with the wretched situation of the person, it gives us a lively idea and sensation of sorrow, which is the passion that *generally* attends it; and this idea becomes still more lively, and the sensation more violent by a contrast with that security and indifference, which we observe in the person himself. A contrast of any kind never fails to affect the imagination, especially when presented by the subject; and 'tis on the imagination that pity entirely depends.*

2. From Adam Smith, *The Theory of Moral Sentiments* (1759)

[Mackenzie's friend Adam Smith analyzed the concept of sympathy in detail in *The Theory of Moral Sentiments*. Though he puts sympathy at the center of his ethical system, he differs from Hume in arguing that sympathetic recreations of the sentiments of others are weaker and more problematic than Hume allows. Smith also stresses some of the problems of an excess of sympathy. The selections are taken from D.D. Raphael and A.L. Macfie's edition (Oxford: Oxford UP, 1976).]

Of Sympathy (I.i.1)

How selfish soever man may be supposed, there are evidently some principles in his nature, which interest him in the fortune of

---

* To prevent all ambiguity, I must observe, that where I oppose the imagination to the memory, I mean in general the faculty that presents our fainter ideas. In all other places, and particularly when it is oppos'd to the understanding, I understand the same faculty, excluding only our demonstrative and probable reasonings.

others, and render their happiness necessary to him, though he derives nothing from it except the pleasure of seeing it. Of this kind is pity or compassion, the emotion which we feel for the misery of others, when we either see it, or are made to conceive it in a very lively manner. That we often derive sorrow from the sorrow of others, is a matter of fact too obvious to require any instances to prove it; for this sentiment, like all the other original passions of human nature, is by no means confined to the virtuous and humane, though they perhaps may feel it with the most exquisite sensibility. The greatest ruffian, the most hardened violator of the laws of society, is not altogether without it.

As we have no immediate experience of what other men feel, we can form no idea of the manner in which they are affected, but by conceiving what we ourselves should feel in the like situation. Though our brother is upon the rack, as long as we ourselves are at our ease, our senses will never inform us of what he suffers. They never did, and never can, carry us beyond our own person, and it is by the imagination only that we can form any conception of what are his sensations. Neither can that faculty help us to this any other way, than by representing to us what would be our own, if we were in his case. It is the impressions of our own senses only, not those of his, which our imaginations copy. By the imagination we place ourselves in his situation, we conceive ourselves enduring all the same torments, we enter as it were into his body, and become in some measure the same person with him, and thence form some idea of his sensations, and even feel something which, though weaker in degree, is not altogether unlike them. His agonies, when they are thus brought home to ourselves, when we have thus adopted and made them our own, begin at last to affect us, and we then tremble and shudder at the thought of what he feels. For as to be in pain or distress of any kind excites the most excessive sorrow, so to conceive or to imagine that we are in it, excites some degree of the same emotion, in proportion to the vivacity or dullness of the conception.

That this is the source of our fellow-feeling for the misery of others, that it is by changing places in fancy with the sufferer, that we come either to conceive or to be affected by what he feels, may be demonstrated by many obvious observations, if it should not be thought sufficiently evident of itself. When we see a stroke aimed and just ready to fall upon the leg or arm of another person, we naturally shrink and draw back our own leg or our own arm; and when it does fall, we feel it in some measure, and are hurt by it as well as the sufferer. The mob, when they are gazing at a dancer on the slack rope, naturally writhe and twist and balance their own bodies, as they see him do, and as they feel that they themselves must do if in his situation. Persons of delicate fibres and a weak constitution of body complain, that in looking on the sores and ulcers which are exposed by beggars in the streets, they are apt to feel an itching or uneasy sensation in the correspondent part of their own bodies. The horror which they conceive at the misery of those wretches affects that particular part in themselves more than any other; because that horror arises from conceiving what they themselves would suffer, if they really were the wretches whom they are looking upon, and if that particular part in themselves was actually affected in the same miserable manner. The very force of this conception is sufficient, in their feeble frames, to produce that itching or uneasy sensation complained of. Men of the most robust make, observe that in looking upon sore eyes they often feel a very sensible soreness in their own, which proceeds from the same reason; that organ being in the strongest man more delicate, than any other part of the body is in the weakest.

Neither is it those circumstances only, which create pain or sorrow, that call forth our fellow-feeling. Whatever is the passion which arises from any object in the person principally concerned, an analogous emotion springs up, at the thought of his situation, in the breast of every attentive spectator. Our joy for the deliverance of those heroes of tragedy or romance who interest us, is as sincere as our grief for their distress, and our fellow-feeling with their misery is not more real than that with their happiness. We enter into their gratitude towards those faithful friends who did not desert them in their difficulties; and we heartily go along with their resentment against those perfidious traitors who injured, abandoned, or deceived them. In every passion of which the mind of man is susceptible, the emotions of the by-stander always correspond to what, by bringing the case home to himself, he imagines should be the sentiments of the sufferer.

Pity and compassion are words appropriated to signify our fellow-feeling with the sorrow of others. Sympathy, though its meaning was, perhaps, originally the same, may now, however, without much impropriety, be made use of to denote our fellow-feeling with any passion whatever.

Upon some occasions sympathy may seem to arise merely from the view of a certain emotion in another person. The passions, upon some occasions, may seem to be transfused from one man to another, instantaneously, and antecedent to any knowledge of what excited them in the person principally concerned. Grief and joy, for example, strongly expressed in the look and gestures of any one, at once affect the spectator with some degree of a like painful or agreeable emotion. A smiling face is, to every body that sees it, a cheerful object; as a sorrowful countenance, on the other hand, is a melancholy one.

This, however, does not hold universally, or with regard to every passion. There are some passions of which the expressions excite no sort of sympathy, but before we are acquainted with what gave occasion to them, serve rather to disgust and provoke us against them. The furious behaviour of an angry man is more likely to exasperate us against himself than against his enemies. As we are unacquainted with his provocation, we cannot bring his case home to ourselves, nor conceive any thing like the passions which it excites. But we plainly see what is the situation of those with whom he is angry, and to what violence they may be exposed from so enraged an adversary. We readily, therefore, sympathize with their fear or resentment, and are immediately disposed to take part against the man from whom they appear to be in so much danger.

If the very appearances of grief and joy inspire us with some degree of the like emotions, it is because they suggest to us the general idea of some good or bad fortune that has befallen the person in whom we observe them: and in these passions this is sufficient to have some little influence upon us. The effects of grief and joy terminate in the person who feels those emotions, of which the expressions do not, like those of resentment, suggest to us the idea of any other person for whom we are concerned, and whose interests are opposite to his. The general idea of good or bad fortune, therefore, creates some concern for the person who has met with it, but the general idea of provocation excites no sympathy with the anger of the man who has received it. Nature, it seems, teaches us to be more averse to enter into this passion, and, till informed of its cause, to be disposed rather to take part against it.

Even our sympathy with the grief or joy of another, before we are informed of the cause of either, is always extremely imperfect. General lamentations, which express nothing but the anguish of the sufferer, create rather a curiosity to inquire into his situation, along with some disposition to sympathize with him, than any actual sympathy that is very sensible. The first question which we ask is, What has befallen you? Till this be answered, though we are uneasy both from the vague idea of his misfortune, and still more from torturing ourselves with conjectures about what it may be, yet our fellow-feeling is not very considerable.

Sympathy, therefore, does not arise so much from the view of the passion, as from that of the situation which excites it. We sometimes feel for another, a passion of which he himself seems to be altogether incapable; because, when we put ourselves in his case, that passion arises in our breast from the imagination, though it does not in his from the reality. We blush for the impudence and rudeness of another, though he himself appears to have no sense of the impropriety of his own behaviour; because we cannot help feeling with what confusion we ourselves should be covered, had we behaved in so absurd a manner.

Of all the calamities to which the condition of mortality exposes mankind, the loss of reason appears, to those who have the least spark of humanity, by far the most dreadful, and they behold that last stage of human wretchedness with deeper commiseration than any other. But the poor wretch, who is in it, laughs and sings perhaps, and is altogether insensible of his own misery. The anguish which humanity feels, therefore, at the sight of such an object, cannot be the reflection of any sentiment of the sufferer. The compassion of the spectator must arise altogether from the consideration of what he himself would feel if he was reduced to the same unhappy situation, and, what perhaps is impossible, was at the same time able to regard it with his present reason and judgment.

What are the pangs of a mother, when she hears the moanings of her infant that during the agony of disease cannot express what it feels? In her idea of what it suffers, she joins, to its real helplessness, her own consciousness of that helplessness, and her own terrors for the unknown consequences of its disorder; and out of all these, forms, for her own sorrow, the most complete image of misery and distress. The infant, however, feels only the uneasiness of the present instant, which can never be great. With regard to the future, it is perfectly secure, and in its thoughtlessness and want of foresight, possesses an antidote against fear and anxiety, the great tormentors of the human breast, from which reason and philosophy will, in vain, attempt to defend it, when it grows up to a man.

We sympathize even with the dead, and overlooking what is of real importance in their situation, that awful futurity which awaits them, we are chiefly affected by those circumstances which strike our senses, but can have no influence upon their happiness. It is miserable, we think, to be deprived of the light of the sun ...

Of the amiable and respectable virtues (I.i.5)

Upon these two different efforts, upon that of the spectator to enter into the sentiments of the person principally concerned, and upon that of the person principally concerned, to bring down his emotions to what the spectator can go along with, are founded two different sets of virtues. The soft, the gentle, the amiable virtues, the virtues of candid condescension and indulgent humanity, are founded upon the one: the great, the awful and respectable, the virtues of self-denial, of self-government, of that command of the passions which subjects all the movements of our nature to what our own dignity and honour, and the propriety of our own conduct require, take their origin from the other.

How amiable does he appear to be, whose sympathetic heart seems to re-echo all the sentiments of those with whom he converses, who grieves for their calamities, who resents their injuries, and who rejoices at their good fortune! When we bring home to ourselves the situation of his companions, we enter into their gratitude, and feel what consolation they must derive from the tender sympathy of so affectionate a friend. And for a contrary reason, how disagreeable does he appear to be, whose hard and obdurate heart feels for himself only, but is altogether insensible to the happiness or misery of others! We enter, in this case too, into the pain which his presence must give to every mortal with whom he converses, to those especially with whom we are most apt to sympathize, the unfortunate and the injured.

On the other hand, what noble propriety and grace do we feel in the conduct of those who, in their own case, exert that recollection and self-command which constitute the dignity of every passion, and which bring it down to what others can enter into! We are disgusted with that clamorous grief, which, without any delicacy, calls upon our compassion with sighs and tears and importunate lamentations. But we reverence that reserved, that silent and majestic sorrow, which discovers itself only in the swelling of the eyes, in the quivering of the lips and cheeks, and in the distant, but affecting, coldness of the whole behaviour. It imposes the like silence upon us. We regard it with respectful attention, and watch with anxious concern over our whole behaviour, lest by any impropriety we should disturb that concerted tranquility, which it requires so great an effort to support.

The insolence and brutality of anger, in the same manner, when we indulge its fury without check or restraint, is, of all objects, the most detestable. But we admire that noble and generous resentment which governs its pursuit of the greatest injuries, not by the rage which they are apt to excite in the breast of the sufferer, but by the indignation which they naturally call forth in that of the impartial spectator; which allows no word, no gesture, to escape it beyond what this more equitable sentiment would dictate; which never, even in thought, attempts any greater vengeance, nor desires to inflict any greater punishment, than what every indifferent person would rejoice to see executed.

And hence it is, that to feel much for others and little for ourselves, that to restrain our selfish, and to indulge our benevolent affections, constitutes the perfection of human nature; and can alone produce among mankind that harmony of sentiments and passions in which consists their whole grace and propriety. As to love our neighbour as we love ourselves is the great law of Christianity, so it is the great precept of nature to love ourselves only as we love our neighbour, or what comes to the same thing, as our neighbour is capable of loving us.

As taste and good judgment, when they are considered as qualities which deserve praise and admiration, are supposed to imply a delicacy of sentiment and an acuteness of understanding not commonly to be met with; so the virtues of sensibility and self-command are not apprehended to consist in the ordinary, but in the uncommon degrees of those qualities. The amiable virtue of humanity requires, surely, a sensibility, much beyond what is possessed by the rude vulgar of mankind. The great and exalted virtue of magnanimity undoubtedly demands much more than that degree of self-command, which the weakest of mortals is capable of exerting. As in the common degree of the intellectual qualities, there is no abilities; so in the common degree of the moral, there is no virtue. Virtue is excellence, something uncommonly great and beautiful, which rises far above what is vulgar and ordinary. The amiable virtues consist in the degree of sensibility which surprises by its exquisite and unexpected delicacy and tenderness. The awful and respectable, in that degree of self-command which astonishes by its amazing superiority over the most ungovernable passions of human nature....

Of the Social Passions (I.ii.4)

As it is a divided sympathy which renders the whole set of passions just now mentioned, upon most occasions, so ungraceful and disagreeable; so there is another set opposite to these, which a redoubled sympathy renders almost always peculiarly agreeable and becoming. Generosity, humanity, kindness, compassion, mutual friendship and esteem, all the social and benevolent affections, when expressed in the countenance or behaviour, even towards those who are not peculiarly connected with ourselves, please the indifferent spectator upon almost every occasion. His sympathy with the person who feels those passions, exactly coincides with his concern for the person who is the object of them. The interest, which, as a man, he is obliged to take in the happiness of this last, enlivens his fellow-feeling with the sentiments of the other, whose emotions are employed about the same object. We have always, therefore, the strongest disposition to sympathize with the benevolent affections. They appear in every respect agreeable to us. We enter into the satisfaction both of the person who feels them, and of the person who is the object of them. For as to be the object of hatred and indignation gives more pain than all the evil which a brave man can fear from his enemies; so there is a satisfaction in the consciousness of being beloved, which, to a person of delicacy and sensibility, is of more importance to happiness, than all the advantage which he can expect to derive from it....

The sentiment of love is, in itself, agreeable to the person who feels it. It sooths and composes the breast, seems to favour the vital motions, and to promote the healthful state of the human constitution; and it is rendered still more delightful by the consciousness of the gratitude and satisfaction which it must excite in him who is the object of it. Their mutual regard renders them happy in one another, and sympathy, with this mutual regard, makes them agreeable to every other person. With what pleasure do we look upon a family, through the whole of which reign mutual love and esteem, where the parents and children are companions for one another, without any other difference than what is made by respectful affection on the one side, and kind indulgence on the other; where freedom and fondness, mutual raillery and mutual kindness, show that no opposition of interest divides the brothers, nor any rivalship of favour sets the sisters at variance, and where every thing presents us with the idea of peace, cheerfulness, harmony and contentment? On the contrary, how uneasy we are made when we go into a house in which jarring contention sets one half of those who dwell in it against the other; where amidst affected smoothness and complaisance, suspicious looks and sudden starts of passion betray the mutual jealousies which burn within them, and which are every moment ready to burst out through all the restraints which the presence of the company imposes?

Those amiable passions, even when they are acknowledged to be excessive, are never regarded with aversion. There is something agreeable even in the weakness of friendship and humanity. The too tender mother, the too indulgent father, the too generous and affectionate friend, may sometimes, perhaps, on account of the softness of their natures, be looked upon with a species of pity, in which, however, there is a mixture of love, but can never be regarded with hatred and aversion, nor even with contempt, unless by the most brutal and worthless of mankind. It is always with concern, with sympathy and kindness, that we blame them for the extravagance of their attachment. There is a helplessness in the character of extreme humanity which more than any thing interests our pity. There is nothing in itself which renders it either ungraceful or disagreeable. We only regret that it is unfit for the world, because the world is unworthy of it, and because it must expose the person who is endowed with it as a prey to the perfidy and ingratitude of insinuating falsehood, and to a thousand pains and uneasinesses, which, of all men, he the least deserves to feel, and which generally too he is, of all men, the least capable of supporting. It is quite otherwise with hatred and resentment. Too violent a propensity to those detestable passions, renders a person the object of universal dread and abhorrence, who, like a wild beast, ought, we think, be hunted out of all civil society.

That though our sympathy with sorrow is generally a more lively sensation than our sympathy with joy, it commonly falls much more short of the violence of what is naturally felt by the person principally concerned (I.iii.1)

Our sympathy with sorrow, though not more real, has been more taken notice of than our sympathy with joy. The word sympathy, in its most proper and primitive signification, denotes our fellow-feeling with the sufferings, not that with the enjoyments, of others. A late ingenious and subtile philosopher thought it necessary to prove, by arguments, that we had a real sympathy with joy, and that congratulation was a principle of human nature. Nobody, I believe, ever thought it necessary to prove that compassion was such.

First of all, our sympathy with sorrow is, in some sense, more universal than that with joy. Though sorrow is excessive, we may still have some fellow-feeling with it. What we feel does not, indeed, in this case, amount to that complete sympathy, to that perfect harmony and correspondence of sentiments which constitutes approbation. We do not weep, and exclaim, and lament, with the sufferer. We are sensible, on the contrary, of his weakness and of the extravagance of his passion, and yet often feel a very sensible concern upon his account. But if we do not entirely enter into, and go along with, the joy of another, we have no sort of regard or fellow-feeling for it. The man who skips and dances about with that intemperate and senseless joy which we cannot accompany him in, is the object of our contempt and indignation.

Pain besides, whether of mind or body, is a more pungent sensation than pleasure, and our sympathy with pain, though it falls greatly short of what is naturally felt by the sufferer, is generally a more lively and distinct perception than our sympathy with pleasure, though this last often approaches more nearly, as I shall shew immediately, to the natural vivacity of the original passion.

Over and above all this, we often struggle to keep down our sympathy with the sorrow of others. Whenever we are not under the observation of the sufferer, we endeavour, for our own sake, to suppress it as much as we can, and we are not always successful. The opposition which we make to it, and the reluctance with which we yield to it, necessarily oblige us to take more particular notice of it. But we never have occasion to make this opposition to our sympathy with joy. If there is any envy in the case, we never feel the least propensity towards it; and if there is none, we give way to it without any reluctance. On the contrary, as we are always ashamed of our own envy, we often pretend, and sometimes really wish to sympathize with the joy of others, when by that disagreeable sentiment we are disqualified from doing so. We are glad, we say, on account of our neighbour's good fortune, when in our hearts, perhaps, we are really sorry. We often feel a sympathy with sorrow when we would wish to be rid of it; and we often miss that with joy when we would be glad to have it. The obvious observation, therefore, which it naturally falls in our way to make, is, that our propensity to sympathize with sorrow must be very strong, and our inclination to sympathize with joy very weak.

Notwithstanding this prejudice, however, I will venture to affirm, that, when there is no envy in the case, our propensity to sympathize with joy is much stronger than our propensity to sympathize with sorrow; and that our fellow-feeling for the agreeable emotion approaches much more nearly to the vivacity of what is naturally felt by the persons principally concerned, than that which we conceive for the painful one....

It is agreeable to sympathize with joy; and wherever envy does not oppose it, our heart abandons itself with satisfaction to the highest transports of that delightful sentiment. But it is painful to go along with grief, and we always enter into it with reluctance....

Of Self-Command (VI.iii.15)

.... The disposition to the affections which tend to unite men in society, to humanity, kindness, natural affection, friendship, esteem, may sometimes be excessive. Even the excess of this disposition, however, renders a man interesting to every body. Though we blame it, we still regard it with compassion, and even with kindness, and never with dislike. We are more sorry for it than angry at it. To the person himself, the indulgence even of such excessive affections is, upon many occasions, not only agreeable, but delicious. Upon some occasions, indeed, especially when directed, as is too often the case, towards unworthy objects, it exposes him to much real and heartfelt distress. Even upon such occasions, however, a well-disposed mind regards him with the most exquisite pity, and feels the highest indignation against those who affect to despise him for his weakness and imprudence. The defect of this disposition, on the contrary, what is called hardness of heart, while it renders a man insensible to the feelings and distresses of other people, renders other people equally insensible to his; and, by excluding him from the friendship of all the world, excludes him from the best and most comfortable of all social enjoyments.

3. From Laurence Sterne, *A Sentimental Journey Through France and Italy* (1768)

[These selections are taken from T. Becket and P.A. De Hondt's edition (London: 1768).]

a) MONTRIUL

When all is ready, and every article is disputed and paid for in the inn, unless you are a little sour'd by the adventure, there is always a matter to compound at the door, before you can get into your chaise; and that is with the sons and daughters of poverty, who surround you. Let no man say, "let them go to the devil"—'tis a cruel journey to send a few miserables, and they have had sufferings enow without it: I always think it better to take a few sous[1] out in my hand; and I would counsel every gentle traveller to do so likewise; he need not be so exact in setting down his motives for giving them—They will be register'd elsewhere.

For my own part, there is no man gives so little as I do; for few, that I know, have so little to give: but as this was the first publick act of my charity in France, I took the more notice of it.

A well-a-way! said I, I have but eight sous in the world, shewing them in my hand, and there are eight poor men and eight poor women for 'em.

A poor tatter'd soul, without a shirt on, instantly withdrew his claim, by retiring two steps out of the circle, and making a disqualifying bow on his part. Had the whole parterre cried out, *Place aux dames*,[2] with one voice, it would not have conveyed the sentiment of a deference for the sex with half the effect.

Just heaven! For what wise reasons hast thou ordered it, that beggary and urbanity, which are at such variance in other countries, should find a way to be at unity in this?

—I insisted upon presenting him with a single sous, merely for his *politesse*.

A poor little dwarfish brisk fellow, who stood over-against me in the circle, putting something first under his arm, which had once been a hat, took his snuff-box out of his pocket, and generously offer'd a pinch on both sides of him: it was a gift of consequence, and modestly declined—The poor little fellow press'd it upon

---

1 Pennies.
2 An imperative to yield place to the women in the group.

them with a nod of welcomeness—*Prenez en—prenez*,[1] said he, looking another way; so they each took a pinch—Pity thy box should ever want one! said I to myself; so I put a couple of sous into it—taking a small pinch out of his box, to enhance their value, as I did it.—He felt the weight of the second obligation more than that of the first—'twas doing him an honour—the other was only doing him a charity—and he made me a bow down to the ground for it.

—Here! said I to an old soldier with one hand, who had been campaign'd and worn out to death in the service—here's a couple of sous for thee. *Vive le Roi!*[2] said the old soldier.

I had then but three sous left: so I gave one, simply *pour l'amour de Dieu*,[3] which was the footing on which it was begg'd—The poor woman had a dislocated hip; so it could not be well upon any other motive.

Mon cher et très charitable Monsieur[4]—There's no opposing this, said I.

My Lord Anglois[5]—the very sound was worth the money—so I gave *my last sous for it.* But in the eagerness of giving, I had overlooked a *pauvre honteux*,[6] who had no one to ask a sous for him, and who, I believed, would have perished, ere he could have ask'd one for himself: he stood by the chaise, a little without the circle, and wiped a tear from a face which I thought had seen better days—Good God! said I—and I have not one single sous left to give him—But you have a thousand! cried all the powers of nature, stirring within me—so I gave him—no matter what—I am ashamed to say *how much*, now—and was ashamed to think, how little, then: so if the reader can form any conjecture of my disposition, as these two fixed points are given him, he may judge within a livre or two[7] what was the precise sum.

---

1 "Take some—take some."
2 (Long) live the king!
3 For the love of God.
4 My dear and most charitable Sir.
5 My English Lord.
6 A poor ashamed man, i.e., ashamed to be begging.
7 I.e., a pound or two, a much more substantial sum than the sous given to the others.

I could afford nothing for the rest, but, *Dieu vous bénisse—Et le bon Dieu vous bénisse encore*[1]—said the old soldier, the dwarf, &c. The *pauvre honteux* could say nothing—he pulled out a little handkerchief, and wiped his face as he turned away—and I thought he thanked me more than them all.

b) MARIA
   MOULINES

.... When we had got within half a league of Moulines, at a little opening in the road leading to a thicket, I discovered poor Maria sitting under a poplar—she was sitting with her elbow in her lap, and her head leaning on one side within her hand—a small brook ran at the foot of the tree.

I bid the postillion go on with the chaise to Moulines—and La Fleur to bespeak my supper—and that I would walk after him.

She was dress'd in white, and much as my friend described her, except that her hair hung loose, which before was twisted within a silk net.—She had, superadded likewise to her jacket, a pale green ribband, which fell across her shoulder to the waist; at the end of which hung her pipe.—Her goat had been as faithless as her lover; and she had got a little dog in lieu of him, which she had kept tied by a string to her girdle: as I looked at her dog, she drew him towards her with the string.—"Thou shalt not leave me, Sylvio," said she. I looked in Maria's eyes, and saw she was thinking more of her [dead] father than of her lover or her little goat; for as she utter'd them, the tears trickled down her cheeks.

I sat down close by her; and Maria let me wipe them away as they fell, with my handkerchief—I then steep'd it in my own—and then in hers—and then in mine—and then I wip'd hers again—and as I did it, I felt such undescribable emotions within me, as I am sure could not be accounted for from any combinations of matter and motion.

.... *God tempers the wind*, said Maria, to the shorn lamb.

Shorn indeed! And to the quick, said I; and wast thou in my own land, where I have a cottage, I would take thee to it and shelter thee: thou shouldst eat of my own bread, and drink of my own cup—I would be kind to thy Sylvio—in all thy weaknesses and wanderings I would seek after thee and bring thee back—when the sun went down I would say my prayers, and when I had done

---

1 God bless you—and the good Lord bless you again.

thou shouldst play thy evening song upon thy pipe; nor would the incense of my sacrifice be worse accepted for entering heaven along with that of a broken heart.

Nature melted within me, as I utter'd this; and Maria observing, as I took out my handkerchief, that it was steep'd too much already to be of use, would needs go wash it in the stream.—And where will you dry it, Maria? said I—I'll dry it in my bosom, said she—'twill do me good.

And is your heart still so warm, Maria, said I?

I touched upon the string on which hung all her sorrows—she looked with wistful disorder for some time in my face; and then, without saying anything, took her pipe, and play'd her service to the Virgin—The string I had touch'd ceased to vibrate—in a moment or two Maria returned to herself—let her pipe fall—and rose up.

And where are you going, Maria? said I.—She said, to Moulines.—Let us go, said I, together.—Maria put her arm within mine, and lengthening the string, to let the dog follow—in that order we enter'd Moulines.

Appendix B: Mackenzie's Correspondence on the Composition and Publication of The Man of Feeling

[Henry Mackenzie conducted a correspondence with his cousin Elizabeth Rose from 1768 until her death in 1815. In the following letters written between July 1769 and April 1770, Mackenzie describes his literary tastes, the process of writing *The Man of Feeling*, and what he hopes to achieve in it. The subsequent exchange with his correspondent James Elphinston 1770-71 focuses primarily on the novel's reception and Mackenzie's reaction.]

1. **Letters to Elizabeth Rose on the Composition of *The Man of Feeling*, 1769-70 [From Henry Mackenzie, *Letters to Elizabeth Rose of Kilvarock on Literature, Events and People, 1768-1815*. Horst W. Drescher, ed. Edinburgh: Oliver and Boyd, 1967.]**

Edin^r 8th July 1769

You cannot envy me, whom you good-naturedly call a Poet, a fertile Imagination, more than I envy you the Subject you have at present to exert yours upon. The Ideas which are confined to those elegant volumes the Statute-Books of Great Britain (as mine have been for this month past) are perhaps of all others the most distant from Sentiment or Fancy ...

.... You will find inclosed a very whimsical Introduction to a very odd Medley. I tell it as a Compliment, that even amidst the Hurry which our Whitsuntide Term has engaged me in of late, I had time to think of entertaining, or at least of attempting to entertain you ...

You must know, then, that I have seldom been in Use to write any Prose, except what consisted of Observations (such as I could make) on Men & Manners. The way of introducing these by Narrative I had fallen into in some detach'd Essays, from the Notion of it's interesting both the Memory & the Affection deeper, than mere Argument, or moral Reasoning. In this way I was somehow led to think of introducing a Man of Sensibility into different Scenes where his Feelings might be seen in their Effects, & his Sentiments occasionally delivered without the Stiffness of regular

Deduction. In order to give myself entire Liberty in the Historical Part of the Performance, & to indulge that desultory Humour of writing which sometimes possesses me, I began with this Introduction & write now and then a Chapter as I have Leisure or Inclination. How I have succeeded I cannot say; but I have found more Pleasure in the Attempt than in any other ...

Edin^r 31st July 1769

You judge as rightly as you do of every thing else, when you will freely let me know your judgement of them, in the Belief, that the worst Fault your Letters could have to me would be Stiffness....

.... This same Mr. Harley will be introduc'd to your Acquaintance by the two Chapters inclosed. But I wou'd premise one thing that I may not dissapoint you. You will remember that I have made myself accountable only for Chapters & Fragments of Chapters; the Curate must answer for the rest: besides from the general Scope of the Performance, which that Gentleman informed you, might be as well called a Sermon as a History, you wou'd find the Hero's Story, even if it were finish'd & I were to send it you entire, simple to Excess; for I would have it as different from the Entanglement of a Novel as can be. Yet I would not be understood to undervalue that Species of Writing; on the contrary, I take it to be much more important & indeed more difficult than I believe is generally imagin'd by the Authors; which is perhaps the Reason why We have so many Novels, & so few good ones. It is a Sort of Composition which I observe the Scottish Genius is remarkably deficient in; except Smollet, & one female Author,[1] I remember none of our Country who have made Attempts in that Way: yet these Performances are the most current of any I know, and need little more than a proper Jumble of Incidents to please those common-Place Beings you mention....

.... I forget to tell you that from the Reason I have assign'd above the two Chapters of the Man of Feeling inclosed are intituled 11th & 12th tho they are in reality the first.... I am

Your affectionate Cousin
Henry Mackenzie

---

1 Jean Marishall. Her novels *History of Miss Clarinda Cathcart and Miss Fanny Renton* (1765) and *History of Alicia Montague* (1767) had been very well-received. See discussion next letter.

... I am glad to find that Harley continues to please. I had intended that you should have heard no more of him till he reach'd the Metropolis; but as the first of the inclosed Chapters is in Connection with one or two in after Parts of the Performance, I have alter'd my Resolution & sent two which precede that period.

You were not much mistaken when you observ'd a Likeness between Mr. Silton & that worthy Uncle of ours you mention. To tell you the Truth ... I had struck out the Character without any Allusion to him: but I had not gone far, when the Resemblance occurr'd to me, as it now does to you & perhaps the Picture was not the worse for it. I believe indeed that, if we except the fantastic Figures of Romance, in this as in the other Species of Painting some Sort of Model will generally be found useful. I would not even draw honest Peter himself (see the last of the inclosed Chapters) without a present Idea; without which in my opinion, our Descriptions may be labor'd but they will hardly be striking. This Mr. Silton you may possibly hear of again.

I think I did not say that any Scotch female Author had *excell'd* in Novel-Writing, but only that She had attempted it. The Lady I meant is Miss Marshall[1] who has wrote the Histories of Clarinda Cathcart, and Alicia Montague ... Of Emily Montague[2] I had a good Character from my Sisters some time ago, & look'd into it then (I had Leisure for no more) with Pleasure: I shall read it attentively very soon. Lady Julia Mandeville[3] I have wept over formerly....

> Your affectionate Cousin,
> Henry Mackenzie

Edin^r 18th October 1769

'Tis a Rule with me (which I preach to my Sister as to singing) to obey my Friends Desires to entertain them immediately;

---

1 Jean Marishall. See preceding letter.
2 *The History of Emily Montague*, a novel by Frances Brooke (1724-89), published 1769.
3 *The History of Lady Julia Mandeville*, a novel by Frances Brooke, published 1763.

because, if the Performance is really good, it's Merit is enhanced, if otherwise, it's Apology is made, by the Willingness to amuse them....

.... I don't know that any particular Preference is due to the two Chapters of the Man of Feeling I sent you last; but I conclude that there is, since you observed it. Let me again remind you, that I expect your sincere opinion, not only of the Parts you most approve, but also of those which admit of Censure.

I am proud of having drawn a female Character so much to your Liking. I have alwise thought that we grave Fellows are commonly more fortunate in our Acquaintances among your Sex, than those, who, from the Study of their Lives being pointed that Way, are called Women's Men; & consequently (tho it may seem an odd Assertion to many of you) that we have a higher Opinion of it than they have.—

Your Approbation of Peter was of the highest Sort that could have been given him. It is an honest Pride in those who make any Pretence to Genius, to dignify worth, & the Feelings attendant on it, in whatever Station they are found; & it must be handled with little Delicacy, if the Impression it makes, is not as pleasant as it is useful.

I believe in a former Letter I desired you not to laugh at me for my Pretensions to Skill in Physiognomy. We can bear to laugh at ourselves, for you will find that Science ridiculed in an Adventure, which is the Subject of one of the Chapters I have now inclosed. The 20th is the Introduction to a Story which I hope will please; for I would not willingly fall off; so soon after the Approbation you have express'd of the last....

Your affectionate Cousin
Henry Mackenzie

Edin^r 24th January 1770

.... I did not mean any Arraignment of your Taste, when I supposed that you might possibly tire of the Man of Feeling; but I have seen Instances which lead me to doubt my own opinion, when it concerns any of my own Performances. Yet I am going perhaps to transgress in this way, when I tell you, that I now send you the first Part of my favorite Passage, The Story of Old Edwards. There are some Strokes in it which I am prouder of than any thing I ever wrote (for there is no writing so mean but it's Author will have some Pride in't). I hope it will introduce to your Acquaintance a new Character which you will be pleas'd with, as well as raise Harley higher in your Esteem, who I flatter myself is already somewhat a Favorite of yours....

I inclose a Letter of my Father's to your Mamma. Believe me sincerely

Your affectionate Cousin
Henry Mackenzie

Edin^r 19th April 1770

...You need not regret the want of the subsequent Chapters of the Man of Feeling. The winding up of a Story is one of the dullest Things in the world. You remember a Miss Walton; you have nothing to do but to imagine him somehow or other wedded to her and made happy;—so must all stories conclude you know; the Hero is as surely married as he was born; because Marriage is a good Thing & made in Heaven. I believe this Harley will be longer of making his public Appearance than I imagined: I have hitherto felt only the Pleasure of Composition; I begin now to experience the Troubles of an Author: Booksellers, & Managers of Play-houses, are of all Men of Business the least to be depended on, & I have a Degree of unbending Pride about me that cannot easily sollicit either Patronage or Introduction....

Believe me ever
Affectionately yours
Henry Mackenzie

2. Correspondence with James Elphinston[1] on the Composition and Reception of *The Man of Feeling*, 1770-71 from *Literature and Literati: The Literary Correspondence and Notebooks of Henry Mackenzie Vol. 1: Letters 1766-1827* Horst W. Drescher, ed.. Frankfurt: Peter Lang, 1989

To James Elphinston

Edinb., July 23, 1770

Dear Sir,
....
There is indeed another performance, the desultory production

---

1 James Elphinston (1721-1809) was a Scots-born educator, author, and campaigner for orthographic reform. His letter below has been translated from the phonetically spelled English he used back into standard English.

of some leisure hours; of more importance (at least, if age give importance), which I might possibly have given you some trouble about, if I had [not] known that your time and attention must have been most justly engrossed by the state of Mrs. Elphinston's health, which, I rejoice to hear, is so much reestablished.

It consists of some episodical adventures of a Man of Feeling; where his sentiments are occasionally expressed and the features of his mind developed, as the incidents draw them forth. It has, however deficient in other respects, I hope something of Nature in it, and is uniformly subservient to the cause of Virtue. You may, perhaps, from the description, conclude it a novel; nevertheless, it is perfectly different from that species of composition. Somewhat too much of this: But you see I deal honestly by my friends, when I give you this apologetic account, why I had not fastened some trouble on you.

...

I beg my respects to Mrs. Elphinston, and am

Dear Sir,
with sincere regard,
your most obedient servant,
Henry Mackenzie

From James Elphinston

[4 May 1771]

Dearest Sir,

I can no longer forbear giving you joy of *The Man of Feeling* who appeared in *London*, almost three weeks ago. Intently have I watched his reception; as well to judge of his receivers, as of himself. In honour to both, it rejoices me to assure you, that every reader of feeling has received him as a brother.

Yet must I no less honestly hint, that the friends he most would value, and those who love him most, have his introductory, or rather unintroduced, manner to forgive: a manner which, totally unworthy of him, can please only those, who cannot taste *The Man of Feeling*; and whose praise, if they should bestow any, would but make him blush. His truly sentimental friends hope therefore to see him, in a more consistent dress; to see him begun, continued (though diversified) and ended, perhaps with more felicity temporal, and with a prospect of similar posterity; however sublime and affecting his departure at last might be. By and by you may have an opportunity, of imagining a separation, as tender and as trying, as that of a lover and his bride!

Noble as are your characters, our heart tells us they are not beyond man; nor can we but make them welcome, abruptly though they burst upon us. Yet can I not help feeling for the coarseness of the curate, and wishing that insensibility had been fixed on a less sacred character. To your honor however I repeat, that you have, not only scorned to copy the imperfect, the motley, heroes of your predecessors; but have generally avoided the vulgar vile characters...; characters, which when painted, as they may be to the life, with not more genius than taste, in the painter; add only fictitious to real bad company; to the exclusion of those, which alone can improve, or rationally delight the mind.

No more therefore, dear Sir, of your fragments: taste demands a regular meal. Nor fear but we rise with an appetite, which as naturally recoils at surprise, as palls by disappointment.

...

I mention not petty inaccuracies, which your own review will correct; perhaps a scotticism here and there, as *make rich*; nor, charmed as I am with *Lavinia*, can I esteem her beyond a trisyllable:

Could *Thomson* and *Shenstone* look down,[1]
Poor *Harley's Lavinia* to see;
His strains would their[s] jealously crown;
Ah! Where shall we find such a three?

...

If aught I have omitted, your ingenuity will supply it: nor requires it much ingenuity, to conceive the affectionate esteem you have so powerfully augmented, in *The Man of Feeling*'[s] sincerest friend,

James Elphinston
Kensington,
May 4, 1771

---

1 James Thomson (1700-48) and William Shenstone (1714-63), mid-century English poets, widely admired for their pastoral and topographical verse.

To James Elphinston

Edin. 9th May, 1771

Dear Sir,

I take the first opportunity of thanking you, for your letter of the 4th instant; which shows so feelingly, the interest you have taken in *The Man of Feeling*. It was the more acceptable to me, as it is the only intelligence I have received of him.

I am sorry, that the manner of his introduction has given offence to those, whose suffrages I am most sollicitous to obtain. I was led into it, partly by accident, partly from wanting to shun the common road of novels; and partly from my opportunities of writing, being of that desultory kind, which such a plan, I imagined, would give me greater liberty to indulge. Let it be considered, to what use the bulk of my time is appropriated; amidst what sort of employment, I allowed myself the avocation of writing these fragments; that the self-same pen, which is now giving language to sentiment, has been just turned from drawing an *Information*, or completing a *Record*; and the same head, which is now occupied in tracing the movements of the heart, and unwinding the delicate thread of susceptibility and feeling, has but a moment before laboured, in settling the place of a *Whereas* or an *Aforesaid*.

This apology I am not entitled to offer to the Public; because it has a right to expect entertainment, and is not obliged to canvas the reasons of its disappointment; but I would plead it in extenuation, to the few, who take any concern in the trifles I write.

You will not, I am sure, nor will any who know me, suspect my wanting regard for the clerical character. I lighted on the person of a curate, because the curate is often the sportsman of the parish; and, amongst curates, I fancy, might easily be found several such (plump, unfeeling, *good sort of men*) as that logician, whose figure I have chanced to bring into my Introduction. Be so good as to explain to me, what the friends of *The Man of Feeling* expect; when they hope to see him in a more consistent dress, begun, continued, and ended.

...

I return my best respects to Mrs. Elphinston, and ever am,

Dear Sir
with sincere esteem,
your very humble servant,
Henry Mackenzie

To James Elphinston

Edin. 24th June, 1771

Dear Sir,

Your two letters ... I received in course ... The sentence of the *Monthly Reviewers*, on *The Man of Feeling*, I had heard of, some time ago: the review itself I saw only on Saturday last.[1] A judgement, so generally delivered, is not easily controverted; nor should it be my business to contradict it, tho I could. They will not allow me *genius*; but they have allotted me inspiration: for otherwise, tho I might easily have learnt Scotticism,[2] I could hardly have acquired *provincial idioms*.

An imitation of Sterne had been early objected to me; yet certain it is, that some parts of *The Man of Feeling*, which bear the strongest resemblance to *The Sentimental Journey*, were written, and even read to some of my friends, before the publication of that ingenious performance.[3] Setting out with this principle, that it was an imitation of Sterne, it was rightly pronounced a lame one; because, in truth, no such imitation was intended.

In case of another edition, I should take it as a singular favour, if you would point out any defects in language, or Scottish idioms, that struck you on a perusal of the book. In giving language to dialogue, one, whose ear is accustomed to hear such in this country, is very apt to slide into colloquial improprieties.
...

I am,
Dear Sir,
with sincere regard,
your obedient servant,
Henry Mackenzie

---

1 See Appendix D.
2 The problem of reconciling "correct" English usage with Scottish idioms was a problem of some importance for many eighteenth-century Scottish writers. Local variation in English usage was a source of vulnerability, as Mackenzie's experience at the hands of the *Monthly Review* demonstrates.
3 Sterne's *A Sentimental Journey* was published in 1768. Though Mackenzie here strongly denies any connection between his work and the earlier novel, Sterne's sentimental novel was published to a warm reception while Mackenzie could not have been very far into the early stages of composition of *The Man of Feeling*. (The earliest references to the novel in Mackenzie's abundant correspondence are in 1769.) Mackenzie's sensitivity to the *Monthly Review*'s charge of simply imitating Sterne is, however, understandable.

To James Elphinston

Dear Sir,

...

I again return you thanks, for the interest you obligingly take, in the second edition of *The Man of Feeling*. Whatever may be the critical estimation of that performance, Candor (I hope) will allow something for its tendency. That is not, nowadays, the most essential quality to many critics; but it is certainly a very important consideration, to authors; at least to those, who conceive themselves answerable for their productions, in moral view: and that is, surely, the most satisfying reputation which a man feels accord with the voice of his conscience.

...

I beg my respects to Mrs. Elphinston,
and am,
Dear Sir,
with sincere esteem,
your most obedient servant,
Henry Mackenzie

Appendix C: Other Fiction and Journalism by Mackenzie

[The following selections from Mackenzie's fiction and journalism are taken from *The Works of Henry Mackenzie in Eight Volumes*. Edinburgh, 1808.]

1. From *Julia de Roubigné* (1777)

[*Julia de Roubigné*, an epistolary novel, recounts the ill-fated romance of the title character and her impoverished lover Savillon. In the two letters excerpted here, Savillon, who has left France in hopes of making a fortune in Martinique, describes his reactions to the French West Indies and to its slavery-based economy.]

LETTER XXVII

Savillon to Beauvaris.

IT is now a week since I reached my uncle's, during all which time I have been so much occupied in answering questions to the curiosity of others, or asking questions for the satisfaction of my own, that I have scarce had a moment left for any other employment.

I have now seized the opportunity of the rest of the family being still a-bed, to write to you an account of this uncle; of him under whose protection I am to rise into life, under whose guidance I am to thrid the mazes of the world. I fear I am unfit for the task: I must unlearn feelings in which I have been long accustomed to delight: I must accommodate sentiments to conveniency, pride to interest, and sometimes even virtue itself to fashion.

But is all this absolutely necessary?—I hate to believe it. I have been frequently told so indeed; but my authorities are drawn either from men who have never entered the scene at all, or entered it, resolved to be overcome without the trouble of resistance. To think too meanly of mankind, is dangerous to our reverence of virtue.

It is supposed, that, in these wealthy islands, profit is the only medium of opinion, and that morality has nothing to do in the system; but I cannot easily imagine, that, in any latitude, the bosom is shut to those pleasures which result from the exercise of goodness, or that honesty should be always so unsuccessful as to have the sneer of the million against it. Men will not be depraved beyond the persuasion of some motive, and self-interest will often be the parent of social obligation.

My uncle is better fitted for judging of this question; he is cool enough to judge of it from experience, without being misled by feeling.—He believes there are many more honest dealings than honest men, but that there are more honest men than knaves everywhere; that common sense will keep them so, even exclusive of principle; but that all may be vanquished by adequate temptation.

With a competent share of plain useful parts, and a certain steady application of mind, he entered into commerce at an early period of life. Not apt to be seduced by the glare of great apparent advantage, nor easily intimidated from his purposes by accidental disappointment, he has held on, with some vicissitude of fortune, but with uniform equality of temper, till, in virtue of his abilities, his diligence, and his observation, he has acquired very considerable wealth. He still, however, continues the labour of the race, though he has already reached the goal; not because he is covetous of greater riches, but because the industry, by which greater riches are acquired, is grown necessary to the enjoyment of life. "I have been long," said he yesterday, "a very happy man; having had a little less time, and a little more money, than I know what to make of."

The opinion of the world he trusts but little, in his judgment of others; of men's actions he speaks with caution, either in praise or blame, and is commonly most sceptical, when those around him are most convinced: for it is a maxim with him, in questions of character, to doubt of strong evidence from the very circumstance of its strength.

With regard to himself, however, he accepts of the common opinion, as a sort of coin which passes current, though it is not always real, and often seems to yield up the conviction of his own mind in compliance with the general voice. Ever averse to splendid project in action, or splendid conjecture in argument, he contents himself with walking in the beaten track of things, and does not even venture to leave it, though he may, now and then, observe it making small deviations from reason and justice. He has sometimes, since our acquaintance began, tapped me on the shoulder, in the midst of some sentiment I was uttering, and told me, with a smile, that these were fine words, and did very well in the mouth of a young man. Yet he seems not displeased with my feeling what himself does not feel; and looks on me with a more favourable eye, that I have something about me for experience and observation to prune.

His plan of domestic oeconomy is regular, but nobody is disturbed by its regularity; for he is perfectly free from that rigid attention to method, which one frequently sees in the houses of old bachelors. He has sense, or *sang-froid* enough, not to be troubled with little disarrangements, and bears with wonderful complacency, and consequently with great ease to his guests, those accidents which disturb the peace of other entertainments. Since my arrival, we have had every day something like a feast, probably from a sort of compliment which his friends meant to pay to him and to me; but at his table, in its most elevated style, the government is nearly republican; he assumes very little, either of the trouble or the dignity of a landlord, satisfied with giving a general assurance of welcome and good-humour in his aspect.

At one of those dinners was a neighbour and intimate acquaintance of my uncle, a Mr. Dorville, with his wife and daughter. The young lady was seated next me, and my uncle seemed to incline, that I should be particularly pleased with her. He addressed such discourse to her, as might draw her forth to the greatest advantage: and, as he heard me profess myself a lover of music, he made her sing after dinner, till, I believe, some of the company began to be tired of their entertainment. After they were gone, he asked my opinion of Mademoiselle Dorville, in that particular style by which a man gives you to understand that his own is a very favourable one. To say truth, the lady's appearance is in her favour; but there is a jealous sort of feeling which arises in my mind, when I hear the praises of any woman but one; and from that cause, perhaps, I answered my uncle rather coldly; I saw he thought so from the reply he made: I made some awkward apology: he smiled, and said I was a philosopher. Alas! he knows not how little claim I have to philosophy in that way; if, indeed, we are so often to profane that word by affixing to it the idea of insensibility.

To-day I begin business. My uncle and I are to view his different plantations, and he is to shew me, in general, the province he means to allot me. I wish for an opportunity to be assiduous in his service: till I can do something on my part, his favours are like debts upon me. It is only to a friend, like my Beauvaris, that one feels a pleasure in being obliged.

LETTER XXVIII

Savillon to Beauvaris.

A THOUSAND thanks for your last letter. When you know how much I enjoyed the unwieldy appearance of the packet, with my friend's hand on the back of it, you will not grudge the time it cost you. It is just such as I wished: your scene-painting is delightful. No man is more susceptible of local attachments than I; and, with the Atlantic between, there is not a stone in France which I can remember with indifference.

Yet I am happier here than I could venture to expect. Had I been left to my own choice, I should probably have sat down in solitude, to think of the past, and enjoy my reflections; but I have been forced to do better. There is an active duty which rewards every man in the performance; and my uncle has so contrived matters, that I have had very little time unemployed. He has been liberal of instruction, and, I hope, has found me willing to be instructed. Our business, indeed, is not very intricate; but, in the simplest occupations, there are a thousand little circumstances which experience alone can teach us. In certain departments, however, I have tried projects of my own: Some of them have failed in the end, but all gave me pleasure in the pursuit. In one I have been successful beyond expectation; and in that one I was the most deeply interested, because it touched the cause of humanity.

To a man not callous from habit, the treatment of the negroes, in the plantations here, is shocking. I felt it strongly, and could not forbear expressing my sentiments to my uncle. He allowed them to be natural, but pleaded necessity, in justification of those severities, which his overseers sometimes used towards his slaves. I ventured to doubt this proposition, and begged he would suffer me to try a different mode of government in one plantation, the produce of which he had already allotted to my management. He consented, though with the belief that I should succeed very ill in the experiment.

I began by endeavouring to ingratiate myself with such of the slaves as could best speak the language of my country; but I found this was a manner they did not understand, and that, from a white, the appearance of indulgence carried the suspicion of treachery. Most of them, to whom rigour had become habitual, took the advantage of its remitting, to neglect their work altogether; but this only served to convince me, that my plan was a good one, and that I should undoubtedly profit, if I could establish some other motive, whose impulse was more steady than those of punishment and terror.

By continuing the mildness of my conduct, I at last obtained a degree of willingness in the service of some; and I was still induced to believe, that the most savage and sullen among them had principles of gratitude, which a good master might improve to his advantage.

One slave, in particular, had for some time attracted my notice, from that gloomy fortitude with which he bore the hardships of his situation.—Upon enquiring of the overseer, he told me, that this slave, whom he called Yambu, though, from his youth and appearance of strength, he had been accounted valuable, yet, from the untractable stubbornness of his disposition, was worth less money than almost any other in my uncle's possession.— This was a language natural to the overseer. I answered him, in his own style, that I hoped to improve his price some hundreds of livres. On being further informed, that several of his fellow-slaves had come from the same part of the Guinea coast with him, I sent for one of them who could speak tolerable French, and questioned him about Yambu. He told me, that, in their own country, Yambu was master of them all; that they had been taken prisoners, when fighting in his cause, by another prince, who, in one battle, was more fortunate than theirs; that he had sold them to some white men, who came in a great ship to their coast; that they were afterwards brought hither, where other white men purchased them from the first, and set them to work where I saw them; but that when they died, and went beyond the Great Mountains, Yambu should be their master again.

I dismissed the negro, and called this Yambu before me.

When he came, he seemed to regard me with an eye of perfect indifference. One who had enquired no further, would have concluded him possessed of that stupid insensibility, which Europeans often mention as an apology for their cruelties. I took his hand; he considered this a prologue to chastisement, and turned his back to receive the lashes he supposed me ready to inflict. "I wish to be the friend of Yambu," said I. He made me no answer: I let go his hand, and he suffered it to drop to its former posture. "Can this man have been a prince in Africa?" said I to myself.— I reflected for a moment.—"Yet what should he now do, if he has?—Just what I see him do. I have seen a deposed sovereign at

Paris; but in Europe, kings are artificial beings, like their subjects.—Silence is the only throne which adversity has left to princes.

"I fear," said I to him, "you have been sometimes treated harshly by the overseer; but you shall be treated so no more; I wish all my people to be happy." He looked on me now for the first time.—"Can you speak my language, or shall I call for some of your friends, who can explain what you would say to me?" "I speak no say to you," he replied in his broken French.—"And you will not be my friend?"—"No."— "Even if I should deserve it?"—"You a white man."—I felt the rebuke as I ought. "But all white men are not overseers. What shall I do to make you think me a good man?"—"Use men goodly."—"I mean to do so, and you among the first, Yambu."—"Be good for Yambu's people; do your please with Yambu."

Just then the bell rung as a summons for the negroes to go to work: he made a few steps towards the door. "Would you now go to work," said I, "if you were at liberty to avoid it?" "You make go for whip, and no man love go."—"I will go along with you, though I am not obliged; for I chuse to work sometimes rather than be idle."—"Chuse work, no work at all," said Yambu.—'Twas the very principle on which my system was founded.

I took him with me into the house when our task was over. "I wrought chuse work," said I, "Yambu, yet I did less than you."—"Yambu do chuse work then too?"—"You shall do so always," answered I; "from this moment you are mine no more!"—"You sell me other white men then?"—"No, you are free, and may do whatever you please!"—"Yambu's please no here, no this country," he replied, waving his hand, and looking wistfully towards the sea.—"I cannot give you back your country, Yambu; but I can make this one better for you. You can make it better for me too, and for your people!" "Speak Yambu that," said he eagerly, "and be good man!"—"You would not," said I, "make your people work by the whip, as you see the overseers do?"—"Oh! no, no whip!"—"Yet they must work, else we shall have no sugars to buy them meat and clothing with."—(He put his hand to his brow, as if I had started a difficulty he was unable to overcome.)—"Then you shall have the command of them, and they shall work chuse work for Yambu."—He looked askance, as if he doubted the truth of what I said; I called the negro with whom I had the first conversation about him, and, pointing to Yambu, "Your master," said I, "is now free, and may leave you when he pleases!"—"Yambu no leave you," said he to the negro warmly.—"But he may accompany Yambu if he chuses."—Yambu shook his head.—"Master," said his former subject, "where we go? leave good white men and go to bad; for much bad white men in this country."—"Then if you think it better, you shall both stay; Yambu shall be my friend, and help me to raise sugars for the good of us all: you shall have no overseer but Yambu, and shall work no more than he bids you."—The negro fell at my feet and kissed them; Yambu stood silent, and I saw a tear on his cheek.— "This man has been a prince in Africa!" said I to myself.

I did not mean to deceive them. Next morning I called those negroes, who had formerly been in his service, together, and told them, that, while they continued in the plantation, Yambu was to superintend their work; that if they chose to leave him and me, they were at liberty to go; and that, if found idle or unworthy, they should not be allowed to stay. He has, accordingly, ever since had the command of his former subjects, and superintended their work in a particular quarter of the plantation; and having been declared free, according to the mode prescribed by the laws of the island, has a certain portion of ground allotted him, the produce of which is his property. I have had the satisfaction of observing those men, under the feeling of good treatment, and the idea of liberty, do more than almost double their number subject to the whip of an overseer. I am under no apprehension of desertion or mutiny; they work with the willingness of freedom, yet are mine with more than the obligation of slavery.

I have been often tempted to doubt, whether there is not an error in the whole plan of negro servitude; and whether whites, or creoles[1] born in the West Indies, or perhaps cattle, after the manner of European husbandry, would not do the business better and cheaper than the slaves do? The money which the latter cost at first, the sickness (often owing to despondency of mind) to which they are liable after their arrival, and the proportion that die in consequence of it, make the machine, if it may be so called, of a plantation, extremely expensive in its operations. In the list of slaves belonging to a wealthy planter, it would astonish you to see the number unfit for service, pining under disease, a burden on their master.—I am talking only as a merchant; but as a man— Good heavens! when I think of the many thousands of my fellow-

---

1 "In the West Indies and other parts of America, ... person[s] born and naturalized in the country, but of European or of African Negro race" (OED).

creatures groaning under servitude and misery!—Great God! hast thou peopled those regions of thy world for the purpose of casting out their inhabitants to chains and torture?—No; thou gavest them a land teeming with good things, and lighted'st up thy sun to bring forth spontaneous plenty; but the refinements of man, ever at war with thy works, have changed this scene of profusion and luxuriance into a theatre of rapine, of slavery, and of murder!

Forgive the warmth of this apostrophe! Here it would not be understood; even my uncle, whose heart is far from a hard one, would smile at my romance, and tell me that things must be so. Habit, the tyrant of nature and of reason, is deaf to the voice of either; here she stifles humanity, and debases the species;—for the master of slaves has seldom the soul of a man.

This is not difficult to be accounted for:—from his infancy he is made callous to those feelings which soften at once and ennoble our nature. Children must, of necessity, first exert those towards domestics, because the society of domestics is the first they enjoy; here they are taught to command, for the sake of commanding; to beat and torture, for pure amusement;—their reason and good-nature improve as may be expected.

Among the legends of a European nursery, are stories of captives delivered, of slaves released, who had pined for years in the durance of unmerciful enemies.—Could we suppose its infant audience transported to the sea-shore, where a ship laden with slaves is just landing; the question would be universal, "Who shall set these poor people free?"—The young West Indian asks his father to buy a boy for him, that he may have something to vent his spite on when he is peevish.

Methinks, too, these people lose a sort of connection, which is of more importance in life than most of the relationships we enjoy. The ancient, the tried domestic of a family, is one of its most useful members; one of its most assured supports. My friend, the ill-fated Roubigné has not one relation who has stood by him in the shipwreck of his fortunes; but the storm could not sever from their master his faithful Le Blanc, or the venerable Lasune.[1]

Oh, Beauvaris! I sometimes sit down alone, and, transporting myself into the little circle at Roubigné's, grow sick of the world, and hate the part which I am obliged to perform in it.

---

1   The novel opens with the heroine's father, Roubigné, losing the bulk of his fortune. LeBlanc and Lasune are servants of the Roubigné family.

2. *The Mirror* nos. 42-44, 19-26 June 1779: "The Effects of Religion on Minds of Sensibility. The Story of La Roche"

[Mackenzie devoted three consecutive issues of his periodical *The Mirror* to a sentimental tale which became well known and widely reprinted as the "story of La Roche." The story describes the growth of a friendship between an English philosopher and skeptic, modeled on David Hume, and a country clergyman (La Roche) and his daughter.]

[*The Mirror* no. 42, 19 June 1779]

WHEN I first undertook this publication, it was suggested by some of my friends, and, indeed, accorded entirely with my own ideas, that there should be nothing of religion in it. There is a sacredness in the subject, that might seem profaned by its introduction into a work, which, to be extensively read, must sometimes be ludicrous, and often ironical. This consideration will apply, in the strongest manner, to any thing mystic or controversial; but it may, perhaps, admit of an exception, when religion is only introduced as a feeling, not a system, as appealing to the sentiments of the heart, not to the disquisitions of the head. The following story holds it up in that light, and is therefore, I think, admissible into the Mirror. It was sent to my editor as a translation from the French. Of this my readers will judge. Perhaps they might be apt to suspect, without any suggestion from me, that it is an original, not a translation. Indeed, I cannot help thinking, that it contains in it much of that picturesque description, and that power of awakening the tender feelings, which so remarkably distinguish the composition of a gentleman, whose writings I have often read with pleasure. But, be that as it may, as I felt myself interested in the narrative, and believed that it would affect my readers in the like manner, I have ventured to give it entire as I received it, though it will take up the room of three successive papers.

TO THE AUTHOR OF THE MIRROR.

SIR,

MORE than forty years ago, an English philosopher, whose works have since been read and admired by all Europe, resided at a little town in France. Some disappointments in his native country had first driven him abroad, and he was afterwards induced to remain there, from having found, in this retreat, where the connections even of nation and language were avoided, a perfect seclusion and retirement highly favourable to the developement of abstract subjects, in which he excelled all the writers of his time.[1]

Perhaps in the structure of such a mind as Mr. ——'s, the finer and more delicate sensibilities are seldom known to have place; or, if originally implanted there, are in a great measure extinguished by the exertions of intense study and profound investigation. Hence the idea of philosophy and unfeelingness being united, has become proverbial, and in common language, the former word is often used to express the latter.—Our philosopher had been censured by some, as deficient in warmth and feeling: but the mildness of his manners has been allowed by all; and it is certain, that if he was not easily melted into compassion, it was, at least, not difficult to awaken his benevolence.

One morning, while he sat busied in those speculations which afterwards astonished the world, an old female domestic, who served him for a housekeeper, brought him word, that an elderly gentleman and his daughter had arrived in the village the preceding evening, on their way to some distant country, and that the father had been suddenly seized in the night with a dangerous disorder, which the people of the inn where they lodged feared would prove mortal: that she had been sent for, as having some knowledge in medicine, the village-surgeon being then absent; and that it was truly piteous to see the good old man, who seemed not so much afflicted by his own distress, as by that which it caused to his daughter.—Her master laid aside the volume in his hand, and broke off the chain of ideas it had inspired. His nightgown was exchanged for a coat, and he followed his gouvernante to the sick man's apartment.

It was the best in the little inn where they lay, but a paltry one notwithstanding. Mr. —— was obliged to stoop as he entered it. It was floored with earth, and above were the joists not plastered, and hung with cobwebs.—On a flock bed, at one end, lay the old man he came to visit; at the foot of it sat his daughter. She was dressed in a clean white bedgown; her dark locks hung loosely

---

1   The character of the philosopher, with his combination of abstruse thought, atheism, and benevolence, is modelled on David Hume.

over it as she bent forward, watching the languid looks of her father. Mr. —— and his housekeeper had stood some moments in the room without the young lady's being sensible of their entering it.—"Mademoiselle!" said the old woman at last, in a soft tone.—She turned, and showed one of the finest faces in the world. It was touched, not spoiled, with sorrow; and when she perceived a stranger, whom the old woman now introduced to her, a blush at first, and then the gentle ceremonial of native politeness, which the affliction of the time tempered, but did not extinguish, crossed it for a moment, and changed its expression.—It was sweetness all, however, and our philosopher felt it strongly. It was not a time for words; he offered his services in a few sincere ones. "Monsieur lies miserably ill here," said the gouvernante; "if he could possibly be moved any where"——"If he could be moved to our house," said her master.—He had a spare bed for a friend, and there was a garret room unoccupied, next to the gouvernante's. It was contrived accordingly. The scruples of the stranger, who could look scruples, though he could not speak them, were overcome, and the bashful reluctance of his daughter gave way to her belief of its use to her father. The sick man was wrapt in blankets, and carried across the street to the English gentleman's. The old woman helped his daughter to nurse him there. The surgeon, who arrived soon after, prescribed a little, and nature did much for him; in a week he was able to thank his benefactor.

By that time his host had learned the name and character of his guest. He was a Protestant clergyman of Switzerland, called La Roche, a widower, who had lately buried his wife, after a long and lingering illness, for which travelling had been prescribed, and was now returning home, after an ineffectual and melancholy journey, with his only child, the daughter we have mentioned.

He was a devout man, as became his profession. He possessed devotion in all its warmth, but with none of its asperity; I mean that asperity which men, called devout, sometimes indulge in. Mr. ——, though he felt no devotion, never quarrelled with it in others. His gouvernante joined the old man and his daughter in the prayers and thanksgivings which they put up on his recovery; for she, too, was a heretic, in the phrase of the village.—The philosopher walked out, with his long staff and his dog, and left them to their prayers and thanksgivings.—"My master,"—said the old woman, "alas! he is not a Christian; but he is the best of unbelievers."—"Not a Christian!"—exclaimed Mademoiselle La

Roche, "yet he saved my father! Heaven bless him for it; I would he were a Christian!"—"There is a pride in human knowledge, my child," said her father, "which often blinds men to the sublime truths of revelation; hence opposers of Christianity are found among men of virtuous lives, as well as among those of dissipated and licentious characters. Nay, sometimes, I have known the latter more easily converted to the true faith than the former, because the fume of passion is more easily dissipated than the mist of false theory and delusive speculation."—"But Mr. ——," said his daughter, "alas! my father, he shall be a Christian before he dies."—She was interrupted by the arrival of their landlord.— He took her hand with an air of kindness:—she drew it away from him in silence; threw down her eyes to the ground, and left the room.——"I have been thanking God," said the good La Roche, "for my recovery."—"That is right," replied his landlord.——"I would not wish," continued the old man, hesitatingly, "to think otherwise; did I not look up with gratitude to that Being, I should barely be satisfied with my recovery, as a continuation of life, which, it may be, is not a real good.——Alas! I may live to wish I had died, that you had left me to die, Sir, instead of kindly relieving me, (he clasped Mr. ——'s hand;)—but, when I look on this renovated being as the gift of the Almighty, I feel a far different sentiment—my heart dilates with gratitude and love to Him: it is prepared for doing His will, not as a duty, but as a pleasure, and regards every breach of it, not with disapprobation, but with horror."—"You say right, my dear Sir," replied the philosopher; "but you are not yet re-established enough to talk much—you must take care of your health, and neither study nor preach for some time. I have been thinking over a scheme that struck me today, when you mentioned your intended departure. I never was in Switzerland: I have a great mind to accompany your daughter and you into that country.—I will help to take care of you by the road; for, as I was your first physician, I hold myself responsible for your cure." La Roche's eyes glistened at the proposal; his daughter was called in and told of it. She was equally pleased with her father; for they really loved their landlord—not perhaps the less for his infidelity; at least that circumstance mixed a sort of pity with their regard for him—their souls were not of a mould for harsher feelings; hatred never dwelt in them.

CONTINUATION OF THE STORY OF LA ROCHE.

THEY travelled by short stages; for the philosopher was as good as
his word, in taking care that the old man should not be fatigued.
The party had time to be well acquainted with one another, and
their friendship was increased by acquaintance. La Roche found
a degree of simplicity and gentleness in his companion, which is
not always annexed to the character of a learned or a wise man.
His daughter, who was prepared to be afraid of him, was equally
undeceived. She found in him nothing of that self-importance,
which superior parts, or great cultivation of them, is apt to con-
fer. He talked of every thing but philosophy or religion; he
seemed to enjoy every pleasure and amusement of ordinary life,
and to be interested in the most common topics of discourse:
when his knowledge or learning at any time appeared, it was
delivered with the utmost plainness, and without the least shadow of dogmatism.

On his part, he was charmed with the society of the good clergyman and his lovely daughter. He found in them the guileless
manner of the earliest times, with the culture and accomplish-
ment of the most refined ones. Every better feeling, warm and
vivid; every ungentle one, repressed or overcome. He was not
addicted to love; but he felt himself happy in being the friend of
Mademoiselle La Roche, and sometimes envied her father the
possession of such a child.

After a journey of eleven days, they arrived at the dwelling of
La Roche. It was situated in one of those valleys of the canton of
Berne, where nature seems to repose, as it were, in quiet, and has
enclosed her retreat with mountains inaccessible.——A stream,
that spent its fury in the hills above, ran in front of the house, and
a broken water-fall was seen through the wood that covered its
sides; below, it circled round a tufted plain, and formed a little
lake in front of a village, at the end of which appeared the spire
of La Roche's church, rising above a clump of beeches.

Mr. —— enjoyed the beauty of the scene; but to his companions, it recalled the memory of a wife and parent they had lost.—
The old man's sorrow was silent; his daughter sobbed and wept.
Her father took her hand, kissed it twice, pressed it to his bosom,
threw up his eyes to heaven; and, having wiped off a tear, that was
just about to drop from each, began to point out to his guest

some of the most striking objects which the prospect afforded. The philosopher interpreted all this; and he could but slightly censure the creed from which it arose.

They had not been long arrived, when a number of La Roche's parishioners, who had heard of his return, came to the house to see and welcome him. The honest folks were awkward, but sincere, in their professions of regard. They made some attempts at condolence; it was too delicate for their handling; but La Roche took it in good part. "It has pleased God," said he; and they saw he had settled the matter with himself. Philosophy could not have done so much with a thousand words.

It was now evening, and the good peasants were about to depart, when a clock was heard to strike seven, and the hour was followed by a particular chime. The country folks, who had come to welcome their pastor, turned their looks towards him at the sound; he explained their meaning to his guest. "That is the signal," said he, "for our evening exercise; this is one of the nights of the week in which some of my parishioners are wont to join in it: a little rustic saloon serves for the chapel of our family, and such of the good people as are with us; if you chuse rather to walk out, I will furnish you with an attendant; or here are a few old books, that may afford you some entertainment within."—"By no means," answered the philosopher; "I will attend Ma'moiselle at her devotions."—"She is our organist," said La Roche; "our neighbourhood is the country of musical mechanism; and I have a small organ fitted up for the purpose of assisting our singing."—"'Tis an additional inducement," replied the other; and they walked into the room together. At the end stood the organ mentioned by La Roche; before it was a curtain, which his daughter drew aside, and, placing herself on a seat within, and drawing the curtain close, so as to save her the awkwardness of an exhibition, began a voluntary, solemn and beautiful in the highest degree. Mr. —— was no musician, but he was not altogether insensible to music; this fastened on his mind more strongly, from its beauty being unexpected. The solemn prelude introduced a hymn, in which such of the audience as could sing immediately joined; the words were mostly taken from holy writ; it spoke the praises of God, and his care of good men. Something was said of the death of the just, of such as die in the Lord.—The organ was touched with a hand less firm;—it paused, it ceased; and the sobbing of Ma'moiselle La Roche was heard in its stead. Her father gave a sign for stopping the psalmody, and rose to pray. He was discomposed at first, and his voice faltered as he spoke; but his heart was in his words, and his warmth overcame his embarrassment. He addressed a Being whom he loved, and he spoke for those he loved. His parishioners catched the ardour of the good old man; even the philosopher felt himself moved, and forgot, for a moment, to think why he should not.

La Roche's religion was that of sentiment, not theory, and his guest was averse from disputation; their discourse, therefore, did not lead to questions concerning the belief of either; yet would the old man sometimes speak of his, from the fullness of a heart impressed with its force, and wishing to spread the pleasure he enjoyed in it. The ideas of his God, and his Saviour, were so congenial to his mind, that every emotion of it naturally awakened them. A philosopher might have called him an enthusiast; but, if he possessed the fervour of enthusiasts, he was guiltless of their bigotry. "Our Father which art in Heaven!" might the good man say—for he felt it—and all mankind were his brethren.

"You regret, my friend," said he to Mr. ——, "when my daughter and I talk of the exquisite pleasure derived from music, you regret your want of musical powers and musical feelings; it is a department of soul, you say, which nature has almost denied you, which, from the effects you see it have on others, you are sure must be highly delightful. Why should not the same thing be said of religion? Trust me, I feel it in the same way, an energy, an inspiration, which I would not lose for all the blessings of sense or enjoyments of the world; yet so far from lessening my relish of the pleasures of life, methinks I feel it heighten them all. The thought of receiving it from God, adds the blessing of sentiment to that of sensation in every good thing I possess; and when calamities overtake me—and I have had my share—it confers a dignity on my affliction, so lifts me above the world!—Man, I know, is but a worm,—yet, methinks, I am then allied to God!"—It would have been inhuman in our philosopher to have clouded, even with a doubt, the sunshine of this belief.

His discourse, indeed, was very remote from metaphysical disquisition, or religious controversy. Of all men I ever knew, his ordinary conversation was the least tinctured with pedantry, or liable to dissertation. With La Roche and his daughter it was perfectly familiar. The country round them, the manners of the villagers, the comparison of both with those of England, remarks on the works of favourite authors, on the sentiments they conveyed, and the passions they excited, with many other topics in which there was an equality, or alternate advantage, among the speakers, were the subjects they talked on. Their hours too of riding and walking were many, in which Mr. ——, as a stranger, was shewn the remarkable scenes and curiosities of the country. They would sometimes make little expeditions, to contemplate, in different attitudes, those astonishing mountains, the cliffs of which, covered with eternal snows, and sometimes shooting into fantastic shapes, form the termination of most of the Swiss prospects. Our philosopher asked many questions as to their natural history and productions. La Roche observed the sublimity of the ideas which the view of their stupendous summits, inaccessible to mortal foot, was calculated to inspire, which naturally, said he, leads the mind to that Being by whom their foundations were laid.—— "They are not seen in Flanders!" said Ma'moiselle, with a sigh. "That's an odd remark," said Mr. ——, smiling.——She blushed, and he inquired no farther.

It was with regret he left a society in which he found himself so happy; but he settled with La Roche and his daughter a plan of correspondence; and they took his promise, that, if ever he came within fifty leagues of their dwelling, he should travel those fifty leagues to visit them.

[*The Mirror* no. 44, 26 June 1779]

CONCLUSION OF THE STORY OF LA ROCHE.

ABOUT three years after, our philosopher was on a visit at Geneva; the promise he made to La Roche and his daughter, on his former visit, was recalled to his mind, by the view of that range of mountains, on a part of which they had often looked together. There was a reproach, too, conveyed along with the recollection, for his having failed to write to either for several months past. The truth was, that indolence was the habit most natural to him, from which he was not easily roused by the claims of correspondence either of his friends or of his enemies; when the latter drew their pens in controversy, they were often unanswered as well as the former. While he was hesitating about a visit to La Roche, which he wished to make, but found the effort rather too much for him, he received a letter from the old man, which had been forwarded to him from Paris, where he had then fixed his residence. It contained a gentle complaint of Mr. ——'s want of punctuality, but an assurance of continued gratitude for his former good offices;

and, as a friend whom the writer considered interested in his family, it informed him of the approaching nuptials of Ma'moiselle La Roche, with a young man, a relation of her own, and formerly a pupil of her father's, of the most amiable dispositions, and respectable character. Attached from their earliest years, they had been separated by his joining one of the subsidiary regiments of the Canton, then in the service of a foreign power. In this situation, he had distinguished himself as much for courage and military skill, as for the other endowments which he had cultivated at home. The time of his service was now expired, and they expected him to return in a few weeks, when the old man hoped, as he expressed it in his letter, to join their hands, and see them happy before he died.

Our philosopher felt himself interested in this event; but he was not, perhaps, altogether so happy in the tidings of Ma'moiselle La Roche's marriage, as her father supposed him. Not that he was ever a lover of the lady's; but he thought her one of the most amiable women he had seen, and there was something in the idea of her being another's for ever, that struck him, he knew not why, like a disappointment. After some little speculation on the matter, however, he could look on it as a thing fitting, if not quite agreeable, and determined on this visit to see his old friend and his daughter happy.

On the last day of his journey, different accidents had retarded his progress: he was benighted before he reached the quarter in which La Roche resided. His guide, however, was well acquainted with the road, and he found himself at last in view of the lake, which I have before described, in the neighbourhood of La Roche's dwelling. A light gleamed on the water, that seemed to proceed from the house; it moved slowly along as he proceeded up the side of the lake, and at last he saw it glimmer through the trees, and stop at some distance from the place where he then was. He supposed it some piece of bridal merriment, and pushed on his horse that he might be a spectator of the scene; but he was a good deal shocked, on approaching the spot, to find it proceed from the torch of a person clothed in the dress of an attendant on a funeral, and accompanied by several others, who, like him, seemed to have been employed in the rites of sepulture.

On Mr. ——'s making inquiry who was the person they had been burying? one of them, with an accent more mournful than is common to their profession, answered, "Then you knew not Mademoiselle, Sir?—you never beheld a lovelier"—"La Roche!"

exclaimed he, in reply—"Alas! it was she indeed!"—The appearance of surprise and grief which his countenance assumed, attracted the notice of the peasant with whom he talked. He came up closer to Mr. ——; "I perceive. Sir, you were acquainted with Mademoiselle La Roche." "Acquainted with her!—Good God!—when—how—where did she die? Where is her father?" "She died, Sir, of heart-break, I believe; the young gentleman to whom she was soon to have been married, was killed in a duel by a French officer, his intimate companion, and to whom, before their quarrel, he had often done the greatest favours. Her worthy father bears her death, as he has often told us a Christian should; he is even so composed, as to be now in his pulpit, ready to deliver a few exhortations to his parishioners, as is the custom with us on such occasions:—Follow me, Sir, and you shall hear him." He followed the man without answering.

The church was dimly lighted, except near the pulpit, where the venerable La Roche was seated. His people were now lifting up their voices in a psalm to that Being whom their pastor had taught them ever to bless and to revere. La Roche sat, his figure bending gently forward, his eyes half-closed, lifted up in silent devotion. A lamp placed near him threw its light strong on his head, and marked the shadowy lines of age across the paleness of his brow, thinly covered with grey hairs.

The music ceased; La Roche sat for a moment, and nature wrung a few tears from him. His people were loud in their grief. Mr. —— was not less affected than they. La Roche arose. "Father of mercies!" said he, "forgive these tears; assist thy servant to lift up his soul to thee; to lift to thee the souls of thy people! My friends! it is good so to do: at all seasons it is good; but, in the days of our distress, what a privilege it is! Well saith the sacred book, 'Trust in the Lord; at all times trust in the Lord.' When every other support fails us, when the fountains of worldly comfort are dried up, let us then seek those living waters which flow from the throne of God. 'Tis only from the belief of the goodness and wisdom of a Supreme Being, that our calamities can be borne in that manner which becomes a man. Human wisdom is here of little use; for, in proportion as it bestows comfort, it represses feeling, without which we may cease to be hurt by calamity, but we shall also cease to enjoy happiness. I will not bid you be insensible, my friends! I cannot, I cannot, if I would (his tears flowed afresh)—I feel too much myself, and I am not ashamed of my feelings; but therefore may I the more willingly be heard; therefore have I prayed God to give me strength to speak to you; to direct you to Him, not with empty words, but with these tears; not from speculation, but from experience,—that while you see me suffer, you may know also my consolation.

"You behold the mourner of his only child, the last earthly stay and blessing of his declining years! Such a child too!—It becomes not me to speak of her virtues; yet it is but gratitude to mention them, because they were exerted towards myself. Not many days ago you saw her young, beautiful, virtuous, and happy; ye who are parents will judge of my felicity then,—ye will judge of my affliction now. But I look towards Him who struck me; I see the hand of a father amidst the chastenings of my God. Oh! could I make you feel what it is to pour out the heart, when it is pressed down with many sorrows, to pour it out with confidence to Him, in whose hands are life and death, on whose power awaits all that the first enjoys, and in contemplation of whom disappears all that the last can inflict! For we are not as those who die without hope; we know that our Redeemer liveth,—that we shall live with him, with our friends, His servants, in that blessed land where sorrow is unknown, and happiness is endless as it is perfect. Go then, mourn not for me, I have not lost my child: but a little while, and we shall meet again never to be separated. But ye are also my children: would ye that I should not grieve without comfort? So live as she lived: that, when your death cometh, it may be the death of the righteous, and your latter end like his."

Such was the exhortation of La Roche; his audience answered it with their tears. The good old man had dried up his at the altar of the Lord; his countenance had lost its sadness, and assumed the glow of faith and of hope. Mr. —— followed him into his house. The inspiration of the pulpit was past; at sight of him the scenes they had last met in, rushed again on his mind; La Roche threw his arms round his neck, and watered it with his tears. The other was equally affected; they went together, in silence, into the parlour, where the evening service was wont to be performed. The curtains of the organ were open; La Roche started back at the sight. "Oh! my friend!" said he, and his tears burst forth again. Mr. —— had now recollected himself; he stept forward, and drew the curtains close—the old man wiped off his tears, and taking his friend's hand, "You see my weakness," said he, "'tis the weakness of humanity; but my comfort is not therefore lost." "I heard you," said the other, "in the pulpit; I rejoice that such consolation is yours." "It is, my friend," said he, "and I trust I shall ever hold it fast; if there are any who doubt our faith, let them think of what importance religion is to calamity, and forbear to weaken its force; if they cannot restore our happiness, let them not take away the solace of our affliction."

Mr. ——'s heart was smitten; and I have heard him, long after, confess, that there were moments when the remembrance overcame him even to weakness; when, amidst all the pleasures of philosophical discovery, and the pride of literary fame, he recalled to his mind the venerable figure of the good La Roche, and wished that he had never doubted.

3. *The Mirror* no. 101, 25 April 1780: "The Effects of Sentiment and Sensibility on Happiness. From a Guardian"

[In the guise of a long letter to the editor of *The Mirror*, Mackenzie offers a cautionary tale about the dangers of excessive sensibility.]

TO THE AUTHOR OF THE MIRROR.

SIR,
IN books, whether moral or amusing, there are no passages more captivating both to the writer and the reader, than those delicate strokes of sentimental morality, which refer our actions to the determination of feeling. In these the poet, the novel-writer, and the essayist, have always delighted; you are not, therefore, singular, for having dedicated so much of the Mirror to sentiment and sensibility. I imagine, however, Sir, there is much danger in pushing these qualities too far; the rules of our conduct should be founded on a basis more solid, if they are to guide us through the various situations of life; but the young enthusiast of sentiment and feeling is apt to despise those lessons of vulgar virtue and prudence, which would confine the movements of a soul formed to regulate itself by finer impulses. I speak from experience, Mr. Mirror; with what justice you shall judge, when you have heard the little family-history I am going to relate.

My niece, Emilia ——, was left to my care by a brother whom I dearly loved, when she was a girl of about ten years old. The beauty of her countenance, and the elegance of her figure, had already attracted universal notice; as her mind opened, it was found not less worthy of admiration. To the sweetest natural disposition, she united uncommon powers both of genius and of understanding: these I spared no pains to cultivate and improve; and I think I so far succeeded, that, in her eighteenth year, Emilia was inferior to few women of her age, either in personal attractions, or in accomplishments of the mind. My fond hopes (for she was a daughter to me, Mr. Mirror) looked now for the reward of my labour, and I pictured her future life as full of happiness as of virtue.

One feature of her mind was strongly predominant; a certain delicacy and fineness of feeling which she had inherited from Nature, and which her earliest reading had tended to encourage and increase. To this standard she was apt to bring both her own actions and the actions of others; and allowed more to its effects, both in praise and blame, than was consistent with either justice or expediency. I sometimes endeavoured gently to combat these notions. She was not always logical, but she was always eloquent in their defence; and I found her more confirmed on their side, the more I obliged her to be their advocate. I preferred, therefore, being silent on the subject, trusting that a little more experience and knowledge of the world would necessarily weaken their influence.

At her age, and with her feelings, it is necessary to have a friend: Emilia had found one at a very early period. Harriet S——— was the daughter of a neighbour of my brother's, a few years older than my niece. Several branches of their education the two young ladies had received together; in these the superiority lay much on the side of Emilia: Harriet was nowise remarkable for fineness of genius or quickness of parts; but though her acquirements were moderate, she knew how to manage them to advantage; and there was often a certain avowal of her inferiority, which conciliated affection the more, as it did not claim admiration. Her manners were soft and winning, like those of Emilia; her sentiments as delicate and exalted; there seemed, however, less of nature in both.

Emilia's attachment to this young lady I found every day increase, till, at last, it so totally engrossed her as rather to displease me. When together, their attention was confined almost entirely to each other; or what politeness forced them to bestow upon others, they considered as a tax which it was fair to elude as much as possible. The world, a term which they applied indiscriminately to almost every one but themselves, they seemed to feel as much pride as happiness in being secluded from; and its laws of prudence and propriety, they held the invention of cold and selfish minds, insensible of the delights of feeling, of sentiment, and of friendship. These ideas were, I believe, much strengthened by a correspondence that occupied most of the hours (not many indeed) in which they were separated. Against this I ventured to remonstrate in a jocular manner, with Emilia; she answered me in a strain so serious, as convinced me of the danger of so romantic an attachment. Our discourse on the subject grew insensibly warm: Emilia at last burst into tears; and I apologized for having, I knew not how, offended her. From that day forth, though I continued her adviser, I found I had ceased to be her friend.

That office was now Harriet's alone; the tie only wanted some difficulty to rivet it closer, some secret to be entrusted with, some distress to alleviate. Of this an opportunity soon after presented itself. Harriet became enamoured of a young gentleman of the name of Marlow, an officer of dragoons, who had come to the country on a visit to her brother, with whom he had been acquainted at college. As she inherited several thousand pounds, independent of her expectations from her father, such a match was a very favourable one for a young man, who possessed no revenue but his commission. But, for that very reason, the consent of the young lady's relations was not to be looked for. After some time, therefore, of secret and ardent attachment, of which my niece was the confident, the young folks married without it, and trusted to the common relentings of parental affection, to forgive a fault which could not be remedied. But the father of Harriet remained quite inexorable: nor was his resentment softened even by her husband's leaving the army; a step which, it was hoped, might have mitigated his anger, as he had often declared it principally to arise from his daughter's marrying a soldier.

After some fruitless attempts to reinstate themselves in the old gentleman's affections, they took up their residence in a provincial town, in a distant part of the kingdom; where, as Harriet described their situation to Emilia, they found every wish gratified in the increasing tenderness of one another. Emilia, soon after, went to see them in their new abode: her description of their happiness, on her return, was warm to a degree of rapture. Her visit was repeated on occasion of Harriet's lying-in of her first child. This incident was a new source of delight to Emilia's friends, and of pleasure to her in their society. Harriet, whose recovery was slow, easily prevailed on her to stay till it was completed. She became a member of the family, and it was not without much regret, on both sides, that she left, at the end of six months, a house from which, as she told me, the world was secluded, where sentiment regulated the conduct, and happiness rewarded it. All this while I was not without alarm, and could not conceal my uneasiness from Emilia; I represented the situation in which her friend stood, whom prudent people must consider as having, at least, made a bold step, if not a blameable one. I was answered rather angrily, by a warm remonstrance against the inhumanity of parents, the unfeelingness of age, and the injustice of the world.

That happiness, which my niece had described as the inmate of Harriet's family, was not of long duration. Her husband, tired of the inactive scene into which his marriage had cast him, grew first discontented at home, and then sought for that pleasure abroad which his own house could not afford him. His wife felt this change warmly, and could not restrain herself from expressing her feelings. Her complaints grew into reproaches, and rivetted her husband's dislike to her society, and his relish for the society of others. Emilia was, as usual, the confident of her friend's distress; it was now increased to a lingering illness, which had succeeded the birth of a second girl. After informing me of those disagreeable circumstances in which her Harriet was situated, Emilia told me she had formed the resolution of participating, at least, if she could not alleviate, her friend's distress, by going directly to reside in her house. Though I had now lost the affections of my niece, she had not yet forced me into indifference for her. Against this proposal I remonstrated in the strongest manner. You will easily guess my arguments; but Emilia would not allow them any force. In vain I urged the ties of duty, of prudence, and of character. They only produced an eulogium on generosity, on friendship, and on sentiment. I could not so far command my temper as to forbear some observations, which my niece interpreted into reflections upon her Harriet. She grew warm on the subject; my affection for her would not suffer me to be cool. At last, in the enthusiasm of her friendship, she told me I had cancelled every bond of relationship between us; that she would instantly leave my house, and return to it no more. She left it accordingly, and set out for Harriet's that very evening.

There, as I learned, she found that lady in a situation truly deplorable: her health declined, her husband cruel, and the fortune she had brought him wasted among his companions at the tavern, and the gaming-table. The last calamity the fortune of

Emilia enabled her to relieve; but the two first she could not cure, and her friend was fast sinking under them. She was at last seized with a disorder which her weak frame was unable to resist, and which, her physicians informed Emilia, would soon put a period to her life. This intelligence she communicated to the husband in a manner suited to wring his heart for the treatment he had given his wife. In effect, Marlow was touched with that remorse which the consequences of profligate folly will sometimes produce in men more weak than wicked. He too had been in use to talk of feeling and of sentiment. He was willing to be impelled by the passions, though not restrained by the principles of virtue, and to taste the pleasures of vice, while he thought he abhorred its depravity. His conversion was now as violent as sudden. Emilia believed it sincere, because confidence was natural to her, and the effects of sudden emotion her favourite system. By her means a thorough re-union took place between Mr. and Mrs. Marlow: and the short while the latter survived, was passed in that luxury of reconcilement, which more than reinstates the injurer in our affection. Harriet died in the arms of her husband; and, by a solemn abjuration, left to Emilia the comfort of him, and the care of her children.

There is in the communion of sorrow one of the strongest of all connections; and the charge which Emilia had received from her dying friend of her daughters, necessarily produced the freest and most frequent intercourse with their father. Debts, which his former course of life had obliged him to contract, he was unable to pay; and the demands of his creditors were the more peremptory, as, by the death of his wife, the hopes of any pecuniary assistance from her father were cut off. In the extremity of this distress, he communicated it to Emilia. Her generosity relieved him from the embarrassment, and gave him that farther tie which is formed by the gratitude of those we oblige. Meanwhile, from the exertions of that generosity, she suffered considerable inconvenience. The world was loud, and sometimes scurrilous, in its censure of her conduct. I tried once more, by a letter written with all the art I was master of, to recall her from the labyrinth in which this false sort of virtue had involved her. My endeavours were vain. I found that sentiment, like religion, had its superstition, and its martyrdom. Every hardship she suffered she accounted a trial, every censure she endured she considered as a testimony of her virtue. At last my poor deluded niece was so entangled in the toils which her own imagination, and the art of Marlow, had spread for her, that she gave to the dying charge of Harriet the romantic interpretation of becoming the wife of her widower, and the mother of her children. My heart bleeds, Mr. Mirror, while I foresee the consequences! She will be wretched, with feelings ill-accommodated to her wretchedness. Her sensibility will aggravate that ruin to which it has led her, and the world will not even afford their pity to distresses, which the prudent may blame, and the selfish may deride.

Let me warn at least where I cannot remedy. Tell your readers this story, Sir. Tell them, there are bounds beyond which virtuous feelings cease to be virtue; that the decisions of sentiment are subject to the controul of prudence, and the ties of friendship subordinate to the obligations of duty.

I am, &c.

LEONTIUS.

4. *The Lounger* no. 20, 18 June 1785: "On Novel-Writing"

[Here Mackenzie warns against the dangers of reading novels—especially sentimental novels with their "sickly sort of refinement"—which he describes as tending to instill a taste for intensity of feeling in place of "real practical duties." Another recantation of sentimentalism.]

Decipit exemplar vitiis imitabile.——Hor.[1]

No species of composition is more generally read by one class of readers, or more undervalued by another, than that of the novel. Its favourable reception from the young and the indolent, to whom the exercise of imagination is delightful, and the labour of thought is irksome, needs not be wondered at; but the contempt which it meets from the more respectable class of literary men, it may perhaps be entitled to plead that it does not deserve. Con-

---

1 Horace, *Epistles*, I. xix.17: "An example whose vices are imitable leads [us] astray." Mackenzie sounds a note of caution, or alarm, on the novel as a form likely to produce imitations by its readers. This was a widespread concern. In his reference later in the essay to the "character of mingled virtue and vice ... in some of the best of our novels," for example, he alludes to the well-known example of Henry Fielding's *Tom Jones* (1749), criticized by Samuel Johnson and many others in the decades after its publication as inviting indulgence and possibly imitation of the vices of its otherwise likeable protagonist.

sidered in the abstract, as containing an interesting relation of events, illustrative of the manners and characters of mankind, it surely merits a higher station in the world of letters than is generally assigned it. If it has not the dignity, it has at least most of the difficulties, of the epic or the drama. The conduct of its fable, the support of its characters, the contrivance of its incidents, and its developement of the passions, require a degree of invention, judgment, taste, and feeling, not much, if at all, inferior to those higher departments of writing, for the composition of which a very uncommon portion of genius is supposed to be requisite. Those difficulties are at the same time heightened by the circumstance, of this species of writing being, beyond any other, open to the judgment of the people; because it represents domestic scenes and situations in private life, in the execution of which any man may detect errors and discover blemishes, while the author has neither the pomp of poetry, nor the decoration of the stage, to cover or to conceal them.

To this circumstance, however, may perhaps be imputed the degradation into which it has fallen. As few endowments were necessary to judge, so few have been supposed necessary to compose a novel; and all whose necessities or vanity prompted them to write, betook themselves to a field, which, as they imagined, it required no extent of information or depth of learning to cultivate, but in which a heated imagination, or an excursive fancy, were alone sufficient to succeed; and men of genius and of knowledge, despising a province in which such competitors were to be met, retired from it in disgust, and left it in the hands of the unworthy.

The effects of this have been felt, not only in the debasement of the novel in point of literary merit, but in another particular still more material, in its perversion from a moral or instructive purpose to one directly the reverse. Ignorance and dulness are seldom long inoffensive, but generally support their own native insignificance by an alliance with voluptuousness and vice.

Even of those few novels which superior men have written, it cannot always be said, that they are equally calculated to improve as to delight. Nor is this only to be objected to some who have been professedly less scrupulous in that particular; but I am afraid may be also imputed to those whose works were meant to convey no bad impression, but, on the contrary, were intended to aid the cause of virtue, and to hold out patterns of the most exalted benevolence.

I am not, however, disposed to carry the idea of the dangerous tendency of all novels quite so far as some rigid moralists have done. As promoting a certain refinement of mind, they operate like all other works of genius and feeling, and have indeed a more immediate tendency to produce it than most others, from their treating of those very subjects which the reader will find around him in the world, and their containing those very situations in which he himself may not improbably at some time or other be placed. Those who object to them as inculcating precepts, and holding forth examples, of a refinement which virtue does not require, and which honesty is better without, do not perhaps sufficiently attend to the period of society which produces them. The code of morality must necessarily be enlarged in proportion to that state of manners to which cultivated æras give birth. As the idea of property made a crime of theft, as the invention of oaths made falsehood perjury; so the necessary refinement in manners of highly-polished nations creates a variety of duties and of offences, which men in ruder, and, it may be (for I enter not into that question,) happier periods of society, could never have imagined.

The principal danger of novels, as forming a mistaken and pernicious system of morality, seems to me to arise from that contrast between one virtue or excellence and another, that war of duties which is to be found in many of them, particularly in that species called the sentimental. These have been chiefly borrowed from our neighbours the French, whose style of manners, and the very powers of whose language, give them a great advantage in the delineation of that nicety, that subtilty of feeling, those entanglements of delicacy, which are so much interwoven with the characters and conduct of the chief personages in many of their most celebrated novels. In this rivalship of virtues and of duties, those are always likely to be preferred which in truth and reason are subordinate, and those to be degraded which ought to be paramount. The last, being of that great cardinal sort which must be common, because they apply to the great leading relations and circumstances of life, have an appearance less dignified and heroic than the others, which, as they come forth only on extraordinary occasions, are more apt to attract the view and excite the admiration of beholders. The duty to parents is contrasted with the ties of friendship and of love; the virtues of justice, of prudence, of economy, are put in competition with the exertions of generosity, of benevolence, and of compassion: and even of these virtues of sentiment there are still more refined divisions, in which the overstrained delicacy of the persons represented always leads them to act from the motive least obvious, and therefore generally the least reasonable.

In the enthusiasm of sentiment there is much the same danger as in the enthusiasm of religion, of substituting certain impulses and feelings of what may be called a visionary kind, in the place of real practical duties, which in morals, as in theology, we might not improperly denominate good works. In morals, as in religion, there are not wanting instances of refined sentimentalists, who are contented with talking of virtues which they never practise, who pay in words what they owe in actions; or, perhaps, what is fully as dangerous, who open their minds to impressions which never have any effect upon their conduct, but are considered as something foreign to and distinct from it. This separation of conscience from feeling is a depravity of the most pernicious sort; it eludes the strongest obligation to rectitude, it blunts the strongest incitement to virtue; when the ties of the first bind the sentiment and not the will, and the rewards of the latter crown not the heart but the imagination.

That creation of refined and subtile feeling, reared by the authors of the works to which I allude, has an ill effect, not only on our ideas of virtue, but also on our estimate of happiness. That sickly sort of refinement creates imaginary evils and distresses, and imaginary blessings and enjoyments, which embitter the common disappointments, and depreciate the common attainments of life. This affects the temper doubly, both with respect to ourselves and others; with respect to ourselves, from what we think ought to be our lot; with regard to others, from what we think ought to be their sentiments. It inspires a certain childish pride of our own superior delicacy, and an unfortunate contempt of the plain worth, the ordinary but useful occupations and ideas of those around us.

The reproach which has been sometimes made to novels, of exhibiting "such faultless monsters as the world ne'er saw," may be just on the score of entertainment to their readers, to whom the delineation of uniform virtue, except when it is called into striking situations, will no doubt be insipid. But, in point of moral tendency, the opposite character is much more reprehensible; I mean that character of mingled virtue and vice which is to be found in some of the best of our novels. Instances will readily occur to every reader, where the hero of the performance has violated, in one page, the most sacred laws of society, to whom, by the mere turning of the leaf, we are to be reconciled, whom we are to be made to love and admire, for the beauty of some humane, or the brilliancy of some heroic action. It is dangerous thus to bring us into the society of vice, though introduced or accompanied by virtue. In the application to ourselves, in which the moral tendency of all imaginary characters must be supposed to consist, this nourishes and supports a very common kind of self-deception, by which men are apt to balance their faults by the consideration of their good qualities; an account which, besides the fallacy of its principle, can scarcely fail to be erroneous, from our natural propensity to state our faults at their lowest, and our good qualities at their highest rate.

I have purposely pointed my observations, not to that common herd of novels (the wretched offspring of circulating libraries) which are despised for their insignificance, or proscribed for their immorality; but to the errors, as they appear to me, of those admired ones which are frequently put into the hands of youth for imitation as well as amusement. Of youth it is essential to preserve the imagination sound as well as pure, and not to allow them to forget, amidst the intricacies of sentiment, or the dreams of sensibility, the truths of reason, or the laws of principle.

5. *The Lounger* no. 90, 21 October 1786: "Letter from Barbara Heartless, the Unfortunate Attendant of a Woman of Extreme Sensibility and Feeling"

[Once more using the device of the fictive letter to the editor, Mackenzie offers a further critique of sensibility as a form of self-indulgence, this time in a humourous mode. Mrs. Sensitive, the "woman of extreme sensibility" of the title, weeps over animals but is indifferent to the suffering of her servants, her relatives, and the poor.]

TO THE AUTHOR OF THE LOUNGER.

SIR,

THOUGH, from my rank in life, being a tradesman's daughter, left an orphan at six years old, I had little title to know any thing about sensibility or feeling; yet having been very kindly taken into a family, where there were several young ladies, who were great readers, I had opportunities of hearing a good deal about these things. By the same young ladies I was made acquainted with your Paper, and it was a favourite employment of mine to read the Lounger to them every Saturday morning. In one of the numbers published some time ago, we met with Mrs. Alice Heartly's account of an old lady with whom she lives; and from the experience of our own feelings, could not help pitying the connection with one so destitute of all tender sentiments as my Lady Bidmore. I had soon after occasion to congratulate myself on a very different sort of establishment, having been recommended by my young patronesses to a lady, who used frequently to visit at their house, whom we all knew (indeed it was her pride, she used to say, to acknowledge her weakness on that side) to be a perfect pattern, or, according to her own phrase, a perfect martyr, of the most acute and delicate sensibility. At our house I saw her once in the greatest distress imaginable, from the accidental drowning of a fly in the cream-pot; and got great credit with her myself, for my tenderness about a goldfinch belonging to one of our young ladies, which I had taught to perch upon my shoulder, and pick little crumbs out of my mouth. I shall never forget Mrs. Sensitive's crying out, "Oh! how I envy her the sweet little creature's kisses!" It made me blush to hear her speak so; for I had never thought of kisses in the matter.

That little circumstance, however, procured me her favour so much that, on being told of my situation, she begged I might, as she was kind enough to express it, be placed under her protection. As I had heard so much of her tender-heartedness and her feeling; as she was very rich, having been left a widow, with the disposal of her husband's whole fortune; as she had nobody but herself in family, so that it promised to be an easy place; all these things made me very happy to accept of her offer; and I agreed to go home to her house immediately, her last attendant having left her somewhat suddenly. I heard indeed, the very morning after I went thither, that her servants did not use to stay long with her, which gave me some little uneasiness; but she took occasion to inform me, that it was entirely owing to their cruelty, and want of feeling, having turned them all off for some neglect or ill usage of her little family, as she called it. This little family, of which I had not heard before, consists of a number of birds and beasts, which it is the great pleasure of Mrs. Sensitive's life to keep and to fondle, and on which she is constantly exercising her sensibilities, as she says. My chief employment is to assist her in the care of them.

The waiting on this family of Mrs. Sensitive's is not so easy a task as I at first had flattered myself it would have been. We have three lap-dogs, four cats, some of the ladies of which are almost always lying-in, a monkey, a flying squirrel, two parrots, a parroquet, a Virginia nightingale, a jack-daw, an owl, besides half a hundred smaller birds, bulfinches, canaries, linnets, and white sparrows. We have a dormouse in a box, a set of guinea-pigs in the garret, and a tame otter in the cellar; besides out-pensioners of pigeons and crows at our windows, and mice that come from a hole in the parlour wainscotting, to visit us at breakfast and dinner time. All these I am obliged to tend and watch with the utmost care and assiduity; not only to take care that their food and their drink be in plenty, and good order; not only to wash the lap-dogs, and to comb the cats, to play on the bird-organ for the instruction of the canaries and goldfinches, and to speak to the parrots and jack-daw for theirs; but I must accommodate myself, as my mistress says, to the feelings of the sweet creatures; I must contribute to their amusement, and keep them in good spirits; I must scratch the heads of the parrots; I must laugh to the monkey, and play at cork-balls with the kittens. Mrs. Sensitive says, she can understand their looks and their language from sympathy; and that she is sure it must delight every susceptible mind to have thus an opportunity for extending the sphere of its sensibilities.

She sometimes takes an opportunity of extending something else with poor me. You can hardly suppose what a passion she gets into, if any thing about this family of hers is neglected; and when she chuses to be angry, and speak her mind to me a little loud or so, her favourites, I suppose from sympathy too, join in the remonstrance, and make such a concert!—What between the lap-dogs, the parrots, the jack-daw, and the monkey, there is such a barking, squalling, cawing, and chattering!—Mrs. Sensitive's ears are not so easily hurt as her feelings.

But the misfortune is, Mr. Lounger, that her feelings are only made for brute creatures, and don't extend to us poor Christians of the family. She has no pity on us, no sympathy in the world for our distresses. She keeps a chambermaid and a boy besides myself; and I assure you it does not fare near so well with us as it does with the lap-dogs and the monkey. Nay, I have heard an old milk-woman say, who has been long about the family, that Mr. Sensitive himself was not treated altogether so kindly as some of his lady's four-footed favourites. He was, it seems, a good-natured man, and not much given to complain. The old woman says, she never heard of his finding fault with any thing, but once that Mrs. Sensitive insisted on taking into bed a Bologna greyhound, because she said it could not sleep a-nights, from the coldness of the climate in this country. Yet she often talks of her dear, dear Mr. Sensitive, and weeps when she talks of him; and she has got a fine tombstone raised over his grave, with an epitaph full of disconsolates, and inconsolables, and what not. To say truth, that is one way even for a human creature to get into her good graces; for I never heard her mention any of her dead friends without a great deal of kindness and tender regrets: but we are none of us willing to purchase her favour at that rate.

As for the living, they have the misfortune never to be to her liking. Ordinary objects of charity we are ordered never to suffer to come near her; she says she cannot bear to hear their lamentable stories, for that they tear her poor feelings in pieces. Besides, she has discovered, that most of them really deserve no compassion, and many sensible worthy people of her acquaintance have cautioned her against giving way to her sensibility in that way: because, in such cases, the compassion of individuals is hurtful to society. There are several poor relations of her husband's, who, if it had not been for a settlement he made in her favour a short while before his death, would have had, I am told, by law, the greatest part of his fortune, to whom she never gave a shilling in her life. One little boy, her husband's godson, she consented to take into the house; but she turned him out of doors in less than a week, because of a blow he gave to Fidele, who was stealing his bread and butter.

Some of the other members of the family are almost tempted to steal bread and butter too. Mrs. Sensitive is an economist, though she spends a great deal of money on these nasty dogs and monkeys, and contrives to pinch it off us, both back and belly, as the saying is. The chambermaid has given her warning already on this score; and the boy says, he will only stay till he is a little bigger. As for me, she is pleased to say, that I am of an order of beings superior to the others; and she sometimes condescends to reason with me. She would persuade me, Sir, that it is a sin to eat the flesh of any bird or beast, and talks much of a set of philosophers, who went naked, I think, who believed that people were turned into beasts and birds; and that therefore we might chance to eat our father or mother in the shape of a goose or a turkey. And she says, how delighted she would be in the society of those naked philosophers, and how much their doctrines agree with her fine feelings; and then she coaxes me, and says, that I have fine feelings too: but indeed I have no such feelings belonging to me; and I know her greens and water don't agree with my feelings at all, but quite to the contrary, that there is such a grumbling about me.——And as for people being changed into birds and beasts, I think it is heathenish, and downright against the Bible; and yet it is diverting enough sometimes to hear her fancies about it; and I can't help having my fancies too: as the other morning, when the great horned owl sat at table by her, on the chair which she has often told me her dear, dear Mr. Sensitive used to occupy, and the poor creature looked so grave, and sat as silent as mum-chance;—but then she was so kind to the owl! I don't know what her squirrel was changed from, but it is always getting into some odd corner or other. It was but yesterday I got a sad scold for offering to squeeze it when it had crept Lord knows how far up my petticoats; and my mistress was in such a flurry, for fear I should have hurt it! She lets it skip all about her without ever starting or wincing, for all her feelings are so fine. But these fine feelings are not like the feelings of any other body; and I wish to get into the service of some person who has them of a coarser kind, that would be a little more useful. If Mrs. Heartly, therefore, continues in her resolution of quitting Lady Bidmore's, on account of that old lady's want of feeling, I would be very much obliged to you to recommend me to the place. I think I can bear a pretty good hand at a rubber and hard brush; and as for keeping the furniture clean, it would be perfect pastime only, in comparison of my morning's cleaning out Mrs. Sensitive's living collection. I hope Lady Bidmore, from her education, has never heard any thing of the naked philosophers; and if any other set have taught her that people are changed into commodes, chests of drawers, or bedsteads, it signifies very little, as we shall take exceeding good care of them, and the belief will have no effect on our dinners or suppers.

I am, &c.
BARBARA HEARTLESS.

Appendix D: Contemporary Reviews and Evaluations

[As an anonymously published first novel, *The Man of Feeling* received scant notice on its first publication. Coverage was mostly limited to a brief paragraph in the monthly catalogue of books received given at the end of the major critical journals. Reviewers' responses to the first edition were lukewarm, and certainly less enthusiastic than that of readers. Mackenzie's disappointment in the criticism of the *Monthly Review* is noted in his correspondence (see Appendix B); but *The Critical Review* offered a moderately positive account.]

1. The *Monthly Review* (vol. 44, p. 418) May 1771

This performance is written after the manner of Sterne; but it follows at a prodigious distance the steps of that ingenious and sentimental writer. It is not however totally destitute of merit; and the Reader, who weeps not over some of the scenes it describes, has no sensibility of mind. But it is to be observed, that the knowledge of men it contains, appears to be rather gathered from books than experience; and that, with regard to composition, it is careless, and abounds in provincial and Scottish idioms. It is probably a first work; and from the specimen it affords of the talents of its Author, we should not be disposed to think that he will ever attain to any great eminence in literature. He may amuse himself at the foot of Parnassus; but to ascend the steps of the mountain must be the task of those on whom their benignant stars have bestowed the rare gifts of true genius.

2. *The Critical Review* (vol. 31, pp. 482-83) June 1771

By those who have feeling hearts, and a true relish for simplicity in writing, many pages in this miscellaneous volume will be read with satisfaction. There is not indeed fable enough in this volume to keep up the attention of the majority of novel readers; there is not business enough in it for the million: but there are several interesting situations, several striking incidents, several excellent reflections, which sufficiently discover the author's invention and judgment, delicacy and taste. The story of Old Edwards is exquisitely affecting: the whole thirty-fourth chapter, indeed, in which it is introduced, is written in a very masterly manner.

3. *The Scots Magazine* (vol. 33, p. 427) August 1771

Written after the manner of Stern [sic]. Not destitute of merit; and the reader who weeps not over some of the scenes it describes, has no sensibility. M.

4. *The London Magazine* (vol. 40, pp. 411–413) August 1771

There is much good sense, but very little order, in this novel; the sentiments do honour to humanity, and the general propriety of the observations give such striking lessons upon life, that we cannot dismiss the article without laying an extract before our readers. [The rest of the review consists of "The Pupil: A Fragment" quoted in its entirety.]

5. Sir Walter Scott, "Henry Mackenzie," *Lives of the Novelists* (1823)

[This memoir was written as a preface to an edition of Mackenzie's novels in Ballantyne's *Novelists' Library* (Edinburgh: 1823). Scott wrote a series of "lives" for Ballantyne between 1821 and 1824. From *Lives of The Novelists* by Sir Walter Scott, Oxford UP, 1906.]

For the biographical part of the following memoir we are chiefly indebted to a short sketch of the life of our distinguished contemporary, compiled from the most authentic sources, and prefixed to a beautiful duodecimo edition of *The Man of Feeling*, printed at Paris a few years since. We have had the further advantage of correcting and enlarging the statements which it contains from undoubted authority.

Henry Mackenzie, Esq., was born at Edinburgh in August 1745, on the same day on which Prince Charles Stuart landed in Scotland. His father was Dr. Joshua Mackenzie, of that city, and his mother, Margaret, the eldest daughter of Mr. Rose of Kilravock, of a very ancient family in Nairnshire. After being educated at the High School and University of Edinburgh, Mr. Mackenzie, by the advice of some friends of his father, was articled to Mr. Inglis of Redhall, in order to acquire a knowledge of the business of the exchequer, a law department in which he was likely to have fewer competitors than in any other in Scotland.

To this, although not perfectly compatible with that literary taste which he very early displayed, he applied with due diligence; and in 1765 went to London to study the modes of English exchequer practice, which, as well as the constitution of the courts, are similar in both countries. While there, his talents induced a friend to solicit his remaining in London, and qualifying himself for the English bar. But the anxious wishes of his family that he should reside with them, and the moderation of an unambitious mind, decided his return to Edinburgh; and here he became, first partner, and afterwards successor to Mr. Inglis, in the office of Attorney for the Crown.

His professional labour, however, did not prevent his attachment to literary pursuits. When in London he sketched some part of his first and very popular work, *The Man of Feeling*, which was published in 1771 without his name; and was so much a favourite with the public as to become, a few years after, the occasion of a remarkable fraud. A Mr. Eccles, of Bath, observing that this work was accompanied by no author's name, laid claim to it, transcribed the whole in his own hand, with blottings, interlineations, and corrections, and maintained his right with such plausible pertinacity that Messrs. Cadell and Strahan (Mr. Mackenzie's publishers) found it necessary to undeceive the public by a formal contradiction.

In a few years after this he published his *Man of the World*, which seems to be intended as a second part to *The Man of Feeling*. It breathes the same tone of exquisite moral delicacy and of refined sensibility. In his former fiction he imagined a hero constantly obedient to every emotion of his moral sense. In *The Man of the World* he exhibited, on the contrary, a person rushing headlong into misery and ruin, and spreading misery all around him, by pursuing a happiness which he expected to obtain in defiance of the moral sense. His next production was *Julia de Roubigné*, a novel in a series of letters. The fable is very interesting, and the letters are written with great elegance and propriety of style.

In 1776 Mr. Mackenzie was married to Miss Penuel Grant, daughter of Sir Ludovick Grant of Grant, Bart., and Lady Ogilvy, by whom he has a numerous family, the eldest of whom, Mr. Henry Joshua Mackenzie, has, while these sheets are passing the press, been called to the situation of a Judge of the Supreme Court of Session, with the unanimous approbation of his country.

In 1777 or 1778 a society of gentlemen of Edinburgh were accustomed at their meetings to read short essays of their composition, in the manner of the *Spectator*, and Mr. Mackenzie being admitted a member, after hearing several of them read, suggested the advantage of giving greater variety to their compositions by admitting some of a lighter kind, descriptive of common life and manners; and he exhibited some specimens of the kind in his own writing. From this arose the *Mirror*, a well-known periodical publication, to which Mr. Mackenzie performed the office of editor, and was also the principal contributor. The success of the *Mirror* naturally led Mr. Mackenzie and his friends to undertake the *Lounger*, upon the same plan, which was not less read and admired.

When the Royal Society of Edinburgh was instituted, Mr. Mackenzie became one of its most active members, and he has occasionally enriched the volumes of its *Transactions* by his valuable communications, particularly by an elegant tribute to the memory of his friend Judge Abercromby, and a memoir on German Tragedy. He is one of the original members of the Highland Society; and by him have been published the volumes of their *Transactions*, to which he has prefixed an account of the institution and principal proceedings of the Society, and an interesting account of Gaelic poetry.

In the year 1792 he was one of those literary men who contributed some little occasional tracts to disabuse the lower orders of the people, led astray at that time by the prevailing frenzy of the French Revolution. In 1793 he wrote the *Life of Dr. Blacklock*, at the request of his widow, prefixed to a quarto edition of that blind poet's works. His intimacy with Blacklock gave him an opportunity of knowing the habits of his life, the bent of his mind, and the feelings peculiar to the privation of sight under which Blacklock laboured.

The literary society of Edinburgh, in the latter part of last century, whose intimacy he enjoyed, is described in his *Life of John Home*, which he read to the Royal Society in 1812, and, as a sort of Supplement to that Life, he then added some Critical Essays, chiefly on Dramatic Poetry, which have not been published.

In 1808 Mr. Mackenzie published a complete edition of his works in eight volumes octavo, including a tragedy, *The Spanish Father*, and a comedy, *The White Hypocrite*, which last was once performed at the Theatre Royal, Covent Garden. The tragedy had never been represented, in consequence of Mr. Garrick's opinion that the catastrophe was of too shocking a kind for the modern stage; though he owned the merit of the poetry, the force of some of the scenes, and the scope for fine action in the character of Alphonso, the leading person of the drama. In this edition also is given a carefully corrected copy of the tragedy of *The Prince of Tunis*, which had been represented at Edinburgh, in 1763, with great success.

Among the prose compositions of Mr. Mackenzie is a political tract, *An Account of the Proceedings of the Parliament of 1784*, which he was induced to write at the persuasion of his old and steady friend, Mr. Dundas, afterwards Lord Melville. It introduced him to the countenance and regard of Mr. Pitt, who revised the work with particular care and attention, and made several corrections in it with his own hand. Some years after Mr. Mackenzie was appointed, on the recommendation of Lord Melville and Right Hon. George Rose, also his particular friend, to the office of Comptroller of the Taxes for Scotland, an appointment of very considerable labour and responsibility, and in discharging which this fanciful and ingenious author has shown his power of entering into and discussing the most dry and complicated details, when that became a matter of duty.

The time, we trust, is yet distant when, speaking of this author as of those with whom his genius ranks him, a biographer may with delicacy trace his personal character and peculiarities, or record the manner in which he has discharged the duties of a citizen. When that hour shall arrive we trust few of his own contemporaries will be left to mourn him; but we can anticipate the sorrow of a later generation when deprived of the wit which enlivened their hours of retirement, the benevolence which directed and encouraged their studies, and the wisdom which instructed them in their duties to society. It is enough to say here that Mr. Mackenzie survives, venerable and venerated, as the last link of the chain which connects the Scottish literature of the present age with the period when there were giants in the land—the days of Robertson, and Hume, and Smith, and Home, and Clerk, and Fergusson; and that the remembrance of an era so interesting could not have been entrusted to a sounder judgment, a more correct taste, or a more tenacious memory. It is much to be wished that Mr. Mackenzie, taking a wider view of his earlier years than in the *Life of Home*, would place on a more permanent record some of the anecdotes and recollections with which he delights society. We are about to measure his capacity for the task by a singular standard, but it belongs to Mr. Mackenzie's character. He has, we believe, shot game of every description which Scotland contains (deer, and probably grouse, excepted), on the very grounds at present occupied by the extensive and splendid streets of the New Town of Edinburgh; has sought for hares and wild ducks where there are now palaces, churches, and assembly-rooms; and has witnessed moral revolutions as surprising as this extraordinary change of local circumstances. These mutations in manners and in morals have been gradual indeed in their progress, but most important in their results, and they have been introduced into Scotland within the last half-century. Every sketch of them, or of the circumstances by which they were produced, from the pen of so intelligent an observer, and whose opportunities of observation have been so extensive, would, however slight and detached, rival in utility and amusement any work of the present time.

As an author Mr. Mackenzie has shown talents both for poetry and the drama. Indeed we are of opinion that no man can succeed perfectly in the line of fictitious composition without most of the properties of a poet, though he may be no writer of verses; but Mr. Mackenzie possesses the powers of melody in addition to those of conception. He has given a beautiful specimen of legendary poetry in two little Highland ballads, a style of composition which becomes fashionable from time to time on account of its simplicity and pathos, and then is again laid aside, when worn out by the servile imitators to whom its approved facility offers its chief recommendation. But it is as a novelist that we are now called on to consider our author's powers; and the universal and permanent popularity of his writings entitles us to rank him among the most distinguished of his class. His works possess the rare and invaluable property of originality, to which all other qualities are as dust in the balance, and the sources to which he resorts to excite our interest are rendered accessible by a path peculiarly his own. The reader's attention is not riveted, as in Fielding's works, by strongly marked character, and the lucid evolution of a well-constructed fable; or, as in Smollett's novels, by broad and strong humour, and a decisively superior knowledge of human life in all its varieties; nor, to mention authors whom Mackenzie more nearly resembles, does he attain the pathetic effect which is the object of all three, in the same manner as Richardson or as Sterne. An accumulation of circumstances, sometimes amounting to tediousness, a combination of minutely-traced events, with an ample commentary on each, were thought necessary by Richardson to excite and prepare the mind of the reader for the affecting scenes which he has occasionally touched with such force; and without denying him his due merit, it must be allowed that he has employed preparatory volumes in accomplishing what has cost Mackenzie and Sterne only a few pages, perhaps only a few sentences.

On the other hand, although the last two named authors have, in particular passages, a more strong resemblance to each other than those formerly named, yet there remain such essential points of difference betwixt them, as must secure for Mackenzie the praise of originality which we have claimed for him. It is needless to point out to the reader the difference between the general character of their writings, or how far the chaste, correct, almost studiously decorous manner and style of the works of the author of *The Man of Feeling* differ from the wild wit, and intrepid contempt at once of decency and regularity of composition, which distinguish *Tristram Shandy*. It is not in the general conduct or style of their works that they in the slightest degree approach; nay, no two authors in the British language can be more distinct. But even in the particular passages where both had in view to excite the reader's pathetic sympathy, the modes resorted to are different. The pathos of Sterne in some degree resembles his humour, and is seldom attained by simple means; a wild, fanciful, beautiful flight of thought and expression is remarkable in the former, as an extravagant, burlesque, and ludicrous strain of thought and language characterises the latter. The celebrated passage where the tear of the recording angel blots the profane oath of Uncle Toby out of the register of heaven, a flight so poetically fanciful as to be stretched to the very verge of extravagance, will illustrate our position. To attain his object—that is, to make us thoroughly sympathise with the excited state of mind which betrays Uncle Toby into the indecorous assertion which forms the ground-work of the whole, the author calls Heaven and Hell into the lists, and represents, in a fine poetic frenzy, its effects on the accusing spirit and the registering angel. Let this be contrasted with the fine tale of *La Roche*, in which Mackenzie has described, with such unexampled delicacy and powerful effect, the sublime scene of the sorrows and resignation of the deprived father. This also is painted reflectively; that is, the reader's sympathy is excited by the effect produced on one of the drama, neither angel nor devil, but a philosopher, whose heart remains sensitive, though his studies have misled his mind into the frozen regions of scepticism. To say nothing of the tendency of the two passages, which will scarce, in the mind of the most unthinking, bear any comparison, we would only remark that Mackenzie has given us a moral truth, Sterne a beautiful trope; and that if the one claims the palm of superior brilliancy of imagination, that due to nature and accuracy of human feeling must abide with the Scottish author.

Yet, while marking this broad and distinct difference between these two authors, the most celebrated certainly among those who are termed sentimental, it is but fair to Sterne to add, that although Mackenzie has rejected his license of wit and flights of imagination, retrenched, in a great measure, his episodical digressions, and altogether banished the indecency and buffoonery to which he had too frequent recourse, still their volumes must be accounted as belonging to the same class; and, amongst the thousand imitators who have pursued their path, we cannot recollect one English author who is entitled to the same honour. The foreign authors Riccoboni and Marivaux belong to the same department; but of the former we remember little, and the latter, though full of the most delicate touches, often depends for effect on the turn of phrase, and the protracted embarrassments of artificial gallantry, more than upon the truth and simplicity of nature. The *Heloise* and *Emile* partake of the insanity of their author, and are exaggerated, though most eloquent, descriptions of overwhelming passion, rather than works of sentiment.

In future compositions, the author dropped even that resemblance which the style of *The Man of Feeling* bears, in some particulars, to the works of Sterne; and his country may boast that, in one instance at least, she has produced in Mackenzie a writer of pure musical Addisonian prose, which retains the quality of vigour without forfeiting that of clearness and simplicity.

We are hence led to observe that the principal object of Mackenzie, in all his novels, has been to reach and sustain a tone of moral pathos, by representing the effect of incidents, whether important or trifling, upon the human mind, and especially on those which were not only just, honourable, and intelligent, but so framed as to be responsive to those finer feelings, to which ordinary hearts are callous. This is the direct and professed object of Mackenzie's first work, which is in fact no narrative, but a series of successive incidents, each rendered interesting by the mode in which they operate on the feelings of Harley. The attempt had been perilous in a meaner hand; for, sketched by a pencil less nicely discriminating, Harley, instead of a being whom we love, respect, sympathise with, and admire, had become the mere Quixote of sentiment, an object of pity, perhaps, but of ridicule at the same time. Against this the author has guarded with great skill; and, while duped and swindled in London, Harley neither loses our consideration as a man of sense and spirit, nor is subjected to that degree of contempt with which readers in general regard the misadventures of a novice upon town, whilst they hug themselves in their own superior knowledge of the world. Harley's spirited conduct towards an impertinent passenger in the stage-coach, and his start of animated indignation on listening to Edwards's story, are skilfully thrown in, to satisfy the reader that his softness and gentleness of temper were not allied to effeminacy, and that he dared, on suitable occasions, do all that might become a man. We have heard that some of Harley's feelings were taken from those of the author himself, when, at his first entrance on the dry and barbarous study of municipal law, he was looking back, like Blackstone, on the land of the Muses, which he was condemned to leave behind him. It has also been said that the fine sketch of Miss Walton was taken from the heiress of a family of distinction, who ranked at that time high in the Scottish fashionable world. But such surmises are little worth the tracing; for we believe no original character was ever composed by any author, without the idea having been previously suggested by something which he had observed in nature.

The other novels of Mr. Mackenzie, although assuming a more regular and narrative form, are, like *The Man of Feeling*, rather the history of effects produced on the human mind by a series of events, than the narrative of those events themselves. The villainy of Sindall [in *The Man of the World*] is the tale of a heart hardened to selfishness, by incessant and unlimited gratification of the external senses; a contrast to that of Harley, whose mental feelings have acquired such an ascendancy as to render him unfit for the ordinary business of life. The picture of the former is so horrid that we would be disposed to deny its truth, did we not unhappily know that sensual indulgence, in the words of Burns,

hardens a'within,
And petrifies the feeling[1]

---

1   Robert Burns, "Epistle to a Young Friend," 1786.

and that there never did, and never will exist, anything permanently noble and excellent in a character which was a stranger to the exercise of resolute self-denial. The history of the victims of Sindall's arts and crimes, particularly the early history of the Annesleys, is exquisitely well drawn; and, perhaps, the scene between the brother and sister by the pond equals any part of the author's writings. Should the reader doubt this, he may easily make the experiment, by putting it into the hands of any young person of feeling and intelligence, and of an age so early as not to have forgotten the sports and passions of childhood.

The beautiful and tragic tale of *Julia de Roubigné* is of a very different tenor from *The Man of The World*; and we have good authority for thinking that it was written in some degree as a counter-part to the latter work. A friend of the author, the celebrated Lord Kames, we believe, had represented to Mr. Mackenzie in how many poems, plays, and novels the distress of the piece is made to turn upon the designing villainy of some one of the *dramatis personae*. On considering his observations, the author undertook, as a task fit for his genius, the composition of a story in which the characters should be all naturally virtuous, and where the calamities of the catastrophe should arise, as frequently happens in actual life, not out of schemes of premeditated villainy, but from the excess and over-indulgence of passions and feelings, in themselves blameless, nay, praiseworthy, but which, encouraged to a morbid excess, and coming into fatal though fortuitous concourse with each other, lead to the most disastrous consequences. Mr. Mackenzie executed his purpose; and as the plan fell in most happily with the views of a writer, whose object was less to describe external objects than to read a lesson on the human heart, he has produced one of the most heart-wringing histories which has ever been written. The very circumstances which palliate the errors of the sufferers, in whose distress we interest ourselves, point out to the reader that there is neither hope, remedy, nor revenge. When a Lovelace or a Sindall comes forth like an evil principle, the agent of all the misery of the scene, we see a chance of their artifices being detected; at least the victims have the consciousness of innocence, the reader the stern hope of vengeance. But when, as in *Julia de Roubigné*, the revival of mutual affection on the part of two pure and amiable beings, imprudently and incautiously indulged, awakens, and not unjustly, the jealous honour of a high-spirited husband,—when we see Julia precipitated into misery by her preference of filial duty to early love, Savillon, by his faithful and tender attachment to a deserving object, and Montauban, by a jealous regard to his spotless fame, we are made aware, at the same time, that there is no hope of aught but the most unhappy catastrophe. The side of each sufferer is pierced by the very staff on which he leant, and the natural virtuous feelings which they at first most legitimately indulged, precipitate them into error, crimes, remorse, and misery. The cruelty to which Montauban is hurried may, perhaps, be supposed to exempt him from our sympathy, especially in an age when such crimes as that of which Julia is suspected are usually borne by the injured parties with more equanimity than her husband displays. But the irritable habits of the time, and of his Spanish descent, must plead the apology of Montauban, as they are admitted to form that of Othello. Perhaps, on the whole, *Julia de Roubigné* gives the reader too much actual pain to be so generally popular as *The Man of Feeling*, since we have found its superiority to that beautiful essay on human sensibility often disputed by those whose taste we are in general inclined to defer to. The very acute feelings which the work usually excites among the readers whose sympathies are liable to be awakened by scenes of fictitious distress, we are disposed to ascribe to the extreme accuracy and truth of the sentiments, as well as to the beautiful manner in which they are expressed. There are few who have not had, at one period of life, disappointments of the heart to mourn over, and we know no book which recalls the recollection of such more severely than *Julia de Roubigné*.

We return to consider the key-note, as we may term it, on which Mackenzie has formed his tales of fictitious woe, and which we have repeatedly described to be the illustration of the nicer and finer sensibilities of the human breast. To attain this point, and to place it in the strongest and most unbroken light, the author seems to have kept the other faculties with which we know him to be gifted in careful subordination. The northern Addison, who revived the art of periodical writing, and sketched, though with a light pencil, the follies and lesser vices of his time, has showed himself a master of playful satire. The historian of the Homespun family may place his narrative, without fear of shame, by the side of *The Vicar of Wakefield*.[1] Colonel Caustic and

---

1   Oliver Goldsmith's popular novel, published 1766.

Umfraville are masterly conceptions of the *laudator temporis acti*;[1] and many personages in those papers which Mr. Mackenzie contributed to the *Mirror* and *Lounger* attest with what truth, spirit, and ease he could describe, assume, and sustain a variety of characters. The beautiful landscape painting which he has exhibited in many passages (take, for example, that where the country seat of the old Scottish lady and its accompaniments are so exquisitely delineated) assures us of the accuracy and delicacy of his touch in delineating the beauties of nature.

But all these powerful talents, any single one of which might have sufficed to bring men of more bounded powers into notice, have been by Mackenzie carefully subjected to the principal object which he proposed to himself—the delineation of the human heart. Variety of character he has introduced sparingly, and has seldom recourse to any peculiarity of incident, availing himself generally of those which may be considered as common property to all writers of romance. His sense of the beauties of nature, and his power of describing them, are carefully *kept down*, to use the expression of the artists; and like the single straggling bough which shades the face of his sleeping veteran, just introduced to relieve his principal object, but not to rival it. It cannot be termed an exception to this rule, though certainly a peculiarity of this author, that on all occasions where sylvan sports can be introduced, he displays an intimate familiarity with them, and, from personal habits, to which we have elsewhere alluded, shows a delight to dwell for an instant upon a favourite topic.

Lastly, the wit which sparkles in his periodical essays, and, we believe, in his private conversation, shows itself but little in his Novels; and, although his peculiar vein of humour may be much more frequently traced, yet it is so softened down, and divested of the broad ludicrous, that it harmonises with the most grave and affecting parts of the tale, and becomes, like the satire of Jaques, only a more humorous shade of melancholy.[2] In short, Mackenzie aimed at being the historian of feeling, and has succeeded in the object of his ambition. But as mankind are never contented, and as critics are certainly no exception to a rule so general, we could wish that, without losing or altering a line that our author has written, he had condescended to give us, in addition to his

---

1 Praiser of time gone by.
2 An allusion to the character of Jaques in Shakespeare's *As You Like It* (1599).

stores of sentiment, a romance on life and manners, by which, we are convinced, he would have twisted another branch of laurel into his garland. However, as Sebastian expresses it,

What had been, is unknown; what is, appears:[1]

we must be proudly satisfied with what we have received, and happy that, in this line of composition, we can boast a living author of excellence like that of Henry Mackenzie.

---

1 The reference is to John Dryden's play *Don Sebastian* (1690). In Samuel Johnson's "Preface to *Dryden*," part of his ten-volume *Prefaces Biographical and Critical to the Works of the English Poets* (London: 1779-81), Johnson quotes the line, much as Scott does here, to underscore the futility of speculating about works never written.

Select Bibliography

Works by Henry Mackenzie

[The eight volumes of the official *Works* published by Mackenzie in 1808 have recently been reprinted by Routledge / Thoemmes Press. They omit some material, including his *Life* of John Home and notes towards a memoir. These unpublished notes on his life and times were edited a century later into *The Anecdotes and Egotisms of Henry Mackenzie* by Harold William Thompson (below). In his biography of Mackenzie, Thompson lists over twenty-five known editions of *The Man of Feeling*, including French and American editions and Collected Works, in the fifty years after its first publication in 1771. I list only the first three of these early editions below, along with the 1808 *Works of Henry Mackenzie*.]

Letters to Elizabeth Rose of Kilravock on Literature, Events and People 1768-1815. Ed. Horst W. Drescher. Edinburgh: Oliver and Boyd / Munster: Verlag Aschendorff, 1967.

Literature and Literati: The Literary Correspondence and Notebooks of Henry Mackenzie. 2 vols.

—Vol. 1: *Letters 1766-1827*. Ed. Horst W. Drescher. Publications of the Scottish Studies Centre of the Johannes Gutenberg Universitat Mainz in Germersheim. Frankfurt am Main: Verlag Peter Lang, 1989.

—Vol 2: *Notebooks 1763-1824*. Ed. Horst W. Drescher. New York: Peter Lang, 1999.

The Man of Feeling. First edition, London, April 1771.

The Man of Feeling. Second, corrected, edition, London, August 1771.

The Man of Feeling. Third edition, London, 1773.

The Man of Feeling. Ed. Brian Vickers. London: Oxford UP, 1967.

The Works of Henry Mackenzie, Esq., In Eight Volumes. Edinburgh and London, 1808.

Report of the Committee . . . Appointed to Inquire into . . . Ossian. Edinburgh, 1805.

An Account of the Life and Writings of John Home, Esq. Edinburgh, 1822.

Thompson, Harold William, ed. *The Anecdotes and Egotisms of Henry Mackenzie*. London: Oxford UP, 1927.

Biography

Scott, Walter. "Henry Mackenzie," *Lives of the Novelists*. London: Oxford UP, 1906. 163-76.

Thompson, Harold William, *A Scottish Man of Feeling: Some Account of Henry Mackenzie, Esq. of Edinburgh and of the Golden Age of Burns and Scott*. London: Oxford UP, 1931.

Sentimentalism and Eighteenth-Century Literature and Culture

Alexander, David. *Affecting Moments: Prints of English Literature Made in the Age of Romantic Sensibility 1775-1800*. York: U of York P, 1993.

Armstrong, Nancy. *Desire and Domestic Fiction: A Political History of the Novel*. New York: Oxford UP, 1987.

Barker, Gerard A. "David Simple: The Novel of Sensibility in Embryo." *Modern Language Studies* 12:2 (Spring 1982): 69-80.

Barker-Benfield, G.J. *The Culture of Sensibility: Sex and Society in Eighteenth-Century Britain*. Chicago: U of Chicago P, 1992.

Bell, Michael. *Sentimentalism, Ethics, and the Culture of Feeling*. New York: Palgrave, 2000.

Benedict, Barbara. *Framing Feeling: Sentiment and Style in English Prose Fiction 1745-1800*. New York: AMS Press, 1994.

Boulukos, George. "The Grateful Slave: A History of Slave Plantation Reform in the British Novel, 1750-1780." *The Eighteenth-Century Novel* 1 (2001): 161-79.

Braudy, Leo. "The Form of the Sentimental Novel." *Novel* 7 (1973): 5-13.

Bredvold, Louis I. *The Natural History of Sensibility*. Detroit: Wayne State UP, 1962.

Brissenden, R.F. *Virtue in Distress: Studies in the Novel of Sentiment from Richardson to de Sade*. Basingstoke: Macmillan, 1974.

Brown, Marshall. *Preromanticism*. Stanford: Stanford UP, 1991.

Conger, Syndy McMillen, ed. *Sensibility in Transformation: Creative Resistance to Sentiment from the Augustans to the Romantics*. London: Associated UP, 1990.

Crane, R.S. "Suggestions toward a Genealogy of the 'Man of Feeling.'" *ELH* 1:3 (1934): 205-30.

Dwyer, John. *Virtuous Discourse: Sensibility and Community in Late Eighteenth-Century Scotland*. Edinburgh: J. Donald, 1987.

Dwyer, John and R.B. Sher, eds. *Sociability and Society in Eighteenth-Century Scotland*. Edinburgh: Mercat, 1993.

Dwyer, John. "Clio and Ethics: Practical Morality in Enlightened Scotland." *The Eighteenth Century: Theory and Interpretation* 30:1 (Spring 1989): 45-72.

Ellis, Markman. *The Politics of Sensibility: Race, Gender, and Commerce in the Sentimental Novel*. Cambridge: Cambridge UP, 1996.

Ellison, Julie. *Cato's Tears and the Making of Anglo-American Emotion*. Chicago: U of Chicago P, 1999.

Friedman, Arthur. "Aspects of Sentimentalism in Eighteenth-Century Literature." *The Augustan Milieu: Essays Presented to Louis A. Landa*. Ed. Henry Knight Miller *et al*. Oxford: Clarendon, 1970. 247-61.

Frye, Northrop. "Towards Defining an Age of Sensibility." *ELH* 23:2 (1956): 144-52.

Garside, P.D. "Henry Mackenzie, the Scottish Novel, and *Blackwood's Magazine*." *Scottish Literary Journal* 15:1 (May 1988): 25-48.

Greene, Donald. "Latitudinarianism and Sensibility: The Genealogy of 'The Man of Feeling' Reconsidered." *Modern Philology* 75 (1977): 159-83.

Hagstrum, Jean. *Sex and Sensibility: Ideal and Erotic Love from Milton to Mozart*. Chicago: U of Chicago P, 1980.

McGann, Jerome. *The Poetics of Sensibility: A Revolution in Literary Style*. Oxford: Clarendon, 1996.

McGuirk, Carol. "Sentimental Encounter in Sterne, Mackenzie and Burns." *SEL: Studies in English Literature 1500-1900* 20 (1989): 505-15.

Markley, Robert. "Sentimentality as Performance: Shaftesbury, Sterne, and the Theatrics of Virtue." *The New Eighteenth Century: Theory, Politics, English Literature*. Ed. Felicity Nussbaum and Laura Brown. New York: Methuen, 1987. 210-30.

Motooka, Wendy. *The Age of Reasons: Quixotism, Sentimentalism and Political Economy in Eighteenth-Century Britain*. London: Routledge, 1998.

Mullan, John. "The Language of Sentiment: Hume, Smith and Henry Mackenzie." *The History of Scottish Literature*, Vol. II: 1660-1800. Ed. Andrew Hook. Aberdeen: Aberdeen UP, 1987. 273-89.

—. *Sentiment and Sociability: The Language of Feeling in the Eighteenth Century*. Oxford: Oxford UP, 1988.

Novak, Maximillian and Anne Mellor, eds. *Passionate Encounters in a Time of Sensibility*. Newark: U of Delaware P, 2000.

Paulson, Ronald. *Satire and the Novel in Eighteenth-Century England*. New Haven: Yale UP, 1967.

Phillips, Mark Salber. *Society and Sentiment: Genres of Historical Writing in Britain, 1740-1820*. Princeton: Princeton UP, 2000.

Rawson, Claude, *Satire and Sentiment 1660-1830*. Cambridge: Cambridge UP, 1983.

Rousseau, G.S. "Nerves, Spirits, and Fibres: Towards Defining the Origins of Sensibility." *Studies in the Eighteenth Century*. Ed. R.F. Brissenden and J.C. Eade. Canberra: Australian National UP / Toronto: U of Toronto P, 1976. 137-57.

Sheriff, John K. *The Good-Natur'd Man: The Evolution of a Moral Ideal, 1660-1800*. University, Alabama: U of Alabama P, 1982.

Spacks, Patricia Meyer. *Desire and Truth: Functions of Plot in Eighteenth-Century English Novels*. Chicago: U of Chicago P, 1990.

Starr, G.A. "Only a Boy: Notes on Sentimental Novels." *Genre* 10:4 (1977): 501-27.

Starr, G.A. "Sentimental Novels of the Later Eighteenth Century." *The Columbia History of the British Novel*. Ed. John Richetti *et al*. New York: Columbia UP, 1994. 181-98.

Todd, Janet. *Sensibility: An Introduction*. London: Methuen, 1986.

Tompkins, J.M.S. *The Popular Novel in England 1770-1800*. Lincoln: U of Nebraska P, 1961 (1932).

Van Sant, Ann Jessie. *Eighteenth-Century Sensibility and the Novel: The Senses in Social Context*. Cambridge: Cambridge UP, 1993.

Wright, Walter F. *Sensibility in English Prose Fiction 1760-1814: A Reinterpretation*. Urbana: U of Illinois P, 1937.

Zimmerman, Everett. "Fragments of History and the Man of Feeling: From Richard Bentley to Walter Scott" *Eighteenth-Century Studies* 23:3 (Spring 1990): 283-300.

Studies of Mackenzie and *The Man of Feeling*

Bandiera, Laura. *L'Ilusione Sentimentale: Saggio sulla Narrativa di Henry Mackenzie*. Bologna: Cooperativa Libraria Universitaria Editrice Bologna, 1987.

Barker, Gerard A. *Henry Mackenzie*. Boston: Twayne, 1975.

Burling, William J. "A 'Sickly Sort of Refinement': The Problem

of Sentimentalism in Mackenzie's *The Man of Feeling*."
Studies in Scottish Literature 23 (1988): 136-49.

Burnham, R. Peter. "The Social Ethos of Mackenzie's *The Man of Feeling*." *Studies in Scottish Literature* 18 (1983): 123-37.

Dykstal, Timothy. "The Sentimental Novel as Moral Philosophy: The Case of Henry Mackenzie." *Genre* 27: 1-2 (1994): 59-81.

Fairer, David. "Sentimental Translation in Mackenzie and Sterne." *Essays in Criticism* 49:2 (April 1999): 132-51.

Gerard, W.B. "Benevolent Vision: The Ideology of Sentimentality in Contemporary Illustrations of *A Sentimental Journey* and *The Man of Feeling*." *Eighteenth-Century Fiction* 14: 3-4 (2002): 533-74.

Harkin, Maureen. "Mackenzie's *Man of Feeling*: Embalming Sensibility." *ELH* 61:2 (Summer 1994): 317-40.

London, April. "Historiography, Pastoral, Novel: Genre in *The Man of Feeling*." *Eighteenth-Century Fiction* 10:1 (October 1997): 43-62.

McDaniel, Dale. "Henry Mackenzie's Harley: A Reaction Against Commercialism." *Studies in Scottish Literature* 33-34 (2004): 62-70.

Manning, Susan. "Enlightenment's Dark Dreams: Two Fictions of Henry Mackenzie and Charles Brockden Brown." *Eighteenth-Century Life* 21:3 (November 1997): 39-56.

Michasiw, Kim Ian. "Imitation and Ideology: Henry Mackenzie's Rousseau." *Eighteenth-Century Fiction* 5:2 (January 1993): 153-76.

Platzner, Robert L. "Mackenzie's Martyr: The Man of Feeling as Saintly Fool." *Novel* 10 (1976): 59-64.

Skinner, Gillian. "'Above Oeconomy': Elizabeth Griffith's *The History of Lady Barton* and Henry Mackenzie's *The Man of Feeling*." *Eighteenth-Century Life* 19:1 (February 1995): 1-17.

Sühnel, Rudolf. "A Plea for *The Man of Feeling*: Henry Mackenzie's Minor Classic in Context." *Das Achtzehnte Jahrhundert: Facetten einer Epoche. Festschrift fur Rainer Gruenter.* Ed. Wolfgang Adam. Heidelberg: Carl Winter UP, 1988. 181-87.

Ware, Elaine. "Charitable Actions Reevaluated in the Novels of Henry Mackenzie." *Studies in Scottish Literature* 22 (1987): 132-41.

Wildermuth, Mark E. "The Rhetoric of Common Sense and Uncommon Sensibility in Henry Mackenzie's *The Man of Feeling*." *Lamar Journal of the Humanities* 23:2 (Fall 1997): 35-47.